THE ORPHAN IN THE PEACOCK SHAWL

ANNEMARIE BREAR

Boldwood

First published in Great Britain in 2022 by Boldwood Books Ltd.

1

Copyright © AnneMarie Brear, 2022

Cover Design by Colin Thomas

Cover Photography: Colin Thomas

A CIP catalogue record for this book is available from the British Library.

Paperback ISBN: 978-1-80415-672-8

Ebook ISBN: 978-1-80162-750-4

Kindle ISBN: 978-1-80162-751-1

Audio CD ISBN: 978-1-80162-758-0

Digital audio download ISBN: 978-1-80162-749-8

Large Print ISBN: 978-1-80162-753-5

Boldwood Books Ltd.

23 Bowerdean Street, London, SW6 3TN

www.boldwoodbooks.com

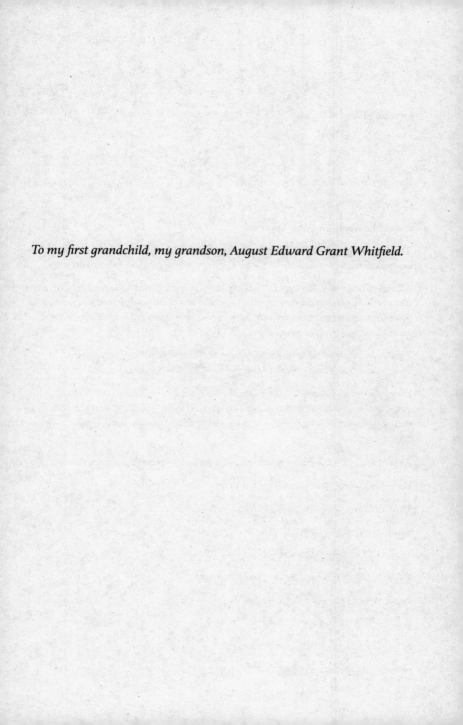

To my first grandchild, my grandson, August Edward Grant Whitfield.

1

YORKSHIRE, ENGLAND, JULY 1850

'Annabelle!'

Hearing her name called, Annabelle Wallis gathered the cut lavender and placed it in her basket along with the cuttings of catnip and camomile. The hot summer sun beat down on the herb garden, burning her skin through the thin linen of her blue dress as fat bees hummed crazily from flower to flower. In contrast, lazy butterflies of brown and gold rested on petals for long periods, until Annabelle passed by them and sent them into the air about her before they calmed and landed again.

The herb and flower garden stretched twenty yards from the cottage, then swept around the potting shed and ended where the vegetable garden began. The small walled plot, cultivated with a variety of vegetables, was hemmed in by fruit trees until finally the path stopped at the beck, running freely at the bottom of the garden. Beyond the beck, the land inclined up a high slope and opened out into wide pastures for the nearby estate's sheep to feed upon.

This little piece of paradise was Annabelle's home in the countryside on the outskirts of the village of Hartleydale, thirteen miles from York. A home she shared with Widow Wallis, the elderly woman who, twenty-two years earlier, had carried Annabelle home from a nearby market as a newborn baby and brought her up like her own daughter.

The people of the small village of Hartleydale accepted the widow's decision with only a ripple of gossip, for Widow Wallis was well respected and, if she had taken in a poor orphaned child, who were they to comment? Hadn't Widow Wallis saved many of them from death or aided them in sickness, delivered their babies into the world, or healed their injuries with her doctoring ways?

Besides, the child would give Widow Wallis the family she'd never had, and she deserved some company, being all alone in the cottage on the edge of the village.

So Annabelle grew up cheerful and content, helping her adopted mother, whom she called 'Ma', in growing her produce to sell to the village shops and slowly learning some of her ways to heal.

'There you are.' Widow Wallis hobbled along the path that snaked through the abundant garden beds. She wore all black, as was her custom. Her grey hair was covered by a black straw hat in summer and a black felt bonnet in winter. Annabelle had never seen her in another colour, nor did Ma own anything but black clothing. Yet the old woman happily bought material of different hues for Annabelle and delighted in her wearing the dresses she created for her.

'I was coming.' Annabelle picked up the two baskets she'd filled, ready to sell tomorrow.

'Dickie has called in to see you.'

Annabelle smiled wryly. 'I did tell him I would be busy today. He knows we always are the day before we go into the village.'

'Aye, well, the lad is smitten with you and would be here every day if he could get away from his duties at the estate.'

Walking through the back door of the cottage, which led straight into the kitchen, Annabelle dumped her baskets on the floor by the large pine table, which was dotted with dried flower posies and bunches of herbs tied with twine.

'Good day to you, Annabelle.' Dickie stood up from where he'd been sitting drinking a cup of tea.

'It's nice to see you, Dickie, though unexpected. You know how busy I am.' She smiled to take the sting out of her rebuke.

'Aye, but I had an hour spare and thought to bring you some news.' His brown hair was damp at the ends, as though he'd recently had a wash.

'News?' Widow Wallis's eyebrows rose. 'What would that be?'

'The estate is agog with the news of Mr John Hartley returning from his trip abroad.'

'John Hartley?' Annabelle poured a glass of elderflower cordial. 'I remember him.'

'You'd only have been a young girl. He left about seven years ago.' Ma placed the dried flower posies into a shallow basket.

'I would have been fifteen.' Annabelle sipped her drink, trying to place the third son of the important Hartley family in her mind. She vaguely recalled seeing him ride across the fields of the estate with his father and older brothers, Desmond and Arthur. But that had been such a long time ago, and the image was blurred.

'Well, he's returned,' Dickie said, accepting one of Ma's delicious jam tartlets. 'Apparently, he's been in London for the last six months, escorting his sister about now she's been presented to court.'

'Miss Eliza has been presented?' Annabelle wondered what it might be like to meet Queen Victoria. She'd seen Miss Eliza over the years, riding through the village or across the estate. A few times they'd come across each other and nodded politely, said good day. By all accounts, Miss Eliza was a lovely young lady.

Widow Wallis sorted through the bunches on the table. 'Miss Hartley must miss her parents at such time. For them not to see her special day would be a sad time for her.'

Dickie nodded. "Tis a shame they died before she was presented. Miss Eliza is rarely home now. She prefers spending all her time in London. They say she's grown wild. The ladies' boarding school she was dispatched to did little to tame her.'

'You know a lot about it,' Annabelle teased with a grin.

A flush brightened Dickie's cheeks. 'You know how it is, estate gossip reaches all ears. Being born on the estate, I know them as well as I know me own family.'

'Is that why Mr John is home?' Widow Wallis asked. 'Because his father died or because Miss Eliza had grown wild?'

'Both, or so we all assume. Mr Desmond is a decent enough master, but the family's concerns are wide and varied. He's doing his best to take care of everything, but his young wife is frail. She's not regained her strength after delivering their baby at Christmas. Mr Desmond must need one of his brothers home to help him now as Mr Arthur is away with the army in India.'

'It'll be strange having him about the place after him being abroad so long,' Annabelle said, sorting the herbs into piles on the table.

'I doubt he'll be around much. The Hartleys have estates all around Yorkshire. That's where he'll be sent.' Dickie finished his tea. 'I'd best be getting back. Will you walk with me a bit, Annabelle?'

She hesitated. There was so much to prepare before tomorrow.

'Go on,' he pleaded with a grin.

She looked at Ma, who nodded. 'Don't be long, mind.'

'I won't, Ma. I'll fetch some water at the same time.' Annabelle picked up one of the empty buckets near the door, and Dickie grabbed the other.

Walking along the path, the heat of midday scorched them. Annabelle pulled up her bonnet, where it dangled on her back by ribbons around her neck.

'Me mam wanted to know if you'd like to come for tea on Sunday after church?' Dickie asked.

'That's kind of her.' Annabelle didn't commit, for she knew that Dickie was becoming too involved with her and she wasn't ready just yet to know what she wanted.

'Will you come, then?'

'I don't know...'

'Please, Annabelle.'

At the edge of the beck, she knelt and settled the bucket in the water to fill. 'I was there last week.'

'Aye, and what's wrong with that?' He placed his bucket in the water beside her.

'People will talk. The village women already assume we're courting, no matter how many times I inform them we aren't.'

'Why don't we, then? You know I like you. I'd marry you tomorrow if I could.' He took the full bucket from the water for her and set it on the grass.

'I'm not ready for that, Dickie. I keep telling you.'

'Why? Most of my friends are married now. Why can't we be?'

She shrugged and picked up a bucket in each hand. 'Not yet.'

He groaned, running his hand through his light-brown hair. 'How long do I have to wait for?'

'I don't know,' she snapped and then felt guilty as he stomped away through the trees. Then, using the stepping stones, he crossed the beck and marched up the slope without a wave.

She watched him leave, his long legs striding through the high grass. He was tall and lean, with an impish grin and a kind heart. He had a secure position as a shepherd on the Hartley estate and would be a good husband.

Yet she faltered and didn't know why.

In the last few months, they'd shared kisses, which she had enjoyed. Occasionally, she'd encouraged Dickie's wandering hands to feel her body over her clothes. The secret meetings in the estate's forest gave her a shiver of excitement and she'd eagerly matched Dickie's urgency to kiss. But he required more, a future she wasn't able to accept. The thought of being married to Dickie didn't fill her with joy, and it should, for she liked him a lot. He was her best friend, only friend, and his kisses promised something else that she was interested to explore, but none of it was enough for her to promise herself to him.

Annabelle sat on the grass in the dappled shade of an enormous chestnut tree and, drawing her knees up, rested her chin on them. The gentle flow of water and the soft melody of it trickling over the rocks soothed her. What held her back from becoming Dickie's wife? She couldn't find one defining reason, except she didn't want to leave this cottage or Ma. Her happiness was all within this one-acre plot, her home, and she didn't wish to leave it.

A rustle in the grass behind her made her look around.

Ma stood gazing up at the branches of the tree's canopy. 'He won't wait forever, you know.'

Annabelle scrambled to her feet and clutched the bucket handles.

'Why do you delay, lass?'

'I admire him, a lot, but...'

Ma sighed. 'Dear girl. I fear for you.'

'Why?' She frowned. 'I've given you no reason to worry. I've been good all my life.'

'Aye, you have. But you're growing older. *I'm* getting older. I want you happy and settled before I die.'

'I *am* happy and you're *not* going to die for years yet.' Annabelle stomped ahead, the heavy buckets making it awkward to go fast.

Once in the kitchen, Annabelle set to work packing the crates with wet moss to keep the herbs alive for tomorrow when they'd trade them to local shops. At dawn, they'd pick the fresh flowers and add them to the cart, which was drawn by their little moor pony, Bobby.

The afternoon dwindled into evening and candles were lit. They finished packing and ate a simple meal of mutton stew and bread.

Annabelle yawned. The newspaper she was reading, although a few days old, still hadn't been read from front to back, for she simply fell asleep each evening before she could finish it.

'Go on up, lass,' Ma said, banking the fire down for the night. 'We've an early start in the morning.'

Yawning, Annabelle kissed Ma's cheek. 'I'll be up in time.'

'Lass?'

Annabelle turned on the first rung of the ladder that led up to the loft where she slept.

Ma placed the fireguard around the fire. 'Consider Dickie.'

'I am doing,' she replied, noticing the grey exhaustion on Ma's face. 'Shall I just go into the village tomorrow? You can stay home and work in the potting shed.'

Ma seemed to ponder on the suggestion. 'There is a lot to be done in the shed, but you can't handle the cart on your own with Bobby.'

'Of course I can.' For the last year, Annabelle had been doing more of the selling and handling of the produce as each shop-keeper bought their required order.

'I'll decide in the morning.' Ma dismissed her by opening the cupboard near the fireplace and pulling out her bedding, which she used on the old blue velvet chaise longue that had always been her bed in the corner of the room, and which had been repaired more times than Annabelle could count.

In the loft, Annabelle bent slightly so as not to bang her head on the roof and undressed. In the moonlight, she washed herself from the hot water in the jug she'd brought up earlier and which was still warm. The scorching temperature of the day remained trapped in the loft. The one little window cut into the roof shingles did little to allow the heat to escape.

Wearing only her shift, Annabelle stood on a small stool and stuck her head out of the window. An owl hooted from the trees lining the beck and further away the eerie bark of a fox echoed around the quiet countryside. She knew every hollow and dip of the land around the cottage and every tree and bush. She craned her neck to look along the dirt path that led to the village road and noticed a little dark object, a hedgehog, slowly sauntering across it.

Daisy, the milking cow, and Bobby, the little moor pony, were dozing in the small enclosure next to the potting shed and Annabelle prayed the pony wouldn't be cantankerous tomorrow. Sometimes, when he was in a rebellious mood, only Ma could soothe Bobby.

Yawning again, Annabelle stepped off the stool and climbed into bed. After blowing out the candle, she snuggled down in the dipping mattress, a single blanket thrown over her legs.

Should she marry Dickie and make Ma happy? Did she want to be a shepherd's wife with a child every year, living on the estate surrounded by strangers?

Unless Dickie could live here?

But did she want that? There were times when she liked his company so much, but there were also times when she was pleased to see him slap his hat on his head and go home.

Groaning in frustration at what to do, she turned over and thumped the pillow.

Why did she even have to make a decision? She wanted nothing in her life to change.

As an owl hooted again, she closed her eyes, remembering it was Ma's birthday the day after next, and she'd need to buy her something tomorrow.

* * *

'I've put a bunch of carrots in the cart in case Bobby decides to be difficult,' Ma said the following morning as they loaded the small cart attached to Bobby.

A streak of pink showed over the trees in the distance as dawn broke. As the land awoke, birds swooped and dived, their calls adding to Daisy's bellow to be milked.

'He'll get a slap if he starts his nonsense,' Annabelle warned. She eyed the pony, his shaggy coat a mixture of white and cream, and he eyed her back with a toss of his pretty head.

'Now, don't be doing any of that or it'll just be making him fussy even more. Don't lose your temper with him.' Ma stroked his neck. 'Remember, Mrs Arnold wants her order first.'

'Yes, I remember.'

'You look bonny. Smile at Mr Nugent and he'll buy even more.'

'Ma!' She grinned, smoothing down the blue and white printed skirt. The bodice of her dress was cut low for summer and edged with a frill of white lace, the sleeves also short and edged the same.

'Well, is it my fault the man has more brass than sense, I ask you? He sees you and loses what little brains he has.' Ma shrugged as though men and their ways were stupid to her. 'Are you sure you can do this without me?'

'Yes. Haven't I been by your side for twenty-one years?'

'Folk will wonder why I'm not with you.'

'And I'll tell them that you're busy at home.'

'They'll think it odd. Maybe I'll come with you.'

Annabelle gazed at Ma, knowing that even as she said the

words, Ma didn't mean it. 'Go inside and have a cup of tea. I'll be back before you know it.'

'Watch Mr Kilburn's dog, it'll snap at your heels when you knock on the door.'

'I know.' Annabelle double-checked she had everything on the cart and her money in the small leather purse dangling from her wrist. 'By the way, how old will you be tomorrow?'

Ma gave her an irritated glare. 'Younger than the moon and older than my boots. Now, off you go.'

Annabelle laughed at the often-repeated phrase whenever she asked Ma her age. 'See you later.'

'Mind as you go, lass.'

Anne took hold of Bobby's lead rope and he contentedly walked beside her along the path. At the road she turned right towards the village of Hartleydale; left would take her to Hartley Manor's gates and onwards to York. The dirt road followed the curve of the fields flowing out from the Hartley estate. Tenanted farms clung to the edge of the estate's boundary walls, doing their best to eke out livings year in year out. Like Widow Wallis, they depended on the village for sale of their produce and animals, though some of the larger farms sold in York.

With a pale golden light shimmering over the landscape, Annabelle strolled the road, offering a wave to Farmer Lipton who was leaving his farmhouse to start his day of work, his sheepdog beside him. Another cart came down the road, the driver doffing his cap to Annabelle as he passed.

Closer to the village, Annabelle slowed Bobby in front of a whitewashed cottage belonging to Mr Kilburn. From one basket, she took out the bottle of dried bilberry powder and knocked on the old wooden door.

A dog's frantic barking broke the silence and as the door

opened, to much yelling and swearing, the little terrier ran around Annabelle's feet dementedly.

'Will tha shut tha trap, tha mongrel dog!' Mr Kilburn bent with age and arthritic pain, booted the dog back into the house and shut the door. 'Sorry, lass.'

'He's an excited one, for sure.' The terrier could still be heard making a commotion behind the door.

'More trouble than he's worth.'

Annabelle handed the small brown bottle to Mr Kilburn. 'Ma says next month we'll have fresh bilberries to pick, and she'll make you a pie.'

'Thank thee kindly, lass. Widow Wallis not with thee?'

'No, not today. In summer we've too much to do in the potting shed and garden.'

'And it saves her legs.' He smiled in the kind way of old men, his pale eyes watery, his grey whiskers out of control the same as his bushy eyebrows.

'How is your son in Leeds?'

'Fine and well. He wrote to me two days ago and sent me some money for the rent. He's a good boy.'

'Does he still ask you to go and live with him?'

'Aye, but I'll not leave here. I was born in this cottage, and I'll die in it.' Mr Kilburn held out a few pennies to her. 'I've coins left over. Take it.'

'No. Ma wouldn't take your money, and neither am I going to.' She stepped back with a smile. 'You take care now, Mr Kilburn.'

'Oh, lass, next week will you drop by a bottle of willow bark oil for me?'

'Yes, of course. I have some in the cart but it's for Mr Tremaine.'

'Nay, I've enough to last until I see thee again.'

'I'll bring you some, then. Take care.'

'And thee, lass.'

Taking a pencil and paper from the satchel in the cart, Annabelle added willow bark oil for Mr Kilburn.

The village's main street was a hive of industry when she reached it. Shop owners were sweeping the front steps, washing windows and putting out their wares. Annabelle chatted to some, sold from the cart to others before focusing on their regular clients.

Mrs Arnold, the baker's wife, checked her order on the bench in the kitchen behind the bakery. 'Widow Wallis didn't forget my sage. Good. That's a large bunch of rosemary, has she charged me extra for it?'

'No, Mrs Arnold. It's a bit extra for a regular customer.' Annabelle knew how to sweet-talk the rotund woman who baked pies to serve in the bakery alongside the bread.

'Is that so? Delightful.' Mrs Arnold beamed. 'Thyme, fennel, mint... What else do you have in the cart?' Mrs Arnold walked out to the cart and peered at the contents. 'Has anyone ordered something different?'

Annabelle hid a grin. Mrs Arnold liked to be the first customer in the village so she could peep into the baskets and see what everyone had ordered. She was the village gossip and woe betide anyone who did something a little unusual or exciting before she did.

'Mrs Elton has asked for a dandelion root tonic. Her son's got a liver complaint.'

'Her son should give up drinking the volume of ale that he does, that might help.'

Annabelle glanced over at the baskets' contents without replying to that comment. 'Nothing different from our ordinary orders.'

'The dried flower posies are for the church?'

'Yes.'

'What is this?' Mrs Arnold held up a small green bottle.

'Dried heartsease.' She took the bottle from the woman and put it back with the order for Mrs Finch.

'Heartsease is for women's problems, isn't it?' Mrs Arnold pounced like a cat on a rat. 'Whose order is that?'

'I couldn't say, Mrs Arnold. It's private business between us and our client.'

Mrs Arnold folded her arms, her expression one of annoyance. 'I bet it's Mrs Finch. She's always complaining about pains. I doubt that bottle will help. Instead, she should put something in her husband's tea to stop him... well... you know... no, maybe you don't, being an innocent... but, well, eleven babies in fourteen years is just irresponsible.'

'I'd best be off.' Annabelle placed the empty basket in the cart. 'Same order next time?'

'Aye, but add some lavender and a bottle of peppermint tea to the order, too.'

Annabelle wrote it down on the piece of paper and then led Bobby away. Further down the street, she stopped outside Mr Nugent's house. He came at once to her knock, grinning like a fool, despite usually being a serious man of law who was renting his house for a year to write a book.

'Miss Wallis. How wonderful to see you!'

'I have your order. A bottle of borage oil.' She handed him the bottle, and he held her hand within both of his own.

'Will you not come in for a cup of tea?' he insisted.

'No, thank you, but I have much to do.' She gently tugged her hand away.

'I must pay you.' He disappeared inside the house and returned with coins. 'I have been needing to stay awake longer to finish writing my book. What would you suggest for me to take?'

'Um... Well, I would suggest a strong cup of ginger tea and—'

'Do you have some in your cart?' he asked hopefully, taking a step nearer to her.

She leaned back. 'I have ginger, yes. You can add it to your tea. Also, a sniff of rosemary oil will awaken you when you're feeling drowsy.'

'Rosemary oil. Yes, very good. I'll take both the ginger and the rosemary oil.' He walked close beside her as she went back to the cart and selected the items for him. He paid her generously, standing so close to her she could smell the staleness of his breath.

'Thank you, Mr Nugent. See you next week.'

'Ah, Miss Wallis, perhaps after church on Sunday we could go for a walk?' His small eyes didn't blink as he waited for her to answer.

'That's not possible, Mr Nugent. I've promised Dickie Smithers I'd go walking with him,' she lied.

'Indeed.' His face fell. 'Perhaps the Sunday after, or during the week, one afternoon? I'm free each day. I could come to your cottage?'

'No! No, I'm very busy. Busy all day, every day. Good day.' She tugged at Bobby's rope to hurry away. Once away from the house, she burst out laughing.

'He's impossible, isn't he?' a young woman about her own age called to Annabelle from across the road.

'A bit, yes.' Annabelle chuckled.

'I'm sure he's asked every single woman in the village to go walking with him. He's desperate.' The young woman gasped. 'Sorry, I didn't mean he was desperate to pick you! I wasn't being rude. Any man would be lucky to have you with that beautiful hair of yours.'

'I know what you meant.' Annabelle smiled.

The woman let out a breath. 'Me and my big mouth. It's always getting me into trouble. You're Widow Wallis's daughter, aren't you?'

'Yes, Annabelle.'

'I'm Ginny Hilbraith. I'm in service up at Hartley Manor. I've seen you a few times at church and several times walking with Dickie Smithers.'

Annabelle blushed. 'We're just friends.'

Ginny shrugged, pushing a tendril of brown hair into her bonnet. 'I don't blame you if you wanted more. He's a decent fellow.'

'But I don't. Friends is enough for now.'

'Don't keep him hanging too long or he'll find another.'

'You?' she asked defensively.

Ginny laughed, a great loud sound. 'God, no. Me and Dickie? No, thank you. I want to do better than being a shepherd's wife.'

'Me, too!' Annabelle said in surprise. 'I always wondered if I was odd to feel that way.'

Ginny fell into step with her. 'Then you and me are alike in that. All the girls at the manor are gushing about getting a beau, their wedding days, having babies.' Ginny pulled a face. 'I'd rather stay single than settle for any fellow who gives me a wink, you know?'

'I do, yes.'

'And with your handsome looks, you can do better than a shepherd, that's for certain.'

'Thank you,' she replied, embarrassed, for no one had ever spoken to her about her appearance, except the odd occasion when Ma said she looked bonny. Even Dickie didn't mention she was attractive so she assumed she wasn't anything special and most of the time she was digging in the garden and covered in dirt, so who could blame him?

At the corner of the High Street and Bernard Street, they halted.

Ginny sighed, taking off her grey shawl. 'I'd best be getting back. I'm on an errand for Mrs Hartley's lady's maid, Miss Nevin. Mrs Hartley is feeling low in spirits again and Miss Nevin wanted something to pick her up a bit. She asked me to come to the village and find something from the shops, some kind of tonic, as Mrs Hartley's doctor is away in London for a week. Only the shops had the same things we have already tried, like smelling salts.'

'She needs some St John's wort. Ma swears by it for when someone is feeling low in spirit.'

'Do you have some?' Ginny glanced into the cart. 'I have money to pay for it.'

'No. There's none on the cart, but we have some at home. I could make up a bottle and bring it to the manor.'

'No, I'll come and collect it. Miss Nevin doesn't want Mr Hartley finding out his wife still needs her little pick-me-ups.' Ginny's voice lowered. 'Mrs Hartley was liking the laudanum a little too much after the baby was born. Everyone was a bit concerned and Mr Hartley, bless him, threw the bottle away and instructed that no more laudanum was to enter the house.'

'Yes, laudanum can become a problem. Ma stays clear of it when anyone asks for it.'

'I can slip away after luncheon tomorrow, hopefully. If that's all right by you?'

Annabelle nodded. 'I'll have it ready for you. You know of the cottage?'

'Everyone knows Widow Wallis's cottage.' Ginny grinned.

'I'll see you then.'

'Aye, about two.'

When she'd finished dropping off her orders, Annabelle went to the back along the High Street to the Horse and Horn Inn. Pulling Bobby around to the stables at the back, she left him there and went into the inn's scullery.

'It's nice to see you, Annabelle. What can I do for you?' The landlord, Mr Tremaine, was rolling a barrel from the taproom down the narrow aisle to the scullery.

'I'd like to buy a bottle of sweet sherry, please, Mr Tremaine, for Ma. It's her birthday tomorrow.'

'Is that so?' He straightened and winced, rubbing his back. 'I'll make you a deal. Do you happen to have some of that willow tree bark oil?'

Smiling, Annabelle produced a bottle of it. 'I brought you some as I know how much you suffer from your back.'

'Then we'll make a swap. That oil for a bottle of sweet sherry. What do you say?'

'I was hoping to make such a deal.' She laughed.

'A wise young woman you are, Miss Annabelle.'

The exchange done, Annabelle led Bobby out of the stables and onto the street for home. Ma didn't want fripperies and useless tat about the house, but she did enjoy a nice glass of sherry on special occasions.

Satisfied the day had gone well, Annabelle gave Bobby a pat on the neck. 'And you've been a good boy, too.'

Suddenly, Mr Kilburn's terrier ran out from under the fence, barking like a crazy thing. Bobby reared on his stumpy hide legs.

'Whoa!' Annabelle held on to the lead rope as Bobby thrashed his head while the dog snapped and snarled at Bobby's legs.

'That bleedin' mongrel!' Mr Kilburn came hobbling out of his cottage, brandishing a walking stick.

Bobby skipped and pranced sideways, dragging the cart across the road.

'Steady, boy. Steady, boy.' She tried to soothe the pony, but the whites of his eyes showed, and he jerked forward, ripping the rope out of her hands.

Free, Bobby cantered down the road, the terrier chasing after him.

'Stop! Bobby!' Angry, Annabelle took off after him. She rounded the curve in the road which was hidden by a belt of trees and ran up to Bobby, who was being held by a man leaning from his horse.

'Oh, thank you!' Annabelle gushed, torn between anger at Bobby and gratitude to the rider.

The man dismounted, raised his whip to the terrier and yelled at it, which thankfully put him off from attacking Bobby again. The dog ran up the road, turned and gave another vicious bark before running off around the bend.

'You're all right now,' Annabelle spoke in a soft voice to Bobby. 'He's gone.'

Bobby tossed his head and stomped his hooves, agitated.

Annabelle quickly grabbed a carrot and held it out to him. It calmed him enough to stand still.

'Are you injured?' the man asked.

She turned to him, able to focus on him now Bobby didn't look ready to bolt again. Her heart, thumping already at the incident, beat like a drummer's tattoo under her corset. Clear grey eyes stared at her in concern from a face as handsome as she'd ever seen.

'Shall I walk you and your pony home?'

It took a moment for her to speak, to even make her mind work in his presence.

'Miss?' He raised his eyebrows at her, a look of worry in his expression.

'I'm fine...' she whispered, horrified by her reaction to this tall, black-haired stranger who'd come to her rescue.

'Are you certain?'

She nodded, taking in his well-cut suit of expensive fawn-coloured material, his brown polished riding boots, the white cravat at his throat, the strong jawline...

'Then I'll be on my way.' He hesitated, as though expecting her to faint at his feet any moment.

She swallowed, blinked rapidly, and gathered her scattered wits. 'Thank you for your help,' she said in a rush and blushed.

He smiled slowly, a smile that reached his eyes. 'What is your name?'

'Annabelle Wallis.'

He bowed. 'John Hartley, at your service.' After a lingering look, he turned and swiftly mounted his horse and cantered out of sight.

Letting out a slow breath, Annabelle tugged on the rope for Bobby to walk on. Her mind replayed the meeting. 'So, that is Mr John Hartley, then...'

2

John Hartley rode down the beech-lined drive of Hartley Manor, the dazzling sun provided dappled shade, giving some respite from the heat. Still, he preferred to be riding horseback than in a hot, stuffy carriage. The deer park to the right of him was bare of animals and humans, but to the left, behind the high-walled garden, hammering rang out.

The drive curved in a long, graceful arch, affording all guests a view of the splendid two-storied sandstone house that had been built by his ancestors three hundred years ago. Over the centuries, wings on either side of the main building had been added as the family's wealth grew. Luscious gardens, sweeping lawns and specimen trees from around the world created a soft mellow frame to the house. A home that he'd not seen for years.

Dismounting at the front steps, John nodded to the groom who came running from around the side of the house, and whose job it was to take family and guests' horses through the arch between the house and service areas and care for them in the stables.

'She's hired,' John told the lad, not recognising him. 'She needs to go back to Jones's Livery, Tanner Row, in York.'

'Yes, sir.'

John paused before going inside and gazed around. Not a lot had changed in the seven years he'd been away. Perhaps some of the trees had grown taller, new garden beds made, but red geraniums grew in the large pots on either side of the steps just as they always had done in summer since he was a boy. And, of course, old Havers, the family butler, opened the door.

'Mr John.' Havers stood in shock. 'We weren't expecting you, sir. Welcome home.'

'It's good to be home.' John smiled. The butler knew the family better than they knew themselves, having been in service at the manor since he was a boy, seventy years ago.

'You've been missed, sir. It's been too long.'

John stepped into the house and gave his gloves and hat to Havers. 'I am glad you are still around, Havers.'

'Only a grave would be my next home, sir.'

John noted the new green silk wallpaper above the wood panelling in the wide entrance. New red carpet swept up the staircase in front of him. Though the same paintings hung on the wall and flowers still filled the crystal vases on the centre hall table.

'Did you have a good journey, sir?'

'Yes, tolerable. The train journey was interesting. I was able to see the changes in the countryside and towns as I made my way north. Though, riding on the road to the village, I nearly collided with a runaway horse.'

'Oh dear, sir, were you hurt?'

'No. I managed to avoid the animal and actually stop the pony and cart.'

'Pony and cart?'

'Yes. A shaggy-looking pony pulling a small cart.'

'Ah, Widow Wallis, I would presume, sir.'

'I remember Widow Wallis as an old woman, the young woman chasing after the pony certainly was not Widow Wallis.'

'It'll be her ward, sir.'

'Her ward?' John mused, barely remembering that Widow Wallis had taken in an orphaned baby.

'Will you be staying long, sir?' Havers asked.

'Yes. I have spent six months in London, and I am in no rush to return there. I am home for a while.'

'Very good, sir. I'll have your room prepared. Will I need to engage a valet for you?'

'No, thank you, Havers. I am happy to share you with my brother, or an under-butler will do.'

'Your trunks?'

'They should be arriving within the hour from the train station. I rode on ahead. I need to go up to wash and change. I take it my old clothes have remained?'

Havers smiled. 'Indeed, sir. Nothing has been removed from your room. However, may I remind you, sir, that when you left Hartley Manor seven years ago, you were a young man of twenty-three...'

Grinning, John took a step towards the staircase. 'Are you suggesting, Havers, that I've grown fat?'

The old butler jerked. 'Fat? Forgive me, sir. No, not at all. You have no fat on you, sir. I merely meant that seven years ago, your shoulders weren't as wide as they are now. You may find your shirts uncomfortable.'

'Just a wash it is, then. I'll change when my trunks arrive.'

'Very good, sir. I'll send up some warm-water jugs.'

John mounted the stairs but turned back halfway up. 'Havers, where were my things put that I have sent home over the years?'

'In the east wing, sir. So much arrived that we gave a whole room to it. The former Rose Bedroom holds your treasures.'

'Thank you.'

Making his way along the gallery, John noticed nothing had changed. His ancestors' portraits lined the walls. He paused to look at one painted of himself, Des and Arthur when they were boys in frilly white shirts and knee-length breeches. His sister, Eliza, hadn't been born then. At his feet, painted in an adoring pose, was his black Labrador, Dash, who had refused to leave him as they were being painted and so the artist included Dash in the scene. How he had loved that dog. They'd been a pair. Always together before he went to school, and returning home on holidays he knew Dash would be waiting at the door for him.

He would get a dog again now he was home. That decided, he walked along to his bedroom, which remained exactly as he left it. Green patterned wallpaper covered the walls and the bed's rich bronze brocade cover was neat and flat. The maids obviously dusted the furniture, but his childhood belongings still lined the shelves, then, as he had grown older, added to those knick-knacks were more serious books on geography and history. His writing desk's drawers were filled with old letters, paper and ink, envelopes and diaries.

Opening the wardrobe doors, he studied the shirts and trousers hanging up. Taking out one white shirt, he put it up against his chest and, yes, Havers was right. He'd grown wider while being away. Likely all those hours hacking away the jungles in India and Africa. The rowing along rivers in America, trekking in Switzerland and all the other adventures he'd enjoyed.

A knock preceded a footman who brought up two jugs and held fresh towels over his arm. 'Your water, sir.' The young man, tall and immaculately dressed in black livery, placed the jugs on the wash-stand by the window.

John didn't know him. 'Thank you. You are?'

'Stevens, sir, the first footman. Mr Havers told me that I am to be your valet, unless you'd prefer Mr Havers himself?'

'No, no. You will do fine. Thank you, Stevens. I would like a bath before dinner, please. My luggage should be arriving any time.'

'Very good, sir. I'll see to it.'

'Oh, and my old shirts hanging up. They do not fit. You may have them, if you wish. I will leave that up to you to sort out.'

'That's kind of you, sir. Thank you.'

Left alone, John washed and tidied himself. He would have liked to change his travelling clothes, but it would have to wait.

Downstairs, John wandered the drawing room, picking up a small book of poetry and putting it down again.

Havers came to stand at the opened double doors to wait for any instructions.

'Where is my brother?' John asked him, glancing up at the portrait of his mother. Elizabeth Hartley had been a beautiful, delicate woman. Small, only five feet tall, and petite. How she'd bred three strapping sons, John didn't know. The portrait showed her as a married woman and mother, yet somehow, she kept her youthful looks, the dark hair and clear grey eyes John had inherited.

'Mr Hartley is visiting the Home Farm today.'

It took a second for John to accept that Mr Hartley was Desmond and not his father. He hadn't heard Desmond addressed that way before, but naturally he would be now he was head of the family.

John gazed at the portraits of his father and mother, painted not long after their marriage. His mother had died three years ago and his father two years ago. John had been away for both of their deaths. He'd missed their funerals, the shared family grief. He'd also missed Desmond's wedding to Penny.

Instead, he'd been travelling the globe. Exploring countries most people only read about. His last stop had been India to meet up with his brother Arthur. They spent as much time as they could hunting, drinking, partying until Arthur's regiment was posted to the south of India and John finally sailed home to England.

On arriving in London, he'd found Eliza at their Mayfair townhouse, ready to start her season with Desmond to chaperone her, but Des, as they all called him, wanted to return to Yorkshire and the estate and his wife, who was due to give birth to their first baby. John became the one to escort Eliza to balls and soirées, to accompany her on rides in the parks, garden parties and to the theatre. At first, he'd enjoyed the entertainments, meeting new people and reaffirming old friendships.

Eventually, though, after six months, the dizzying round of activities grew stale. He became tired of seeing the same faces and hearing the same tales. He was champing at the bit to leave London society and go home, too. Thankfully, Aunt Martha, their mother's sister, took Eliza into her own home and, much to Eliza's happiness, she was allowed to stay in London.

'Oh!' a female voice gasped.

John spun on his heel and bowed.

The woman, only in her mid-twenties and dressed in a gown of pale mauve linen edged with white lace, studied him. 'John?'

'Yes. It's lovely to meet you at last, sister-in-law.' He walked to Penelope Hartley, his brother's wife, and kissed her on both cheeks.

'And you, dear brother. I knew I would recognise you. You look like your dear mama.' She glanced up at her mother-in-law's portrait. 'Yes. You have her eyes.' She turned to Havers. 'Tea, please.'

He bowed and left them.

Penny fiddled with her lace sleeve. 'Shall I send for Des?'

'No, leave him to his business. I am home now. We have plenty of time to talk.' John waited for Penny to sit on the blue-and-cream-striped sofa. 'You are well? Des wrote to Eliza and myself that the birth weakened you considerably.'

'I am gaining strength every day.' She arranged her skirts neatly. 'Being with child and then the birth, well, it was harder than I imagined. But I shan't bore you with such intimate details.' She smiled self-consciously.

'How is my niece?' He sat on the leather wingback chair opposite her.

'Clementine is beautiful, naturally.' Penny smiled softly. 'I suppose all mothers say that, but it's true. Clemmie is adorable. Shall we have some tea and then go up and see her?'

'I would like that.'

'Des will be so happy you are home. Are you glad to be back?'

'I am. I did not think I would be as pleased as I am. I have enjoyed my time away, but... on hearing of Papa's death while in India, I believed it was time I returned.'

'Perhaps with you home, I will see more of my husband,' she murmured.

Guilt filtered through him. 'I will play my part in running the family businesses. I know from speaking to Des in London that Papa had extended his interests greatly before his death.'

'Yes. He was excited when Des and I married and when I became with child...' Her face fell. 'Sadly, we lost that baby only a few weeks after the doctor told me I was with child.'

'Yes, Des wrote and told me.'

'Anyway, your papa decided that the next generation would need more... well, more of everything. He told me once that having four surviving children was a great blessing to him, but also worrying as they needed to be provided for and this estate wouldn't be enough as it had been for him, being an only child, and his father before him.'

John relaxed against the softened leather. This had been his father's chair and he felt close to him sitting in it. 'Des told me that Papa had invested widely, road building, shipping, a mill, property.'

'Yes, indeed. I do not know all the details,' she waved a hand as though she didn't want to know, 'but Des has been spending a great deal of time squirrelled away in his study or away at Rosewood Hall, a run-down sheep farm, up on the moors, north of here somewhere. We cannot fathom why your father bought it, the state it is in. Not that I have been there, but Des tells me it needs much work done to it.'

'Papa enjoyed the country far more than the city. I am much like him in that respect.'

'Apparently, your papa had a wild idea of moving to Rosewood and leaving Des and I here to manage the estate. Des would not hear of it, of course.' She sat forward as Havers and a maid brought in the trays of tea, sandwiches and cakes.

John glanced at the maid, not knowing her. In some respects, he felt a little out of place. Once, he'd known all the staff inside the manor and out.

'No doubt Des will fill you in on all the business. I can tell you now, John, that he works too hard.' Penny poured the tea and passed his cup over.

'But not for much longer. I can ease some of the burden from his shoulders.'

'Thank you. He was so relieved to hand Eliza over to you and come home, especially when he has so much to do here. The London social scene is not really for him.'

'Nor me.' John rolled his eyes. 'Being a bachelor myself, suddenly too much attention was on me, too.'

'Poor you. It is a wonder you did not come home with a bride.'

'God forbid!' He ate one of the tiny tarts, suddenly ravenous.

The image of the girl in the road earlier came to mind, but before he could think more on it, Havers appeared again.

'Sir, your luggage has arrived. It's being taken upstairs.'

'Thank you, Havers.'

'John!' Des boomed from the doorway. Des – tall, solidly built – strode over and shook John's hand before kissing his wife. 'Is it good to be finally home?' he asked. 'And what do you make of Penny? Is she not just delightful?' Des beamed down at his wife.

'Stop it, Des. You will embarrass poor John.' She poured a cup of tea for her husband.

John ate another tart. 'My sister-in-law adds to this family in beauty and grace.'

Penny blushed and waved away his comments.

'It is true,' John defended, grinning. 'You were lucky to secure such a woman, brother.'

'Indeed, I was.' Des chuckled, sitting next to Penny. 'Will it be your turn soon or shall you remain a bachelor as we fear?'

'You were thirty when you married,' John reminded him. 'I have only just turned thirty myself last week. I have time.'

'Of course you do,' Penny championed. 'We shall find you a lovely lady, won't we, Des?'

Des held up his hands. 'Leave me out of it. I have enough to worry about trying to investigate all the young bucks that have written regarding Eliza.'

'Are there any she is keen on?' Penny asked them both.

'There were only one or two she thought to consider,' John said. 'Neville Cunningham and Frederick McKinley. Have you received letters from them?'

Des shook his head. 'That sister of ours has received several offers of marriage and she has rejected them all.'

'She is having fun. Leave her be,' Penny said, sipping her tea.

'She is beautiful and young and so full of life. Why would she take the first offer?'

'It is true that the ones she has rejected are from older men,' Des mused.

John stared into his cup. His thoughts on Eliza differed. He felt she needed marriage, the sooner the better. For months, he'd watched her flirt with every man in her vicinity. No male was immune to her fluttering eyes and endearing smile. She bantered and joked with them all, young or old, high or low born. No man was ignored. Eliza was becoming a little wild and reckless and he needed to talk to Des about it.

'Well, I have some work to do in the study.' Des stood and replaced his cup and saucer on the tray. 'There is much for us to discuss, John, but we shall start on it tomorrow. Have today, as it will be your last day of freedom,' he jested.

'I told you in my letter. I am ready to do my bit.'

Des's expression sobered. 'Good, for I need you.'

'I am taking John up to see Clemmie,' Penny said.

'Yes, she needs to meet and get to know her uncle. At least she will have one of them around while she is growing up.' Des sighed.

'Shall we go up?' Penny asked John.

In the large nursery, a nurse was ironing the tiny white clothes Clemmie wore while Perkins, the nanny, fed Clemmie some oatmeal.

'Look, darling, your Uncle John is here,' Penny cooed at the baby, who smiled instantly.

Nanny Perkins stood to attention at the side of the baby's high chair while Penny took her place and fed her daughter.

'She is a cherub.' John lightly kissed the top of Clemmie's head. 'I have had little to do with babies, but she must be the prettiest one I have seen.' He watched Penny feed the baby, who had the Hartley dark hair, and the chubby rosy cheeks babies had.

'I think she may have a tooth soon, madam,' Nanny Perkins told them with pride.

'A tooth.' Penny kissed Clemmie's cheek. 'What a clever girl you are.'

After another ten minutes in the nursery, which had been fully redecorated since John was a child, he and Penny walked along the gallery.

'Are you busy for the next hour?' he asked her.

'No. I have rebuffed all callers for another week.'

'May I ask why?'

She sighed deeply. 'I have not been feeling myself. I have been incredibly low in spirit since the birth. I cannot tell you why, for I do not have the answers. I have a healthy child and should be grateful, but there are days when getting out of bed is a challenge and I find no enjoyment in anything.'

'I am sorry to hear that.'

'Today is a good day.' She smiled reassuringly. 'And I am pleased about that with you returning home. Maybe now my spirits will be lifted having another family member in the house. I wish Eliza would come home, too, for she always cheers me up. She is so full of life.'

'She is that,' he said wryly. 'Would you care to see some of the things I sent home from my travels?'

'Indeed, I would. Ever since I moved into the manor, I have been wondering what were in the crates you sent home. Eliza wrote and told me you had given her some beautiful things when you arrived in London.'

'Yes, I had a trunk of gifts with me.' John led the way to the Rose Bedroom. 'I have brought it with me for there are presents for you and Des and Clemmie, which I shall unpack later, but I am eager to see what I sent home over the years, for I am sure I have forgotten what I bought.'

'How exciting. Eliza wrote that you had presented her with two mother-of-pearl hair combs from India, a perfume set from Egypt, bolts of silk from China.'

'Yes.' He laughed, opening the bedroom door. 'I enjoyed purchasing gifts.' He stopped on the threshold and stared in shock at the number of crates and trunks piled in the room.

Penny stood next to him. 'Yes. You certainly *did* enjoy buying things.'

'I had no idea it was so much.' He gazed around the room. The bed had been removed to make space for the crates and trunks.

'When you have a home of your own, at least you will not be short of items to fill the rooms. I will ring for a footman to bring some tools to open the crates.'

John ran a hand over the nearest trunk, remembering the day he had it shipped from New York. He knew it held a woven blanket he'd bought from a native Indian when he'd travelled west, an American-style saddle...

'You know that in your mama's sitting room, she kept all your letters and postcards?'

His heart twisted with loss. He missed his parents dreadfully. 'Mama used to get so frustrated with me because I did not stay in one place long enough for her letters to reach me.'

'She died only weeks after Des and I started courting. I only met her twice, but with each visit I could tell how much she loved her children. She was terribly proud of you being out in the world, exploring.'

'Perhaps I should have been home instead. I did not think she would be gone so soon. I thought I had years left with her. That I could travel and come home and tell her all my stories of everything I had seen and done.'

'She had your letters. I imagine she would not have wanted you home to sit by her bedside as she grew weaker.'

'No, she would have hated that,' he murmured.

Penny smiled brightly. 'No more talk of sad things. You are home and the world is inside these trunks. I want to see it!'

He straightened and banished the memories from his mind. Later, he would read the letters he sent to his mama, but not today.

3

Annabelle set out the breakfast, paying extra attention to Ma's place at the end of the table. She filled a small vase with flowers, and brought out the best china, which had been a wedding present to Ma and her husband fifty years ago. Sadly, some of the service had broken over the years, but the flower pattern remained cheerfully bright.

Mashing the tea, Annabelle set the teapot on the table and then concentrated on cooking the best eggs and bacon Ma had ever eaten. She knew she'd be tired after being at the Bransons' house all night delivering Mrs Branson's fifth baby. Annabelle had gone with her yesterday evening and helped deliver the baby or, more accurately, she'd been Ma's helper. However, after the birth, Mrs Branson had run a fever and Ma had told Annabelle to go home to rest and she would stay the night and monitor both mother and baby.

The back door opened, and Ma plodded in, grey-faced with fatigue. 'That looks bonny, lass,' she commented on the table setting.

'Happy birthday.'

'Thank you, sweet girl.' Ma hung her shawl over the nail on the back door. 'Breakfast smells good. I'm hungry.'

'Sit down. How are Mrs Branson and the baby?'

'Both well. Mrs Branson's fever went down at dawn and the baby slept a good four hours before needing a feed. I've left them to it, but I said I'd go back and check on them this afternoon. I'll need to take more honey and ginger tea for Mrs Branson. They can't afford to buy such things as ginger and honey themselves. Mr Branson is out of work most of the time.'

'You'll have a nap first?' Annabelle poured her a cup of tea.

'Aye. I'll have something to eat and then get my head down for a bit. Will you make up a willow bark tonic for Mrs Branson?'

'Shall we give her a bottle of our elderflower cordial as well?' Annabelle plated up their eggs and bacon and brought it to the table.

'Aye, I was about to suggest that. The poor woman needs her strength building up.'

'I met one of the maids, Ginny, from the manor in the village yesterday and she was saying Mrs Hartley is low in spirits.'

'Aye, I heard the birth didn't go well. Took a long time to be born, did the little lass.' Ma ate a forkful of bacon. 'Some women have a rough time of it.'

'I said to Ginny to come here, and I'd give her some St John's wort.'

'Did you now?' Ma gave her a raised eyebrow of concern.

'It's all on the quiet. I doubt Mrs Hartley's doctor would care for her maid to be meddling. But Ginny knew she had to do something to help.' Annabelle dipped a piece of bread into her yolk. 'Did I do right?'

Ma nodded. 'Old Dr Henderson is a good man but what does he know of women's problems or how women's bodies feel after giving birth, or our thoughts for that matter? If Mrs Hartley is low in spirit, then she must be given something to pick her up again. Dr Henderson is likely to humour her and say she will be well in time. The best he'd do is give her advice to journey to one of the spa towns and take the waters or go south to somewhere warm for a rest.'

Finishing her breakfast, Ma leaned back in the chair, fighting a yawn. 'This was nice.' She touched the flowers gently. 'You always make a fuss of me.'

'Why wouldn't I?' Annabelle topped up Ma's teacup.

'I suppose it still surprises me that you care about an old woman.'

She frowned. 'Of course I care. You're my mother. You've cared for me all my life.'

'But you must wonder what might have been if your real mother had lived?'

'Sometimes. At odd times I see myself in the mirror and wonder if my mother looked like me.'

'She did. She was just as pretty as you, but she had made some bad choices, lass.'

'It was lucky she had you to turn to.'

'I was the only person she had, the only friend, so she said. Your father had duped her and then abandoned you both.'

'Not a nice person, then, and someone I don't want to think about.' Annabelle shrugged. 'Would it be wise for me to spend my time wishing things had been different? I don't think so. Besides, I have you and a lovely home here. I don't want anything else.'

'Lass, I won't always be around. I'm an old woman. This is my seventy-first year.'

Her eyes widened. Ma had never told her how old she was.

'So, you see. My time left isn't as long as we'd both hope.'

'Why are you talking like this?' She pushed back her chair and started to clear the table. 'You're tired. Have a nap.'

'Lass.' Ma's gnarled hand clasped over Annabelle's. 'You know this cottage belongs to the manor. I have it for my lifetime, rent-free. I was married to Jem Wallis, as you know, the head groom at the manor until he was killed when the carriage overturned.'

Annabelle plopped down on the chair. She knew the cottage belonged to the estate and about Jem's death, but she sensed Ma had more to say.

'When the accident happened, I was pregnant with our second child. Our eldest boy had died the year before, only a few months old.' Ma's gaze became distant as she talked. 'Inside the carriage was Mrs Hartley. She was badly hurt, trapped. I had been walking across the fields when I saw the accident happen. The axle broke as the carriage turned the corner. I ran to help. There was no one else around.' Ma paused for a moment. 'I saw Jem was dead. His neck broken, his eyes staring up at the sky.'

Annabelle gasped. Ma had never spoken of the details before.

'I heard screams and so I ran to the carriage which was upside down in a ditch. Mrs Hartley couldn't get out. I worked hard to free her. I tried to lift the carriage, stupid thing to try to do. The doors were smashed, and I kicked them in some more to make a hole big enough for me to crawl into. Mrs Hartley was bleeding from the chest and head. I did my best to stem the flow. I knew I couldn't leave her to get help. If I took the pressure off the wounds, she'd bleed to death. So, I stayed with her for hours in the cramped upside-down carriage. I suffered labour pains and Mrs Hartley realised what was happening. She told me to go, but I couldn't leave her.'

Ma played with her teaspoon. 'Finally, we heard voices and shouts. Eventually, we were rescued, but it was too late.'

'Too late?'

'Mrs Hartley survived, but I went into labour, far too soon. That day I lost my husband and my second son.'

'Oh, Ma.' Annabelle embraced her, desperately sad for the trauma she must have suffered. To lose a husband and baby on the same day would've been shattering.

Ma let her hold her for only a moment before she gently pushed her away. 'Mr Hartley, the current Mr Hartley's grandfather, gave me this cottage for life as a reward for saving his wife's life.'

'That is the least you deserved.'

Wiping her eyes tiredly, Ma stared at her. 'Lass, it means that when I am dead, this cottage reverts back to the Hartley estate.'

She blinked, taking in the words. 'I'll have to leave?'

'Aye.'

The blow hit Annabelle like a fist in the stomach. To leave her home? The delightful cottage and all the gardens, the beck, the trees...

'You need to think hard on what you want to do, lass.'

'There's time for all that,' she blurted out, taking the plates to the stone sink to wash. The shock made her hands shake.

'No, lass. There isn't time. I'm old and my health is failing.'

'No, it isn't. You're fine!' she snapped, not wanting to acknowledge that Ma might be gone one day soon. She couldn't bear to think about Ma not being with her. She was the only family she had.

'Annabelle.'

She bowed her head but didn't turn around.

'Listen to me, lass. I don't know how much time I have, but we have to make plans for you.'

'It's your birthday. Why are we talking so maudlin? Have your nap.' Annabelle walked outside into the bright sunshine. Her mind swirled with the knowledge that she'd have to leave the cottage one day. What would she do when the time came?

Meandering through the garden beds, her fingers trailed over the bushes. Birds chirped in the branches above her head, enjoying the summer's day. By the edge of the beck, she squatted down in the dabbled shade to gaze at the trickling water, but its beauty was painful today. She'd never expected she'd have to leave here. She thought as long as the rent was paid, the cottage would be her home, even when she married. She had fully expected her husband to move in here and they'd raise their children in the same happy way she had been brought up.

Those dreams seemed childish now. She'd been naïve. A silly girl who needed to grow up. Life was never that easy and she had to be brave and think of a future without Ma in it, as difficult as that was.

'Good day!' Ginny called from the slope on the other side of the beck.

Annabelle straightened and waved. She'd forgotten Ginny was calling. She watched as Ginny leapt over the stepping stones and crossed the water to where Annabelle stood.

'Isn't this a lovely place?' Ginny smiled, looking around, then she noticed Annabelle's sad expression. 'What's wrong?'

'Ma has just told me that when she dies, I'll have to leave the cottage. It goes back to the estate,' she blurted out, not knowing why she was telling a stranger. Her thoughts and emotions were tumbling inside her, frightening her in their intensity.

'That's a shame.' Ginny rubbed Annabelle's arm. 'But she isn't likely to die soon, is she?'

'I don't know. She's an old woman. Seventy-one. Who knows how long she has at that age?'

'My, that's old, but she could live for a few years yet,' Ginny said with a positive tone. 'Cheer up. It's not something you have to worry about today, is it?'

'I think it's something I need to worry about every day now I know that I'll have to leave this place one day. I've been stupid, thinking it would be my home forever.' She sighed.

'You're being hard on yourself. When we are happy, we don't want things to change.' Ginny gave her an encouraging smile. 'Just enjoy the time you do have here while you can. Life has a way of working things out. It's full of twists and turns, I should know. I work in a big house full of servants and some of the awful and sad stories I hear, well, it's incredible, but things can get better for all of us. We just have to take one day at a time, don't we?'

'Yes, I suppose. Thank you for listening. You must find me a little strange to be unburdening myself on you. We barely know one another.'

'Then we shall be friends, and friends tell each other everything,' Ginny joked.

'I'd like that.' Annabelle's mood lightened. Ginny as a friend was an unexpected surprise. 'How's your mistress doing?'

'A bit better, actually. Mr John is back from his travels and that seems to have lifted her spirits up. He makes her laugh and we've not heard her laugh in a long time.'

'I saw him, Mr Hartley, yesterday. Our pony, Bobby, bolted and Mr Hartley stopped him.' She led the way through the garden to the cottage.

'Oh, he's ever so kind and good-looking. He's the handsomest of the three brothers.' Ginny grinned.

At the back door, she hesitated. 'Ma's asleep. She was out all night delivering a baby. I'll go and get the St John's wort.'

'Thank you,' Ginny whispered.

Returning with the small brown bottle, Annabelle gave it to Ginny and told her the instructions on how to administer it.

'Right. Got it. I'd best go before they realise I'm missing.'

They walked back down to the beck together, Ginny commenting on the size of the garden.

Ginny paused to sniff a rose. 'You know, if you have to leave here, you could always go into service. Work at the manor?'

'It's an option, yes.' Though the thought alarmed her a little. She'd never worked for anyone before.

'Or marrying Dickie Smithers?' Ginny teased.

Annabelle grimaced. 'I could...'

Ginny laughed. 'It's servitude, no matter which one you pick, but being married means you have a bit more freedom than a servant.'

'I just want everything to stay the same.' She shrugged, scared that her future was so uncertain. She silently prayed Ma would live for another ten years or more.

'That never happens.' Ginny leapt along the stepping stones to the other bank. 'I'll see you on Sunday at church. I'll sit next to you, if you want?'

'I'd like that.' Annabelle waved. She'd made a female friend for the first time in her life. Now she had two friends, Ginny and Dickie. Only, Dickie wanted more than just friendship and she didn't believe she could give him more. She'd worry about that another day. Today's revelations were more than enough to cope with.

* * *

John ran his hand down the stallion's foreleg and lifted the hoof to inspect it. Neatly trimmed and freshly shod. He dropped the leg and stepped back to study the horse's stance.

'What is your opinion?' Des asked, patting the horse's shiny chestnut rump. 'He is a beauty.'

'I shall ride him, if I may?' John asked the horse breeder who'd brought five horses to him with a view to purchasing one.

'Certainly, sir.' The man gave the reins to John. 'Put him through his paces, sir.'

'I may be gone a while, then.' John mounted easily, settling his weight into the saddle and allowing the horse to adjust to him on his back. 'What is his name?'

'He's called Dash, sir, for as a young colt he always dashed about the stable yard.'

John sat very still. Dash. Like his old dog. He didn't believe in signs but perhaps he should start. 'I shall be back in an hour.'

He clicked his tongue and trotted out of the stable block's gates and into the fields surrounding the back of the manor. Dash pulled at the bit and tossed his head and for a moment he skipped sideways.

'Steady on, boy. It is just you and me now.' John patted his neck and steered him around the deer park and towards the open grazing fields stretching towards the village.

Flocks of sheep and their lambs scattered out of their way and John encouraged Dash to have his head. The stallion needed no second bidding and lengthened his stride, eating up the ground as they raced through the long grass. The enjoyment of the ride exhilarated John. He'd not ridden at such pace since challenging Arthur to a race in India, over a year ago.

He rode over the fields skirting the village and around the Home Farm, slowing Dash gently as they circled back towards the manor. The blazing sun burned them and made John thirsty. He guided Dash to the beck on the edge of the estate's grazing fields. Down a grassy slope, he dismounted in the shade of tall trees and led Dash to drink at the cool water.

On the other side of the beck, he noticed a cottage and remembered it was Widow Wallis's cottage. The woman who had saved his grandmother's life fifty years ago. Movement caught his eye and, in the garden, bent over hoeing, was the young woman he had met on the road.

Watching her, John studied the way she moved, gracefully, her actions fluid, rhythmic. She swiped at a fly and pushed her hair, the colour of the wheat in the fields, under her bonnet.

Suddenly she looked straight at him, her surprise rendering her still. He waved, not wanting to alarm her. Slowly, she walked through the garden beds to the grassy area on the other side of the beck.

'Forgive me, I did not wish to startle you,' he said, taking off his hat and running his fingers through his hair. She was a beauty. Her complexion clear, eyes bright and he studied the graceful lines of her neck. Abruptly, he was hot and bothered and he considered that was more to do with seeing her than the gallop.

'We meet again, Mr Hartley.'

'You remember me?' he asked, surprised and delighted.

'I do, yes.' She smiled shyly.

'And you are Miss Wallis.' Her beautiful smile caught him unawares, jolting him.

She nodded. 'Annabelle.'

He liked her name. It suited her. He couldn't tear his gaze from her. She wore an old brown dress, but it didn't detract from her beauty, which was wholesome, yet refined. She was taller than his sister, but not too tall. Her limbs slim, her waist slender, and he knew from their first meeting that her eyes were hazel, shot with amber. How had he remembered such detail in only a few moments? But he had. She'd caught his attention and he wanted to learn more about her.

'You have a well-kept cottage,' he said, inwardly groaning at the ridiculous words. Why hadn't he spoken of something intelligent? At least he hadn't resorted to mentioning the weather!

'Thank you. Our home is a source of great pride to us. But the gardens are our living, and we work long hours to maintain them.'

'And it shows. Has your pony recovered from his ordeal?'

'Yes, very much. Thank you again for stopping him. I doubt he'd have slowed down until he reached home, and goodness knows what state the cart would have been in then.'

'I am pleased I was of help.'

'Would you care for a drink? Your horse seems thirsty enough.'

John grinned. Dash hadn't lifted his head from the water. 'I would enjoy that very much.'

'I'll be back shortly.'

He watched her return to the cottage and disappear inside. An old woman, obviously Widow Wallis, came out of a shed, peered at him and then went back to her work.

He pulled Dash's head up as Annabelle came back to him. She lightly skipped the stepping stones, not spilling a drop from the jug she carried. Her bonnet fell down her back, revealing a mass of hair held up with combs. He desperately wanted to take the combs out and see it fall about her shoulders.

'It's elderberry cordial,' she told him, head down, pouring him a glassful.

'Thank you.' He reached for the glass and their fingers touched. A tingle of awareness shot up his arm and tightened his chest. Every part of him became alert, conscious of her.

Her own chest heaved above her scallop-shaped bodice. Up close, John saw the blush on her cheeks, staining them rose. Her mouth opened lightly, and her teeth worried her bottom lip. His groin stirred. She didn't even understand what effect she had on him. God, he didn't need this sudden desire to grip him.

He took a step back and downed the drink in one go. He thrust the glass back at her. 'Thank you.'

Alarmed at his reaction to the girl, he slapped on his hat, gathered the reins and swung up onto Dash's back.

'He's a splendid-looking horse,' she said.

John sat stiffly in the saddle and gazed down at her. He desperately wanted to leave for his own sanity, only he wanted to stay, too. 'Do you ride?'

She shook her head with a secretive smile that went straight to his heart. 'No, we only have Bobby, who you met last week.' She gestured to the field next to the shed where the pony dozed in the sun.

He barely glanced in the direction of the pony, for he wanted to keep staring at this picture of loveliness before him. 'Thank you again for the refreshment.'

A sharp tap of his heels into Dash made the horse jerk into motion. They bounded up the slope and away from the beck and Annabelle Wallis.

John gritted his teeth, putting Dash into a gallop back to the stables. What was wrong with him? Had it been so long since he had a woman that he went weak at the knees for a village maid? He was a fool. He'd secured a mistress for the six months he'd been in London, surely he wasn't that sexually starved?

As he rode closer to the stables, he knew that it wasn't just sex that he craved, but a young blonde woman with hazel eyes. How utterly inconvenient!

4

'Can you believe this weather?' Mrs Arnold asked Ma and Annabelle as they came out of church on Sunday. 'Such hot days for weeks on end.'

'Aye, but there'll be a storm soon.' Ma nodded wisely, though above their heads the sun shone from a clear blue sky.

Annabelle searched the gathering as they piled out of the church and shook Reverend Marr's hand. The manor's servants were coming out, and she spotted Ginny, who waved and hurried over.

'Sorry I couldn't sit with you. We were late getting here,' Ginny gushed. 'How are you?'

'I'm well, and you?' Annabelle walked up the path with Ginny to the gate.

'Loving life as usual.' Ginny grinned.

Annabelle liked Ginny's sunny manner. 'How is Mrs Hartley? Did you give the bottle to her lady's maid?'

'Aye, I did. She does seem better. This is the first time Mrs Hartley has attended church since the baby was born. So, she must be feeling better. Miss Nevin was grateful for the St John's wort and said to thank you for it. I look good in Miss Nevin's eyes, too. She's agreed to teach me how to be a lady's maid so if she's ever sick, I can take her place helping the mistress.'

'I'm pleased Mrs Hartley is feeling better.'

'Having Mr John home had cheered her no end. Though it was all happening at the house this morning.'

'Why? What was going on?' Annabelle experienced a trickle of excitement that Ginny might mention John Hartley. Since the day by the beck when they had chatted and she'd given him a drink, that's all she could think about, which was silly really, for a man such as he wouldn't think twice about her. She searched the crowd for him, but Ginny was talking.

Ginny leaned in close to whisper. 'There's word that Miss Eliza Hartley has caused some scandal in London.'

'Scandal?'

'Aye. We don't know all the ins and outs of it, but Miss Nevin heard it from Mrs Knowles, the housekeeper, that Mr Hartley and Mr John will have to go to London on the morning train and try to sort it out, whatever it is. Miss Nevin has been trying to find out more information as she dressed Mrs Hartley this morning, but Mrs Hartley only spoke of new dresses she needed to order for the autumn.'

'Oh dear. It must be bad if both Mr Hartleys have to go.' Annabelle tried to find John Hartley in the dispersing crowd.

'Miss Eliza is a bit wild, always has been, but so nice, too. I once had a toothache, and she noticed I was near crying with it as I was cleaning her bedroom, and she insisted I go up to bed. Later, she came up to the attics and visited me. Actually, sat by *my* bed. Isn't that kind?'

'It is.' Annabelle's stomach flipped as a small family group moved away and there, standing next to Reverend Marr, was John Hartley, along with his brother and sister-in-law. He wasn't facing her, and she willed him to turn around and notice her. Would he wave and acknowledge her or pretend he didn't know her?

'I'd best go. The others are leaving and Mr Havers gets into a mood if we are late back.' Ginny groaned dramatically.

'It was nice to talk to you again.' She tore her gaze away from John Hartley and smiled at Ginny.

'We can meet again if you like?'

'I'd like that.' Annabelle nodded enthusiastically.

'Did you want to come to the village fair next week? We are allowed to go on Wednesday night for a few hours after the family have been served dinner. Mrs Hartley has been kind and said they'll eat at seven and not eight to give the staff time to go. I don't serve dinner, so I can leave earlier than that.'

'I'd have to ask Ma, but I'd like to go at night for a change instead of being there all day serving behind our stall.'

'Well, I'll meet you by the coconut shy about half seven if you can make it.' Ginny ran off to join the other servants who were climbing onto the back of a cart for the trip back to the manor.

'Who's that you've been talking to?' Ma asked, coming alongside.

'Ginny Hilbraith, from the manor. She's an upper housemaid.'

'Is she the one who asked for the St John's wort?'

'Yes. Mrs Hartley seems to be feeling more her old self, apparently.' Annabelle slipped her arm through Ma's for the walk back to the cottage, which was on the other side of the village. 'Ginny has asked me to join her at the fair on Wednesday night. Can I?'

'You'll be at the fair every day for three days working on the stall. Won't you be tired of it to then go back at night?'

'I've never been at night-time. I'll be able to see the fire breathers properly and the colourful lanterns all lit up. They have a band at night, too.'

'Aye, of course you can go. But don't be back too late, mind. And find someone suitable to walk home with, a family, or another woman. I don't want you walking back in the dark through the fields or on the High Street when there's bound to be drunkards about.'

'I'll be careful.' Annabelle could barely contain her excitement. She'd been to the fair each year since she was old enough to enjoy it, but it had always been during the day with Ma, who usually had a stall to sell her herbs and tonics.

'I'm pleased you've made a friend with that Ginny girl,' Ma said as they walked.

'Why?'

'Because I know what it's like to not have a friend you can rely on.'

'You know everyone in the village and miles around.'

'Aye, but they are acquaintances, not friends, true friends. You have Dickie and now this Ginny. It pleases me to know that you won't be alone.'

'Stop talking like that. It upsets me when you do.'

'I'm sorry, but we have to face it.'

Annabelle stopped. 'What is it that you're not telling me?'

Ma's expression closed. 'Nothing. I'm just preparing you for the future, that's all. Come on now, we have much work to do to get ready for the fair.'

When they reached the cottage, Dickie was waiting for them at the gate.

'Why weren't you in church, young man?' Ma asked, leading the way into the cottage.

'I was late and missed the sermon, so I thought to come straight here.' Dickie smiled at Annabelle. 'Do you fancy a walk?'

'Sorry, we have too much to do for the fair next week.'

'Don't be worrying about that today.' Ma didn't meet

Annabelle's eyes. 'You go for your walk and when you come back, we'll have a bite to eat. You'll stay for a meal, Dickie?'

'Aye, thank you.' He grinned at Annabelle, and she inwardly groaned.

'Off you go, then.' Ma shooed them out the door.

Annabelle strode down the garden to the beck. 'We shan't walk for too long. Ma needs my help. I don't want to be away from her.' It irritated her slightly that Ma wasn't telling her everything, and she knew she wasn't, for Ma wasn't good at lying.

'Half an hour is fine then. When the church bells ring the hour, we'll come back.' Dickie leapt across the stepping stones.

Following, Annabelle tried to enjoy the walk along the edge of the estate's grassy fields, but her mind drifted to Ma and the worrying idea she was being kept in the dark about something. Dickie spoke of his week working with the sheep and how his dog, Blackie, had chased a rabbit and caught it. His mam cooked it for their supper.

'My sister Florrie is getting married in a few months. Will you come to the wedding?' Dickie asked.

'I'm not sure...' She didn't want to become a familiar face at Dickie's home, at their family events.

'You like Florrie.'

'I do, yes. She's lovely.'

Dickie bent and snapped off a long blade of grass. 'It'll be a grand day.'

They reached a stone wall and climbed over the stile to the next field. Ahead a horseman rode in full gallop.

'That's Mr John.' Dickie watched in admiration. 'He can ride better than any man I know. That's his new horse, Dash.'

Annabelle's heart thumped as Mr Hartley slowed his horse and trotted towards them. She smoothed down her pink dress, hoping she looked presentable.

'Sir.' Dickie doffed his cap as John Hartley came closer.

'Smithers, the shepherd's son, aren't you?' Mr Hartley asked Dickie.

'I am, sir, but my father died six years ago. I'm the shepherd now.'

'Did he? Forgive me. I did not know.' John's gaze went to Annabelle. 'Miss Wallis.'

'Good day, Mr Hartley.'

'It is a fine day for a walk.' His eyes didn't leave her face.

'It is.' Her corset felt too tight as he stared at her. 'Would you care to come to the cottage for a drink?'

'Thank you, but no. Perhaps another time?'

She wanted to say something to prolong him staying, but with a sharp nod to them both, he clicked his tongue for Dash to walk on.

Dickie sauntered on. 'I heard in the kitchens this morning that Mr John and Mr Hartley are off to London in the morning. Miss Eliza is causing trouble again.'

'Yes, I heard.' She kept her gaze on John Hartley until he disappeared through the trees on the other side of the field.

'I bet they want her married off as soon as possible.' Dickie laughed. 'She'd then become another man's problem.'

'I wonder when they'll be back?' she murmured.

'Pardon?'

'Nothing. We should be heading back now.' The return of John Hartley had awoken something in her and she didn't quite understand it. His looks, his presence caused her body to react to him and her mind to spin with stupid daydreams of what it would feel like to be kissed by him.

'Annabelle.' Dickie took her hand to stop her from walking away. 'Can we speak, properly like?' He leaned in close and gently kissed her lips.

'What do you mean?' She reared back.

'Well, you know I think the world of you, don't you?'

'Aye…' She inwardly groaned, not wanting this conversation.

'And I hope you like me, too?' His hold on her hand tightened.

'Aye…'

'Then why don't we, you know, start courting properly like.' He half-grinned nervously. 'You know I want to marry you. Everyone knows you're the prettiest girl in the district and I want to make you mine.'

'Dickie, please.' She blushed at his comments, but his words were too strong. She didn't want to be his. She didn't want to be his wife.

'Don't decide now. I can wait.' He nodded eagerly. 'At least I'll try to.'

'But—'

'No, don't say anything just yet. I want you to give it a ponder.' He kissed her again, then strode ahead as though afraid of what she might say.

Sighing deeply, Annabelle walked after him, her mind whirling. She liked Dickie but couldn't see herself married to him. He was kind and sweet. Not bad to look at with kind eyes and a cheery manner. Although she enjoyed his kisses, she didn't miss him when he wasn't around, and she supposed she should do if she loved him?

Back at the cottage, Annabelle helped Ma with the midday meal, but she barely ate any of the boiled potatoes and cabbage. Dickie kept the conversation going with Ma and after the meal, while Annabelle washed up the plates, Dickie offered to fill the water buckets from the beck.

'What's up with you, lass?' Ma asked, clearing the table once Dickie had gone to the beck.

'Dickie asked me to go courting with him.'

'Oh, aye?' Ma paused. 'And? What did you say?'

'Nothing. He told me to mull it over before giving him his answer.'

'What do you want to do?'

She shrugged. 'I don't know. No, that's not the truth. I do know. I don't want to court him.'

'Are you sure? Don't mess him about, lass. He's a good man and doesn't deserve it.'

'I understand that.' She smiled brightly when Dickie returned but was pleased when he said he had to leave.

'Marrying Dickie wouldn't be so bad, would it?' Ma asked later that night as they sat at the table, steeping herbs to make tonics.

Annabelle took her time to answer. 'Once, a year or so ago, I thought maybe Dickie was the man for me, but I've changed lately. I don't see myself spending the rest of my life as his wife.'

'You'd be secure, though, married to him, for the estate will always need a shepherd and he has a cottage with the position. Granted, he shares it with his mam and sister.'

'Florrie gets married in a few months.'

'So, it'll only be the mam you have to live with as a married woman.'

'I'd always imagined living here when I was married,' Annabelle said sadly.

'I told you, lass. The cottage is mine for life, not yours. As soon as I'm dead, you have to leave.' Ma's busy hands stilled. 'I want to know you'll be settled.'

Alarmed, Annabelle felt her stomach knot in fear of the unknown. 'Can't we just leave things as they are? I don't want to marry and move out of here. There's no rush, is there? We're fine as we are.'

'But, lass—'

'No, Ma. I'll not talk of you dying. It's morbid.'

'It's life.'

'And I'll deal with it once it happens and not before. You could live for years yet.' She didn't want to think of a world without Ma in it.

'So? Don't you want to be married and have babies? You're twenty-two, Annabelle. It's high time for you to have a husband and a family of your own.'

'Not yet.' She knew by the standards of the young women in the village that she was late to be married. But those girls she'd gone to school with and seen at church every Sunday had been happy to marry the first man who asked them. Many were girls from big families, living hand-to-mouth, sleeping four to a bed. Annabelle didn't have that urgency to leave home and control her own house. She'd rather live at the cottage forever. This was her home. One day Ma would die, she understood that, but if she could stay here, the loss wouldn't be as great for she'd have her memories and this cottage to comfort her.

Perhaps if she went to the manor and asked if she could rent it after Ma died? She could afford to do that. She'd continue to grow and sell herbs and tonics just as Ma had done.

Yes, she'd go to the manor and ask to see Mr Desmond Hartley about the cottage.

* * *

John paced the yellow-and-white-painted drawing room of his Aunt Martha's townhouse in London. He glanced at Des, who stood by the window, staring out, waiting for their sister and aunt to return from their shopping outing.

For scandal to have hit the family jolted him, and Des, out of the cocoon that had settled around them. The estate and family business affairs, which were far more varied and widespread than John had ever imagined, consumed them both, until Des started to receive concerning letters about Eliza.

'Here they come.' Des stepped back from the window. 'Remember, we need to handle the situation carefully.'

John raised an eyebrow. 'Handle it how you want, but we need to have Eliza on the train with us this evening.'

The butler opened the front door and John heard his sister talking as she divested herself of her gloves.

Eliza sailed into the drawing room like a princess, wearing a pale blue dress with gold lace and wrapped around her shoulders was the peacock-coloured silk shawl John had bought her from India. Eliza came to an abrupt halt on seeing her brothers there. 'Des. John.'

Aunt Martha, small and dainty like their late mother, walked in behind Eliza, her expression surprised yet wary. 'My darling nephews. I did not know you were coming to London.'

Both John and Des kissed Aunt Martha and then Eliza.

Eliza frowned at them. 'Are you here on business?'

'Family business, yes,' Des declared.

'Tea, please, Dalton,' Aunt Martha requested from the butler as she sat down on a cream brocade chair. Once the butler had left the room, she gave her attention to Des. 'What family business is this you speak of, nephew?'

Eliza fidgeted on the sofa. 'It is about me, is it not?'

'Indeed. Such reports that I cannot trust them to be true,' Des snapped.

'Reports?' Aunt Martha quizzed. 'What is this?'

Des glanced at John then to Aunt Martha. 'Worryingly, we, John and I, have both received letters from concerned friends about Eliza's behaviour recently.'

Eliza's grey eyes narrowed with hostility. 'You mean to say that nosy troublemakers have tittle-tattled on me for having fun?'

'It has not just been harmless fun, though, has it, sister?' John said calmly. 'It has been reported that you are conducting an affair with a gentleman by the name of Justin Morris-Hippleton. Is this true?'

'An affair? It cannot be!' Aunt Martha defended hotly. 'Eliza is never out of my presence when we are in society and no gentleman of that name has called on her here.'

Des rubbed his forehead in worry. 'He would not call here, Aunt. Morris-Hippleton is a married man. He works in the government at a high level. He is an adviser to one of the parties in parliament. I do not know of the man personally.'

Aunt Martha reddened. She turned to Eliza. 'Is all this true?'

'I have met Mr Morris-Hippleton, yes. We were introduced at a party.'

'Which party?'

'The house party I attended in Gloucester ten months or so ago.'

'Gloucester?' Des frowned. 'Last autumn?'

'Yes. You did not come with me. You accompanied Aunt Martha to visit Kent to see the Fielding cousins, remember? I made a number with the Rogersons' party and went to Gloucester instead.'

'Lady Rogerson said she would be your chaperone,' Aunt Martha declared. 'I shall write to her immediately.'

'Did anything happen between you and Morris-Hippleton?' John asked Eliza.

His sister blushed. 'We became friends, yes.'

'More than that?' he probed, noting her wariness to his questioning.

'Not really.' Eliza's gaze slid away from him to her folded hands in her lap.

'But you must not be friends,' Des declared abruptly. 'For the man is married.'

'Eliza!' Aunt Martha gasped.

'Is the man currently in London?' Des demanded to know. 'For my inquiries suggest that he is.'

'He is,' Eliza admitted, two spots of colour appearing on her cheeks.

'And have you seen him since Gloucester?' John asked, wishing this was all a rather innocent mistake.

'She could not possibly have done,' Aunt Martha said, looking pale.

'Eliza?' John prompted. 'Are you still friends with Morris-Hippleton?'

'I am.' Eliza's chin lifted in defiance.

'So, you see him at balls and parties?'

'Not always,' she hedged, not meeting his eyes.

John was confused. 'I have spent six months escorting you to various balls and parties. How have I not met this fellow?'

A knock on the door preceded Dalton and a maid, who brought in trays of tea and cakes.

Eliza rose. 'Excuse me.' She hurried from the room before anyone could comment.

Des waited until the butler and maid had gone again before he spoke. 'Aunt, I apologise that this horrid business has come about. Eliza will be returning to Yorkshire with us. Today.'

'Yes, of course.' Aunt Martha looked ready to cry and waved a handkerchief in front of her face. 'I do not understand how she could have made a friendship with a man without my knowledge.'

Des paced the room. 'From all accounts I have received, Morris-Hippleton is not a man who can be trusted, but he has many friends in high places and risen high in society. He is a ladies' man, apparently. Loves the secret chase of young debutantes who are flattered and overcome with his good looks and passionate words. His wife is the daughter of a viscount. He has estates in Ireland and

Scotland. He will not give that up for Eliza, nor will the law allow him to, or his wife's family.'

'Indeed.' Aunt Martha dabbed at the corners of her eyes. 'But has it advanced that far, Des? Perhaps this is nothing but an innocent flirtation that the gossips have expanded into something dramatic?'

'Let us hope that it is innocent, Aunt,' John said, but fearing the worst. 'I shall go up and speak to Eliza. She might talk to me.'

'Yes, you do that,' Des said. 'You have always been her favourite brother. Probably because you were never here.'

John ignored the jibe and went up the stairs to the next floor. He had stayed at his aunt's home in the past and knew which were her guest bedrooms. At the second door on the left, he knocked. 'Eliza?'

'Come in, John.'

Inside the bedroom, he found Eliza sitting on the four-poster bed, a letter in her hand. She looked worn out and a little puffy in the face. He noticed she'd gained some weight and the vibrancy she always projected had dimmed somewhat. He sensed she had been enjoying too many late nights. Her time in the capital had worn her out.

He sat beside her. 'Talk to me. I feel I have been a very foolish brother for the last six months to not have noticed any of this.'

'You are not at fault. I made it easy for you not to be aware. I often met Justin when I told you I was having a dress fitting, or meeting friends for tea. I always had my maid, Bridges, with me, well, most of the time...'

'Eliza. I cannot imagine you would be so foolish. A married man? What were you thinking?'

'There's nothing to be said which excuses my behaviour. I only wanted to be with him as much as possible.' She gave a teary smile. 'I love Justin. Dearly. Deeply. He loves me.'

'Christ, Eliza.' John ran a hand through his hair, shocked at how far this torrid affair had gone. 'How did you let that happen? Did you know he was married from the start?'

'Yes. I met his wife.'

'Then what possessed you to allow your feelings to grow for him?'

'I cannot explain it. I behaved as though I was not in control of myself whenever he was around. It was as though a madness took over me. Justin said he would leave his wife for me. I believed him.'

'And now?' He spoke calmly, understanding the madness that could overtake you when you desired another person. For a fleeting moment he thought of Annabelle Wallis and then focused on his sister.

'I have not heard from him for some days.'

'Has he promised to run away with you?'

'We spoke of it.'

John tutted angrily. 'It is impossible. His wife could sue for desertion.'

'I know. She has written to me.' Shaking, Eliza passed the letter she held to him to read.

Miss Eliza Hartley,

It is with considerable regret that I write to you. However, I feel I have no other means in which to convey to you the seriousness of the situation which must be discussed.

I am aware of your love affair with my husband, Justin.

Stunned, John stared at Eliza. 'Dear God. She knows?'

Eliza closed her eyes. 'Read on.'

You are not the first lady to capture my husband's attention, nor will you be the last. Therefore, I do not feel threatened by you. Simply put, Justin will never leave me for you. It is not possible. I will sue him and his career, which he deems very highly, will be reduced to rubble. The life you would live together would be away from all society and privilege. I would not stop at ruining Justin, but you as well. No house in our society would ever welcome either of you again. Every family you know will shun not only you but your entire family. That is my promise.

You are to have no further contact with Justin. Your letters will go unanswered. We are going away. I will keep this secret hidden. However, if word reaches me that you and Justin have met again, I will destroy your reputation without qualm.

Regards,

Mrs Vivian Morris-Hippleton

John folded the letter. 'How did she find out?'

'Justin wrote and told me that we might have been seen.'

'Obviously! I genuinely believe that woman would destroy your reputation and she has every right to do so. Already your name is linked with his and doing the rounds of the drawing rooms, which is how Des and I found out by good friends reporting it to us. Gossip is already gathering pace.'

'I am sorry.' Eliza took the letter from him. 'I feel ashamed to have received such a letter. To be a scarlet woman. Yet I could not stop myself. I love Justin.'

He wrapped an arm around her shaking shoulders. 'You are coming back with us to Yorkshire, and you must put this fellow out of your mind.'

She nodded, her grey eyes so like his own held pain and sadness. 'I shall instruct Bridges to pack.'

'You must forget this whole episode entirely,' he said gently, wishing he could take this pain away from his darling sister.

'It is easier said than done, brother.'

'Undoubtedly. But you are young and have your whole life

ahead of you. Someone else is out there and worthy of you. Morris-Hippleton was not the man for you. He should never have even looked your way.'

'We knew it was wrong but could not help ourselves.'

'He is married. *He* should have known better. You are an innocent.'

She blushed. 'He does not love his wife,' she defended lamely.

'That does not justify his behaviour, Eliza. As a gentleman he had to be the stronger person in this situation. You are naïve and gently reared from a good family. He saw you as prey.' Anger surged in him again.

'You make him sound a monster, John, and he is not!' she cried.

'Listen to yourself, will you? Defending such a cad! He should have never got himself involved. You will *never* contact him again, or he you. Promise me.'

'But—'

'No, Eliza. No buts. You are risking everything for this unworthy fellow. Consider your future, your family. Do you want us to be the butt of jokes, the content of whispers?'

'No.' She stared down at the letter.

He gripped her hands, trying to make her see sense. 'If one of the newspapers were to get a hold of this gossip, the family would be ruined. Do you want our names in print? To be the fodder for breakfast discussion all around our friends' tables? Do you want to be whispered about at the next ball, or for invitations to dry up? This does not simply affect you but also your family. Promise me this is the end of it.'

A tear dripped over her lashes. 'I promise.'

'Dry your eyes.'

'I am deeply sorry to be such a fool. You will forgive me, John? Please say you will.'

He kissed her forehead. 'You are my darling little sister. Yes, you have been foolish, but in time the gossip will die if it has nothing to feed off, and you will get on with your life and marry someone worthy of you. Now, come downstairs and we shall talk to Des and Aunt Martha. We shall catch the evening train.'

They stood and walked to the door, but Eliza hesitated slightly. 'I am so pleased you have come back, John. I have missed you terribly since you left to go home to Yorkshire.'

He gave her a wry look. 'I've only been gone just over a week.'

'A week can be an exceptionally long time in London.' She looked sad. 'I know I did wrong. Please do not think too badly of me.'

John sighed heavily, angry at himself for allowing his sister to be so reckless when under his care. Guilt wracked him. He'd been so eager to leave for Yorkshire he'd not investigated the worrying signs he'd noticed about his sister's conduct. Though he never expected a love affair to be happening right under his nose! That she had deceived him tarnished his love for her and that hurt. 'I was here for six months and knew nothing of what was happening right under my nose. I failed you as a brother. That will be my shame.'

She shook her head. 'No, please do not think that way. I cannot carry that burden, too.'

He shrugged. 'We all make mistakes. I do not blame you as much as I blame Morris-Hippleton.'

'You won't make any trouble for him?'

'Make trouble for him?' John snapped. 'I would like to, definitely, but I feel that would only make the situation worse. Besides, I imagine his wife might sort him out far better than me giving him a bloody nose.' John took her elbow. 'Let us go down and you can apologise to Aunt Martha and Des.'

Tears reddened her eyes. 'How will I face their disappointment?'

'With a stiff back and humility,' John murmured. 'I am pleased that Mama and Papa are not alive to witness your disgrace.'

'Do not mention them, John. I feel dreadful enough as it is.'

'Really? I hope so, Eliza. I really do.' John headed for the stairs. 'Perhaps it is time for you to grow up a little and realise that life is not all flirtations and dancing.'

'You hate me.'

He halted at the top of the stairs. 'No, and that is childish to think so. Stop being a silly girl, Eliza. It is time you matured and acted like the lady Mama would want you to be.'

He turned away from her distraught face and hurried down the stairs, annoyed with himself for not doing his duty as a brother. He had also let down his parents. They would have wanted him to look after her when they died, but instead he had continued travelling, enjoying himself and giving no thought to his family. His selfishness was partly to blame in this situation. Eliza needed a steady hand, she needed her brothers' guidance, and Des had enough to do once Papa died. John knew he should have come home straight away, but he didn't, and the result was Eliza becoming wayward and unruly. Now, it was up to him to steer her back on to the right path and take care of her.

5

'Oh, good throw, Annabelle.' Ginny clapped. 'You're better at it than me.'

Annabelle grinned and threw another ball at the stacked coconuts, knocking them all down.

'Well done, lass.' The man behind the stall nodded. 'Here's your prize.' He handed her a small knitted dog with floppy ears.

'Just what I always wanted,' Annabelle laughed.

Ginny linked arms with her as they left the stall and walked around the fair. 'What shall we do next?'

Despite being on the stall all day with Ma, Annabelle didn't feel tired. Night-time at the fair had a different feel to it than during the day. There seemed to be more excitement, more entertainment, as though the evening was the real time for the fair to come alive.

'Let's see the lion,' Ginny suggested.

'I feel rather sorry for him,' Annabelle said as they peered at the old lion sitting in a red painted cage on wheels. 'He looks bored.'

'I'd be bored in there, too.'

'Look at his mane.' She peered closer just as the scabby lion yawned and she could see his large yellowy teeth.

'He'd eat us alive.' Ginny shivered. 'Talking of eating, I'm starving.'

'There's a soup stall over there.' Annabelle pointed to the right of them. 'Or a potato and butter stall next to it.'

'Let's have a potato and then I'll challenge you at the apple bobbing.'

'Oh, look.' Annabelle stepped backwards as a fire-eater walked by, spitting flames into the air. Enthralled children ran after him, shouting, 'Again! Again!'

'Isn't that Dickie Smithers?' Ginny asked, pointing to the opening of the boxing tent.

'It is.' Annabelle waved to Dickie as he glanced their way.

He hurried over to her. 'Will you come and watch me in my match?'

'You're boxing?' She couldn't believe it. She'd never taken Dickie as a fighter. He'd not mentioned it to her in all the years she'd known him.

'Aye. I thought to give it a go.'

'Dickie, you're not built for boxing. There's nothing to you. You're all arms and legs and as thin as a rake.'

'Aye, but I'm quick.' He danced about on his tiptoes. 'And I have a long reach.'

Ginny laughed. 'You'll get your face smashed in, you daft lump.'

'No, I won't.' Dickie frowned at her. 'I'll win and get a purse of two crowns.'

'Two crowns?' Ginny was impressed.

'I don't think I want to watch you getting punched.' Annabelle went to walk away.

'I'll do much better if I know you're cheering me on, Annabelle. Please come.'

'Why? It'll be brutal.'

'You'll be my lucky charm. I know it!' He grinned like a foolish boy.

A bell was rung outside of the tent.

'That's the next fight bell. I'd best go.' Dickie paused. 'Do come and watch me, please.'

'Oh, all right.' She ignored her inner warnings that told her this was silly. She hated fighting of any kind.

They paid a farthing for the fee and were allowed to enter. Inside the packed tent, men jostled for space to see the roped-off grassed boxing ring. Annabelle and Ginny had to push their way through the working-class men who cheered or jeered depending who their money was on.

'Stay with me,' Annabelle said over her shoulder to Ginny, who was smaller than her.

Finding a spot between two burly men, she pulled Ginny in close, and they watched Dickie square up to a man twice his age and size.

'This is ridiculous.' She fumed. 'Look at the size of his opponent. Dickie's going to get hurt.'

'More fool him, then.' Ginny elbowed the man next to her who jostled for more room.

'Want to place a bet, ladies?' A youth came before them, holding out his hat for them to place their money in.

'No, we do not!' Annabelle snapped.

The bell rang again and suddenly the crowd roared, deafening her. Dickie and his opponent danced around each other as though afraid to make contact.

'Go on, Dickie!' Ginny yelled.

Annabelle was knocked to one side as the man next to her charged forward, shouting encouragement. She watched in horrified fascination as Dickie, shirtless, danced about the older man, trying to tire him out. They jabbed a few times at each other, but

Dickie was right that his reach was longer. He jabbed the other man on the chin and darted backwards.

'He'll win this.' Ginny clapped and jeered. 'Go on, Dickie!'

A sudden blow landed on Dickie's chin, reeling him backwards. He shook his head, focused and then danced forward and punched the other man several times, knocking him back a few strides.

A cheer went up and the crowd behind Annabelle surged, knocking her forward. She reached for Ginny, but they were separated as Dickie was hit hard in the stomach. He bent over, gasping, then he was lost from sight as men rushed towards the ring.

Concentrating on getting back to Ginny, Annabelle pressed the back of the man in front of her, trying to get past him. Someone trod on her foot, and she yelped. An arm bashed the side of her head as a man leapt forward cursing at the fighters. She couldn't breathe in the thick, clawing air of too many people in a compact space.

She couldn't watch as another blow hit Dickie in the eye. He went down on the grass flat on his back. She hated seeing him receiving such heavy punches. She had to get out. The tent seemed too small to hold such a braying mob.

Again, the crowd roared so loud it hurt her ears. Ginny had gone from sight and all she saw was the backs of big men. She searched for Ginny but where her friend had been standing was now a large man, yelling and waving his hat in the air.

Alarmed at the rush of men coming forward, Annabelle tried to make it to the back exit. Suddenly, she was shoved to the side. Crying out, she reached out to steady herself. An old man frowned at her but took her elbow to steady her.

Someone grabbed her by the waist and bodily lifted her from the fray as the fighting intensified, as did the roar of the crowd. She struggled to be free from the hands that held her from behind.

'Miss Wallis, you must leave!'

She turned and stared up into the face of John Hartley. Behind him, the men raged as Dickie fell again.

'What are you doing in here? This is no place for a woman,' Hartley snapped. His grey eyes narrowed as he shielded her from the pushing and shoving.

Another cheer filled the tent, and the crowd grew wilder. Money changed hands quickly. Some men were becoming angry, others jovial. She was pushed from behind, nearly knocking her hat off.

'Come this way.' Mr Hartley took her hand and pulled her behind him, thrusting men aside to make a path for them through the shouting throng.

'My friend, Ginny!' But her words were drowned out.

Outside, behind the back of the tent, the night air was cool. Cheering rose again, and she wondered what was happening to Dickie and where Ginny was. She hoped they were both safe.

'I did not think to see you in there, Miss Wallis, or any woman. It is not a fitting place.' He adjusted his jacket and righted his hat, his tone curt.

She smoothed down the skirt of her best blue dress, feeling she had shamed herself. 'I didn't want to go but my friend, Dickie, asked me to.'

'The young man fighting? I saw him talking to you outside of the tent, was that the estate shepherd?'

'Yes.'

'Do you have an understanding with him? Is that why you watched him?'

'No!' For some reason she didn't want him to think she had a beau.

'Then you should never have been in that tent.' He walked with her around to the front of the tent where the lighted lanterns glowed, and the fair carried on as normal.

Mr Hartley dropped his hand from her elbow. 'Do you feel better now?'

'Yes, thank you.' She liked that he'd held her arm. She wished he hadn't let go.

'Perhaps other amusements will be more entertaining than what will become a blood sport in there.'

'What do you mean?' She stopped near the entrance, wondering where Ginny was.

'The older man fighting is a known boxer. He will beat your friend to a pulp.'

She stared into Mr Hartley's grey eyes. 'Oh, no. We can't let that happen.'

'There is not anything we can do to stop it. It is what happens at these country fairs. Not many rules, I am afraid, not like a proper boxing match.' He gave a grim smile.

'I wish I had never gone inside.' She hoped Ma would never find out. She'd be alarmed at her doing such a thing. Dickie would get a piece of her mind, too, for endangering himself. None of it was worth the money.

'Let us hope your friend is not too injured.' Mr Hartley gazed around. 'Shall I get you something to drink?'

'No, thank you. I should be heading home.' The joy of the night had vanished.

Another cheer filled the air and then men emerged from the tent, either swearing or laughing depending on who they betted on.

'It is over,' Mr Hartley grumbled.

'I must find Ginny.' She searched the men for any sign of her.

'Wait here.' Hartley thrust through the crowd and soon returned with Ginny, who looked shocked and a little dishevelled.

'I was so worried,' Annabelle said. 'Are you hurt?'

'No. I got helped up and taken to the side of the tent. I didn't know where you had gone.'

'Mr Hartley helped me.' She blushed, flicking a glance to him.

'That's kind of you, sir.' Ginny bobbed her head at her employer.

'I do not advise either of you to participate in watching such a spectacle again. The men who frequent those types of events have no courtesy to young women,' Mr Hartley told them, but there was kindness in his voice.

'I can be certain of never entering a boxing tent again,' Annabelle declared.

'Dickie is not in great shape, for sure.' Ginny glanced back at the emptying tent. 'He lost and he'll have some bruises tomorrow.'

'He is lucky he has not come off far worse.' Mr Hartley shook his head. 'They should never have let them fight. It was an unfair contest from the beginning. I will find the organiser and have words.' His gaze held Annabelle's. 'Are you sure you are all right?'

'I am and thank you again.'

He left them and Ginny's eyes widened. 'Heavens, you've got a champion there.'

'Don't be silly.' Though her heart soared at the thought.

'Why am I? You'd not be the first master and village girl to take a liking to one another.'

'He gave me his assistance, Ginny. Nothing more.' Heat flared in her cheeks.

'Then why are you blushing?'

'I'm not. Let us see how Dickie is.' She walked away before Ginny could say any more on the subject of her and Mr Hartley. The very thought gave her palpitations of the heart. A man such as he shouldn't look twice at her. Yet, he had. He *had* looked more than twice at her when she'd met him by the beck, out walking in the field and then again just now. A man of his standing had no need to concern himself with the likes of her. So, what did it mean?

She dismissed it from her mind as they found Dickie sitting on a stool at the back of the tent, his face bloodied and one eye already closing. An older man with a squashed nose was attending to him.

Ginny peered closer to Dickie's damaged face. 'My, you're a mess and no mistake.'

Dickie half-grinned, but it caused the split in his lip to bleed more and for the old man to mutter under his breath.

'Come to the cottage tomorrow, Dickie,' Annabelle said. 'Ma will see to you. Likely you'll need a leech on that swelling around your eye.'

'Did you see me get some good hits in, Annabelle?'

'I saw you make a fool of yourself. That's what I saw, Dickie Smithers. What made you do such a foolish thing?'

His shoulders drooped. 'I thought you'd be impressed if I won.'

'Impressed?' She snorted angrily. 'I'm sorry but fighting will never impress me. Goodnight.'

'Annabelle!'

She ignored his calls and walked away back amongst the stalls and entertainments, though the evening had lost its shine. She was tired and ready for her bed.

'That was harsh.' Ginny giggled, catching up to her. 'Poor fellow is mad over you.'

'I'm not *mad* over *him* and that's the truth.' She sighed, knowing she couldn't pretend any more.

'Then you'd best tell him.'

'I will.' Dickie wanted more from her than she wanted to give and there was no point prolonging the fellow's hopes that they would ever be more than friends.

'Do you want a toffee apple?'

'No, I want to go home. I'm ready for my bed.'

Ginny glanced around. 'There are a few girls from the manor near the roundabout. I should go back with them.'

'Will I see you on Sunday after church?' Annabelle asked hopefully. 'I have enjoyed our time together.'

'Aye, me too. I'll see you after church and we'll plan what to do on my next day off.'

'I'd like that.'

Ginny took a step. 'Will you be all right walking home by yourself?'

'Yes. I'll go through the High Street. People are leaving now. I'll walk with them.'

'Bye, then.'

She watched Ginny join the other housemaids from the manor, who chatted and laughed with her. She was glad she'd made a female friend at last. The girls she went to school with were busy with their own families or had moved away to go into service or had gone to York to work in factories and mills.

Walking behind another family through the quiet village, her mind wandered, replaying the events of the night. Up until the fight, she'd enjoyed herself. Ginny was a laugh, and she realised that she'd missed out on having experiences such as tonight. Her unexciting life with Ma became very apparent. Before this evening, she'd not wished for anything to change in her life, but her days went by in an uninteresting routine with little excitement.

Was there something she was missing from life? If so, what was it?

From her pocket, she took out the little dog she'd won and smiled. The image of Mr Hartley escorting her from the tent filled her mind. The intense stare he gave her, his hands on her body...

'Annabelle, lass, we're turning off here,' Mrs Harris said, looking back to her.

'That's fine, Mrs Harris. I don't have far to go.'

'Our Arnie can walk you to your gate if you want, lass?' Mr Harris offered.

She smiled at the youth of about twelve. 'Thank you, but I'll be all right. It's not far.'

'Right you are then, lass.' Mr Harris waved goodnight.

In the pale moonlight which replaced the light from the numerous house windows left behind in the village, she strolled in the warm evening air. A fox barked somewhere in the fields and an owl hooted, but she wasn't frightened. She knew this road like the back of her hand.

The sound of hooves drumming along the dirt road alerted her to a rider before she saw it. She stepped to the edge of the road and glanced over her shoulder. The darkness hid the face of the rider until he drew alongside.

'Miss Wallis.' Mr Hartley pulled the reins to slow his horse to a walk. 'You are walking alone?'

'I'm perfectly fine, Mr Hartley.'

He dismounted. 'But you should not be alone at night.'

'Who is going to hurt me? I know everyone for miles around.'

'There could always be a vagabond lurking in a ditch.'

'And he could try his luck, I suppose, but he'd not get far for I'd scream and struggle like a rabbit in a sack.'

He chuckled softly. 'I am certain you would.'

They walked together, his horse trailing behind.

'Thank you again for helping me in the boxing tent. I'm embarrassed to be in such a situation.'

'You weren't to know if you've never been to a boxing match before. It can become unruly very quickly.' His smile was warm.

'Ma would be horrified I've done so.'

'She won't hear about it from me,' he teased.

Annabelle relaxed, at ease with him. 'Are you glad to be home from your travels?' she abruptly asked, then wondered if she should have. He was above her in every respect and she had no right to simply engage him in conversation. 'Forgive me for being impertinent.'

'You aren't at all. And yes, I am pleased to be home. I have missed my home, yet I would not change the years I had away. I have seen and done things many men would envy.'

'And women, too, I suspect. I would like to see beyond York-shire. I've never been to London!' She grinned.

'Then you must go. London is full of delights. It is a fine city, but there are many fine cities in the world.'

'Only I can't visit them as you did.' She understood the class divide between them. She was a girl from the village and he a man born to money and privilege. He'd travelled to different countries and she'd only gone as far as York and Harrogate.

'Perhaps one day you might?' he murmured.

'I very much doubt it.' She sighed heavily. 'But it's nice to dream.'

'What are your dreams, Miss Wallis?' His voice was soft, tender, and she liked listening to it.

'My dreams are as varied as the flowers in our garden. There are times when I never want to leave the cottage and then there are times when I wonder what it would be like to explore the world as you did.'

'I had the same dreams. As soon as I finished university I wanted to be away from books and school bells and be free. Yet, when I was far away on the other side of the world, I sometimes longed for home.' He gazed at her, and they stopped walking and were content to just look at each other, to take in the tiny details of the other's face.

She wanted to ask him all about his journeys, to keep him talk-ing, but the path leading to the cottage was a few yards away and she must not linger.

'Shall I walk you to the door?' he asked.

'No, thank you. Ma will be waiting up for me and she'll worry if she sees that you, of all people, have walked me home.'

'Me, of all people.' He chuckled. 'You make me sound like an oddity.'

'I didn't mean to.' She became flustered. 'It's just that—'

He laughed, a delightful sound in the quiet of the night. 'You do not have to explain. I understand. I shall leave you.'

'Thank you for walking me home.'

'It was my pleasure.'

She stared up into his eyes and in the moonlight saw them soften. His smile was warm, inviting. She yearned to kiss him and blushed at her forwardness. 'Goodnight, Mr Hartley.'

He held out his hand and she placed her fingers in his. The contact fired along her skin and straight to her chest, making her heart thump as though she'd run miles.

'Goodnight, Miss Wallis,' he spoke quietly with a slight squeeze of her fingers. 'I hope we meet again.'

Catching her breath, she took the path between the tall trees edging the field where the house cow and Bobby were kept. She wanted to dawdle, to ponder every word said between them, but a lamp in the front window lighted her way to the gate. Ma would be waiting. She turned back and saw that Mr Hartley still stood in the shadows of the moonlit road. He raised a hand, and she answered the same.

Smiling, she entered the cottage to find Ma dozing before the fire. She shook her shoulder gently.

'Did you have a nice time, lass?' Ma asked, rising slowly from the chair.

'I did. I'll tell you all about it tomorrow.' She kissed Ma on the cheek. 'Sleep well.'

Ma patted her hand and went to her bed in the corner of the

cottage. Annabelle placed a fireguard around the hearth and then took the lamp up with her to the loft.

Undressing, she yawned sleepily, happily. The warmth of the loft and the long day and events of the night ushered her to bed like the hand of a ghost. She snuggled down, smiling to herself as she thought of Mr Hartley. How kind he was, and how handsome. She didn't know why he'd taken an interest in her, but she couldn't help but be thankful for it.

6

Annabelle woke to the cockerel crowing. Dawn had broken and a pinkish light filtered into the room. She snuggled down, warm and comfy, not wanting to get out of bed just yet and start the day. Her eyes caught sight of the little knitted dog on her bedside table, and she smiled. Perhaps at the fair today she could leave the stall for a bit and have another go at the coconut shy. She might win a stuffed animal for Ginny. It was the last day of the fair and she knew Ginny wouldn't be able to attend. Perhaps Mr Hartley would be in the village today?

She listened for any movement downstairs. Nothing. Was Ma being quiet or still asleep? It was unlike Ma to not be calling for her to get up. Throwing back the blankets, she washed and dressed in a plain brown skirt and bodice. She rolled her hair into a bun and pinned it into place.

Climbing down the loft ladder, her thoughts on manning the stall, she frowned on seeing Ma still in bed. 'Ma. You've overslept. We've got to get a move on.'

She pulled on her boots, raked the embers in the range and set more kindling on top. With the fire going, she poured water into the kettle from the bucket and set it on the stovetop to boil. 'Do you want eggs and bacon, or kippers?'

Annabelle glanced at Ma, who hadn't moved from the bed. 'Ma. We're going to be late.'

She set the table with the breakfast things. 'It's a good job we restocked the baskets yesterday afternoon.'

Going back to the dresser, she took down the brown earthenware teapot and held it to her chest. For some minutes she stood, not daring to move or even breathe.

'Ma?' she whispered, afraid. Ma never slept in late... 'Ma, will you not wake up?'

Heart beating, she spooned tea leaves into the teapot. The kettle boiled and she took it off the heat. For several moments she stood there, not moving. To move would mean change, loss, pain.

Slowly, taking each step as though her feet were weighted with stones, she edged around the table, past the large wingback chair to Ma's bed. Fear and dread churned her stomach.

When she looked down at Ma, she gasped. The old woman looked much younger than Annabelle had ever seen her. Ma looked serene.

The pale face and blue lips told her the truth, however, but her heart and mind didn't want to accept it, not yet.

'Please wake up, Ma. You can't leave me yet.' Her throat tightened, choked with emotion.

She knelt beside the bed and held Ma's cold hand in her warm one. 'Why did you have to go? I wasn't ready. It's too soon.' Tears blurred her vision and she blinked them away.

Gently, she kissed Ma's thin cheek. She desperately wanted to cry, but she dared not. The pain of Ma never talking to her again or smiling at her stabbed like a dagger in her chest. Her mind spiralled at the enormity of what she faced. The rest of her life without Ma in it. How would she cope? She'd never suffered any loss in her life, for she'd been only a baby when Ma rescued her, and she knew nothing of her parents. But Ma's love had sustained her all her life and she had grown up happy and sheltered by Ma's care. How would she live without her? Who would she talk to?

She was all alone in the world and for a moment she was paralysed by the immensity of the thought.

'Ma... I wasn't ready. It's too soon.' Her chin trembled and a wave of desolation washed over her, consuming her until she couldn't breathe. Sobs broke from her, bending her over Ma's body. She clutched Ma's hand, not wanting to ever let go. 'Please don't leave me.'

Eventually, the storm of emotion passed enough for her to straighten up, wipe her eyes and hear the noise outside. Daisy was bellowing to be milked.

Without thought, Annabelle collected the milk bucket from the small scullery and went out into the morning sunshine. After letting the chickens out to roam, she grabbed an armful of hay for Daisy to eat while she milked her.

Bobby nudged her arm as she entered the small field beside the garden, wanting his share of the hay. Daisy happily let her tie her up and begin the milking, but Annabelle's mind was elsewhere.

The dreadful idea of having to notify someone about Ma made the tears fall again. Reverend Marr needed to be contacted and Dr Henderson. Mrs Evans, the local village woman who laid out the deceased, would have to come.

Suddenly, she didn't want people here. Ma was such a private person. No one came to the cottage unless it was to buy a tonic or herbs or to pay a few pennies for Ma's advice for some illness. To fill the cottage now while she was at peace seemed wrong, a betrayal.

Satisfied she'd milked enough for Daisy to be comfortable, Annabelle untied her and took the bucket inside to pour the milk into the cold jug which was always placed on a marble slab in the larder and covered with a piece of damp linen.

The quietness of the cottage sounded loud. Usually, they were both so busy either inside or out, that she never noticed any quiet times. Even at night as they sat before the fire reading or sewing, they would chat, or the logs would crackle and shift. There was always some noise. But even the birds weren't singing.

Blinking back more tears, Annabelle put on her bonnet. She'd have to go into the village. The thought of leaving Ma alone stopped her from walking out the door. She stood by Ma's bed and tidied the blankets.

'I have to go to Reverend Marr and Dr Henderson. You'll be all right, won't you, Ma?'

A knock on the back door frightened her.

'Annabelle?' Dickie stuck his head in with a grin. 'Morning.'

Seeing a friendly face brought her undone. She ran to him and threw her arms around his neck and cried.

'What's happened?' Dickie pulled her away. 'Are you hurt?'

'It's Ma.' She buried her face into her hands and turned away from him.

'Ma?' Dickie walked into the room properly and over to Ma's bed in the corner. 'Oh, dear God. Is she...?'

'Yes.' She wiped her eyes.

'I'm sorry, Annabelle. Really, I am. She was a fine woman.' Dickie pulled off his cap. He could only see out of one eye, the other closed with swelling. 'How did it happen?'

'When I came down this morning, she was still in bed. I thought she was sleeping...'

'And isn't that the best way to go?' he said kindly.

'She's been talking about dying so much recently. I never expected her to actually die so soon.'

'Has she been ill?'

'Not that I know of, or that she has told me.' Another tear dripped over her lashes. 'Knowing Ma, she'd have hidden any pain from me to not upset me. What if she's been sick for months and never told me?' She hated the thought that Ma would not share her pain with her.

'That's the kind of woman she was, though. She'd help anyone but never want help in return, you know that.'

'Yes, that's exactly what she would have done.' Annabelle took a deep shuddering breath. 'I was going to the village to see Reverend Marr and the doctor, though it's too late for his assistance.'

'Nay, I'll go for you. You stay here. I'll make you a cup of tea first.'

'No. I can make it. I need something to do.' Her hands shook as she emptied the cold tea into a bucket.

Dickie added wood to the fire. 'I'll go into the village for you now. I'll be as quick as I can.'

'What about your work?'

'Nay, the sheep will be fine for an hour or so. They won't miss me.' He smiled gently. 'They're having a good time up on the moors.'

'I don't want you getting into any trouble.'

'The steward never knows where I am. If the sheep are healthy and the lambs are safe from foxes and growing fine, that's all he cares about. I know my job, don't worry.'

When Dickie had gone, she busied herself with making tea.

'I'm going to set the table, Ma,' she said, wanting to talk and feel less alone. She set the table with the tea service. 'I've put the good service out, for the cottage will be visited more times today than it has in weeks. I'm sorry about that, but they have to come.' She glanced at Ma but turned away as the pain in her heart cut deep.

She cleaned and scrubbed the kitchen, opened the windows, straightened the curtains.

Unable to take being inside a minute longer, she went out the back into the warm sunshine. Lifting her face to the sun, she listened to the birds singing. In a spirit of energy, she cut roses, hollyhocks and dahlias and took them inside. She placed them in jugs and vases, which she placed around the cottage. Ma wasn't one for show, but Annabelle wanted the cottage to look pretty. People would be coming, and she wanted them to see the cottage at its best.

Dickie returned with both Dr Henderson and the Reverend.

Dr Henderson examined Ma and pronounced her dead and wrote in his notebook. 'Widow Wallis came to me a few months ago.'

'She did?' Annabelle couldn't have been more surprised if he'd said Ma was a witch. Ma never sought medical advice.

'She had tried everything she could to ease the pain she'd been feeling in her chest. I gave her some medicine and examined her but we both knew it was only a matter of time. It was her heart.'

'She never told me.' Betrayed, her hands shook as she poured out the tea and passed it to the two men and Dickie.

'No, she wouldn't have wanted to worry you.' Dr Henderson took off his glasses and wiped them with a cloth from his pocket. 'I'm terribly sorry for your loss.'

Reverend Marr gave a small prayer, then took Annabelle's hand in his. 'My child, I am most sorry. Widow Wallis was a decent, self-less woman who cared for many people from birth unto death. She helped all those that came to her. She will be greatly missed in the village.'

Annabelle nodded her thanks, biting her lip to stop the tears.

'Widow Wallis had spoken to me about her funeral.'

'She had?' Again, she was shocked at what Ma had kept from her.

'It is all paid for.'

'It is?' She felt stupid.

'And she wishes to be buried in the corner of the churchyard near the boundary wall.'

'Why there?'

'She wanted to be laid to rest under the beech tree that grows over the other side of the wall, but its branches hang over. You know the spot.'

Annabelle smiled. 'Ma loves... loved trees.'

Reverend Marr patted her hand. 'Indeed, she said as much when we talked. Now, would you like for her to be buried on Sunday after the church service?'

'Sunday?'

'Unless you wish to wait? Are there relations to contact?'

'No, no one. Just me.'

'I have no funerals on Sunday. I can have the grave dug tomorrow. Visit Mr Rayburn for the coffin. Widow Wallis has already paid him for one.'

Dr Henderson sipped his tea. 'The entire village will turn out for the funeral, I would expect. Holding the funeral after Sunday service would benefit many who would want to pay their respects while they are already away from their farms and homes.'

'Yes, it makes sense,' she agreed, but it all seemed too sudden. In three days, Ma would be gone, buried, and she'd be alone...

'Mrs Evans will lay her out respectfully.' Reverend Marr replaced his teacup and stood. 'I must be going, my dear Annabelle. Mr Murray at Little Beck Farm is extremely ill. I promised I would sit with him while his daughter goes into the village and does her shopping. Visit Mr Rayburn as soon as you can, unless you'd like me to call on him?'

'No, thank you. I'll go.'

'He can take Widow Wallis back with him. Mrs Evans can do her work there.'

'Not here?'

'Only if you wish for that, but perhaps having her elsewhere tonight will ease your suffering somewhat?' Reverend Marr's tone was gentle, yet his expression showed that keeping Ma in the cottage would be difficult for her.

'Yes, you're right. I hadn't thought.' She hadn't thought about Ma's funeral because she never wanted to face it, and now she must. She hoped she'd have the strength to do Ma proud.

'No, my dear girl. It is all a new experience for you.'

'Thank you, Reverend.'

Dr Henderson stood. 'I shall also leave you. Again, I am sorry for your loss.'

She showed both gentlemen to the door. None of it seemed real. She gazed at Ma on the bed and wished with all her heart she'd wake up.

'You got through that bit.' Dickie cleared away the table. 'I'll come with you to Rayburn's.'

'No, it's fine, Dickie, really. I can do it.' She began washing up the teacups.

'But you shouldn't be alone.'

'I think I'd rather be by myself, if that's all right with you? I need some time...'

'Aye. If you think so. I'll call again this evening.'

'No. You can't come now I'm here alone. People will talk.'

'No, they won't. I'll just pop in and stay a few minutes. We can stand outside if it'll make you feel better about it.' He came and kissed her cheek. 'I'll be up on the moor for the rest of the day, but I'll be back down around seven.'

Once he'd gone, she stood by Ma's bed and bent to kiss her cold cheek. 'I'll be back shortly.' She paused, hating to leave her. 'I'll be as quick as I can.'

Rayburn's funeral shop was down a small side street off the

High Street. Annabelle walked quickly, keeping her head down and avoiding as many people as possible. Some called out a greeting to her, and she'd wave in response, but she had no wish to chat politely today. She didn't want to tell them about Ma or to hear their kind words and sympathy. She wasn't ready to face them.

Mr Rayburn and his oldest son were in an office when a maid showed Annabelle into the house. They shook her hands warmly while speaking of their condolences as she told them her news.

'Widow Wallis was a well-liked and considerate woman, Miss Wallis.' Mr Rayburn ushered her to a seat. 'She delivered my three, including Reggie here.'

Reggie, whom she knew from seeing about the village, filled the room with his large frame. 'Who could ever see me as a little baby, hey?'

'My late wife praised Widow Wallis for always being someone she could talk to about anything, and sage advice would be offered.' Mr Rayburn opened his ledger. 'Now, I know that Widow Wallis paid for her funeral in advance. Clever woman that she was. So, if you're saying Reverend Marr can bury her after Sunday service then we should be collecting her body in the next few hours so we can have her here to be prepared by Mrs Evans.'

'Shall I visit Mrs Evans?'

'No, no. Reggie will do that for you.'

'I'll go now, Father.' Reggie bowed his head at Annabelle and left the room.

Mr Rayburn wrote something down in his ledger. 'Are we able to come to the cottage at any time?'

'Yes.'

'Good. Let's say in an hour?'

She nodded, feeling a little adrift. Everything had been planned without her. She felt as though she wasn't a part of it. 'What do you need me to do?'

'Perhaps select a dress that she'd want to wear?' he said lightly.

'Oh, I see.'

'Her Sunday best is usually what people choose.'

'Of course.'

Mr Rayburn stood, bringing the meeting to an end. 'I shall see you in an hour, Miss Wallis. Take care now.'

He led her to the door and, with a grave smile, saw her out.

Annabelle stood for a moment, not knowing what to do next. The cheery sounds of the fair drifted on a gentle breeze, but she was dead inside.

Had it only been last evening when she'd played at the coconut shy and watched the fire-eater light up the night sky with his flames? Less than a day had gone by since she'd laughed with Ginny and then, last night, she'd walked with John Hartley and talked to him nearly as an equal. In the moonlight, she'd stared into his intense gaze and thought him the most handsome man she'd ever seen.

It seemed a lifetime ago.

Now her world had tilted, shifted in sense and purpose. Ahead stretched impossible days to get through, starting with the funeral and saying goodbye to the only person who'd ever truly loved and cared for her.

Suddenly, her life seemed to be meaningless and filled with uncertainty. Ma had been her rock, the rudder to steer her through life. From now on she was alone and the idea was unimaginable.

7

John sat on the hard wooden pew between Penny and Eliza, listening to Reverend Marr's sermon. Not that he was paying much attention. All sermons bored him. Attending church was expected, a routine, but after all his travels to different countries, he found religion a strange thing. So many other races and creeds believed differently. No one was right or wrong, in his humble opinion, but privately he challenged the church's ideals – not that he could officially announce this to anyone. His family were leaders in this village and surrounding district. Law and order came from Des being the local magistrate, as their father had been before him and all the males in their line for centuries. John understood his place in the world, but that didn't mean he must blindly follow.

His attention was brought back to the present as Reverend Marr finished, but before he let them leave, he held up his hands.

'A final word, if you please. I shall be presiding over the funeral of Widow Wallis shortly. Those of you who wish to stay and pay your respects, please remain seated.'

Nobody moved as whispers grew louder.

Shocked, John turned in his seat and searched the congregation for Annabelle Wallis. He had no idea the widow had died. How had he not known? Miss Wallis must be beside herself with grief.

'Widow Wallis?' Penny whispered beside him. 'The old herbalist lady in the cottage at the edge of the estate?'

'Yes,' Des replied. 'Yardley told me this morning.'

'How did the steward find out?' John asked, spotting Miss Wallis as she stood at the back of the church.

The coffin was carried in, but John watched her, not the coffin. She was dressed all in black and looked slight and pale. The young woman had been on his mind a lot, especially since the night of the fair.

'The shepherd, Smithers, told him,' Des informed them. 'It's all been very sudden.'

'Poor woman,' Eliza murmured. 'She was greatly respected in the village. The maids swore by her tonics.'

'Is that her daughter?' Penny asked.

'Her ward,' John said, not taking his eyes off Miss Wallis as she was ushered to a pew at the front opposite their own. The black mourning she wore drained the creamy colour from her skin.

'Is she an herbalist, too?' Eliza asked, studying her. 'I have seen her over the years. She's very pretty.'

John swallowed, his heart beating rapidly. Miss Wallis looked so forlorn, he wanted to sit with her, hold her hand and assure her she would be fine, that he would help her.

Reverend Marr began the ceremony, which was short, and before long the coffin was carried out again to the graveyard.

John and his family were the first out of the church after Annabelle.

At the door, Des shook hands with Reverend Marr and once his family had done so, he guided his wife and sister along the path. 'Right, let us be getting back. The Broughtons are visiting this afternoon.'

'I shall stay.' John watched Miss Wallis walk behind the coffin to the far side of the graveyard.

'In God's name, why?' Des was astonished.

'Widow Wallis was an important person in the village. She saved the life of our grandmother. I think one of us should attend the burial.'

'Really?' Des frowned. 'I hardly think so. They would not expect one of us to attend.'

'Nevertheless, out of respect, I shall.' John turned away, wanting to join Miss Wallis.

'I shall, too,' Eliza said. 'I see some servants are staying behind. We should show our faces. Send the carriage back for us.' She linked her arm with John, and they walked towards the grave.

John stood with Eliza on one side of the grave while Miss Wallis stood on the other. As Reverend Marr spoke, John kept his gaze on her. She remained straight backed, but her chin wobbled as she tried to keep her emotions in check. He wanted to comfort her. How she must be suffering. He wished they were better acquainted, proper friends even, so he could be the one to stand beside her. Instead, holding her elbow was the estate's shepherd, Smithers, the one who'd lost at the boxing match. Were they a couple, despite Miss Wallis's protest the other night? The young man looked attentive enough. One of the manor's upper maids, Ginny, the one he'd met at the boxing, had her arm around Annabelle's waist.

Annabelle.

Yes, in his mind from now on she was Annabelle, not Miss Wallis, and he'd do what he could to help her. He didn't examine why he felt inclined to help her. Only that he felt an urge to be by her side, to help her when she was so vulnerable. She was alone in the world now and how frightened she must be feeling. He wanted to make her aware that he was there for her if she needed him.

Finally, the coffin was lowered into the ground. Many of the congregation had stayed and were only just now leaving after giving their condolences to Annabelle. She smiled gratefully to those who stopped and had a word with her, and she shook hands with Dr Henderson and the Reverend.

John waited until everyone had gone and then, with Eliza, he stepped around the grave to where she stood.

'Miss Wallis, you have our sincere condolences,' Eliza said.

'Thank you, Miss Hartley.' She looked as delicate as a butterfly's wings. Her large hazel eyes were red with weeping and the black she wore drew all colour from her beautiful face.

'If there is anything we can do, please let us know.' John desperately wanted to take her hand but knew it would be odd to do so. 'I understand this must be a difficult time for you.'

'I will manage, Mr Hartley.' She bit her lip in distress and it went straight to his heart.

'Widow Wallis was very respected. You can gain comfort from that,' Eliza said kindly. 'She would be proud of the turnout today and obviously in you. I understand she taught you everything she knew about herbs and so forth?'

John glanced at Eliza. How did she know that?

Annabelle sighed sadly. 'I wish she had, Miss Hartley. But she had more knowledge than I could ever hope to learn. Perhaps if we had more time...'

'But you know enough to earn a living?'

'Eliza,' John murmured, frowning at the inquisitive question.

'Forgive me, Miss Wallis.' Eliza gave her a soft smile. 'I simply meant that the village will be lost without her and perhaps you will be able to take her place?'

'I hope so, Miss Hartley.'

'Then I am sure you will.' Eliza gave Annabelle's hand a light touch. 'You will continue her good work. I am sure of it.'

'We should be going,' John said, seeing how uncomfortable Annabelle had become.

'Thank you for attending.' Annabelle stepped back, allowing them to pass her.

John wished he could stay but Smithers and the housemaid, Ginny, came to Annabelle's side and started talking to her.

'She is delightful, isn't she? To be so pretty, yet she's working class. If you put a fine dress on her, she could carry it off in any drawing room,' Eliza said as they made the short walk to the gate.

'Beauty is not distributed to only the wealthy and high-born, Eliza.'

'Oh, you know what I mean. Well, anyway, the poor thing is all alone now. I wonder if she'll stay in the village or move to a town? I hope she can continue Widow Wallis's work and not have to leave.'

'Why would she want to leave?' John opened the gate.

'Why would she want to stay?' Eliza gave him a look that spoke volumes. 'She has nothing to stay for, has she? She might want to leave this village and see what is beyond it.'

Annabelle's words from the other night mentioning her wish to see beyond Yorkshire came back to haunt him. The thought of her going away left him cold, which was nonsense for the girl meant nothing to him... He shook his head at his own foolishness. She meant something to him and had done since the first moment he met her. But, God help him, what could he do about it? Should he do anything about it? Was she just an itch he needed to scratch or something more? Unfortunately for his state of mind, he believed she was beginning to become a great deal more than just a beautiful young woman he wanted to kiss. Annabelle Wallis had got under his skin, into his heart and mind and he didn't have a clue how to overcome it.

'I've been meaning to mention something,' Eliza said as they strolled along the lane past the vicarage.

'Oh?' He brought his attention back to his sister.

'Yes. I thought I might visit a friend next month.'

The carriage was coming along the High Street and John waited for it to stop before handing Eliza up into it. 'Which friend?' he asked as they settled.

'Joanna Pritchard. Well, she's Freeman now.'

'I've not heard you mention her for some time.'

'We caught up in London and she's recently married. She's moved to a fine estate near Leeds, and she's invited me to stay for a few days.'

He raised an eyebrow at her. 'Are you telling me the truth?'

'Indeed, I am. I can show you her letter if you like.' She winced as though in pain.

'Are you all right?'

'Yes. I think I twinged something when I climbed into the carriage just now.'

'You need to start riding again. Spending a year sitting in drawing rooms is hardly good for you.'

'Yes, I shall start riding again now I am home. Though I did dance in London. Some exercise was taken.' She gave him a lofty look. 'So, will you smooth it over with Des for me to go to Joanna's, please?'

'And this is not just a ruse to meet a certain someone?'

Eliza scowled. 'No. I told you it is over, and it is. We have not been in contact since I left London.'

'I shan't be hoodwinked again, Eliza.' John glared at her, daring her to lie to his face.

'I am not meeting anyone there. You have my word.' She sounded sincere.

'Then I will talk to Des.' He looked out of the window, wondering if his sister was telling the truth. His thoughts drifted to Annabelle Wallis. Would she stay in the village? Would it be beneficial to him for her to go away? Perhaps then he could stop thinking about her and wanting what he could never have.

* * *

'I can stay for the rest of the day,' Dickie told her, putting on his hat.

'That's kind of you, but it wouldn't be right.' Annabelle smiled and turned to Ginny. 'Thank you for coming. I hope you'll not be in trouble at the manor for staying so long.'

'No, Mrs Knowles is a decent housekeeper, and she knows we are friends.' Ginny pinned on her hat. 'I don't make a habit of asking for time off and she knows it. I wouldn't have been needed much this morning, not on a Sunday, and as long as I'm back before mid-afternoon she won't care so much.'

'I'm so pleased you were both there. It made the funeral less difficult.' Annabelle gave Ginny a hug and she kissed Dickie's cheek.

She walked with them through the garden and down to the beck.

'I'll call tomorrow,' Dickie said, delaying a moment longer.

'I'll be fine,' she reassured him.

Ginny skipped across the stepping stones to the other side. 'I'll see you next Sunday at church unless I can get an hour off during the week. I might be able to run an errand into the village and, if so, I'll call by.'

Annabelle waved them off and turned back to the garden. Clouds covered the sun and she shivered in the shade of the tall trees. At the fence, she patted Bobby, who enjoyed a good rub around the ears. Then she strolled through the garden beds, picking the odd vegetable that was ripe.

Collecting a basket from the potting shed, she continued to work in the garden. She picked strawberries, cut some ripe rhubarb, pulled carrots from the soil and tied up the beans which had fallen away from the trellis. Tomatoes, red and juicy, were added to the basket, and a couple of lettuces.

As she worked, she let the tears fall. Ma would never be in this garden again. Never would Annabelle ask her a question about a certain herb or chat with her about the latest baby she'd brought into the world. Never again would they sit in the sun and shell peas, or pluck a chicken, or dry herbs for tonics.

How would she go on in life without Ma?

'Miss Wallis.'

The male voice made her jump and spin around. She stared at John Hartley, who stood at the end of the garden. His horse was tied to a low tree branch on the other side of the beck.

'Forgive me, I did not mean to frighten you.' He held out a hand in apology.

'I was lost to my thoughts.' She wiped her eyes with the back of her hand.

He walked closer, skirting the bed of potatoes. 'I apologise for intruding. I simply wanted to check you were well, after this morning.'

'I am, thank you for your concern.' She winced at the state of her appearance. She'd not changed from her black mourning into her work clothes and dirt smudged her hem. Her hands were filthy, and her hair had drifted loose from under her bonnet. 'Would you care for some tea?'

He smiled. 'Would that be an inconvenience?'

'Not at all.' She collected two full baskets as the sun came out from behind a large white cloud.

'Allow me.' He took the baskets from her instantly.

She led him into the cottage, pleased she'd cleaned it within an inch of its life yesterday, mainly to give her something to do. She'd also moved the furniture around. Ma's bed had been dismantled and stored in the potting shed, for she couldn't stand to see it empty. The bookshelves were dust-free, and the books lovingly rearranged, for books were Ma's special treasures. The fireplace and the cooking range had been blackleaded. The stone floor and windows were washed, and fresh flowers filled every surface. Cleaning the cottage from top to bottom had given her something to do and tired her out so that she slept deeply that night. Keeping busy had kept the thoughts of the funeral at bay.

John placed the baskets in the scullery and followed her into the cottage. 'This is a pleasant home.'

'I think so.' She poured water into the kettle and added more wood to the range. Nervous at having him here, she avoided looking at him. She set the teacups out on the table and cut more slices of fruit cake that Mrs Arnold had sent.

'Funerals can be difficult,' he said. 'Once they are over, there is a sense of time dragging on.'

'Yes. I agree.' She added fresh tea leaves to the teapot. 'Would you care to sit at the table, or would you prefer to sit out in the garden?'

'Shall we go out into the garden? The sun is out again.'

She nodded, wanting to stare at him. Why was he here?

Quickly, she placed the tea service and cake plates on a tray and took it outside to a small square wooden table where she and Ma liked to sit on a summer's evening. Wisteria vine grew over this side of the cottage and framed the windows. A garden bed of roses flowered along the wall. In the sunshine, it was the perfect spot to relax, but relaxing wasn't something Annabelle could do. Her hands shook slightly as she placed his teacup and saucer on the table.

'Do you have any other family?' he asked.

'No, none. I am an orphan.'

'Yes, I remember the story of Widow Wallis taking you in as a baby.'

She poured out the tea and passed the slice of cake to him. 'Yes. Ma knew my mother. I know little more than that.'

'Are you curious to know more?'

'Perhaps, but what good would it do me? There is no one to tell me about my real mother or father.' She sat opposite him, her thoughts whirling. A handsome man such as him from a wealthy family should have better things to do with his time than be seated in the garden with someone like her.

'Have you thoughts on what you'll do next?' he asked, sipping his tea.

'I would like to continue as I am, but that is not up to me.'

He sat forward, intrigue in his grey eyes. 'Why is that?'

'This cottage was Ma's for her lifetime. I need to ask your brother if I can stay. I will pay rent, of course. I can still sell Ma's tonics, for I know how to make them and what they are used for. I can sell the herbs and give advice for their medicinal purposes.'

'I do not see why my brother would not allow you to stay.'

She sagged against the back of the chair. 'That would be so good, Mr Hartley. I can't tell you how much it means to me to stay.' Suddenly, she burst into tears, surprising herself and Mr Hartley, who hurried around to her and knelt beside her chair.

'Miss Wallis, please do not become distressed. You are welcome to stay in the cottage. I shall speak to my brother about it.' He gave her a folded white handkerchief from his own pocket. Their fingers touched and they stared at each other, their eyes speaking messages their lips couldn't utter.

Distraught, Annabelle dabbed her eyes. 'I'm so sorry, Mr Hartley. Today has been hard and I've been worrying about the cottage.'

'Then worry no more.'

Annabelle stared into his face. The urge to kiss him consumed her. She gripped her hands together to stop herself from reaching for him.

Abruptly, he stood. 'I must go.'

She rose also, her heart pumping with some emotion she couldn't identify but which she had to control. What was she thinking? She couldn't be drawn to this gentleman. He wasn't of her world.

'Thank you for the tea,' he said gruffly, his gaze locked with hers.

Before she could answer he strode away down the garden, jumped the stepping stones and mounted his horse.

As he rode away the sun went behind the clouds and cast a shadow over her.

* * *

John finished the dessert of fresh fruit and whipped cream and wiped the corners of his mouth with a linen napkin. Eliza sat opposite him at the dining table, talking to Ernest Broughton, while Mrs Broughton sat next to John. Des was at the head of the table and Penny at the other end.

'Your travels have tanned you considerably, John.' Mrs Broughton placed her spoon down. 'You must have seen some sights indeed.'

'I have been extremely fortunate,' John answered.

'And what shall you do now you are home? Is it time to take a wife and make a home of your own?'

'In time, yes. For now, I am helping Des with the family concerns.'

'You must find Yorkshire exceedingly dull in comparison to the rest of the world.'

'Oh, I would not say that. Yorkshire has a beauty all of its own and there is more than enough to keep me occupied.'

'You must come to the ball we are having next month. I did not put your name on Des and Penny's invitation because I did not know you had returned to Yorkshire.'

'Thank you, I would be delighted to attend.'

'I am sure you will find enough dance partners. Alison will be home from visiting a cousin in Scotland. She always thought so highly of you when you were both younger.' Her shrewd pale eyes captured his gaze.

John sipped his glass of wine. Alison Broughton had been a good friend when he was a youth, but if Mrs Broughton wanted him for her son-in-law, then she'd have to rethink her plans. He had no wish to marry Alison. 'I fully expected Alison to be married by now, seeing as we are the same age.'

Mrs Broughton sighed and patted the grey hair at her temple. 'No one is good enough, apparently. Alison refuses all offers. At thirty years of age, she is running out of time, and we are running out of patience with her.'

'I am sure she has her reasons.'

'None which explain adequately why she is still unwed. Unless she is waiting for someone... someone who has been away and out of reach?'

John grinned. 'Do not send your Cupid's bow my way, Mrs Broughton. I am not ready for it.'

'When is one ever ready for love, Mr Hartley?' she asked with raised eyebrows.

'Shall we go through, ladies?' Penny asked, rising.

Glad to escape more in-depth talk on his marital views, John rose and pulled out Mrs Broughton's chair for her with a small bow.

Mrs Broughton paused. 'Think on it, dear fellow. Alison comes with a sizeable dowry.'

Left alone with Des and Mr Broughton, John accepted the glass of port Havers poured for the men and regained his seat.

While Des and Broughton talked of law and parliamentary

seats, John's thoughts flew in another direction. To Annabelle and her cottage. He needed to speak to Des about it. Confirming she could stay in the cottage would ease some of her burden and he could call on her tomorrow and tell her the good news. It mattered to him a great deal that he be the one to help her, to ease her worries. He knew he should stop, none of this would end well if he kept going. Annabelle, as lovely as she was, didn't come from his social circle. Would the leap be even considered by her, if he did decide to pursue her?

He threw back a mouthful of port, wanting something harsher like whisky.

What was he doing? Dreaming of a woman he couldn't have. He was behaving like a youth in the first flush of love. The poor young woman had lost her only family. He doubted she'd be thinking of him as anything other than someone from the manor who had been kind to her. Yet, deep inside he wanted her to notice him, to think of him. God, he was mad, insane. He had to stop this nonsense. Annabelle Wallis wasn't for him. He would talk to Des about the cottage and leave it at that. No more could he visit her.

Another port later, Des rose, indicating for them to join the ladies. John hung back and tapped Des's arm. 'Can I have a word?'

Broughton inclined his head and left them.

'What is it?' Des asked, snubbing out his cigar.

'Widow Wallis's cottage. It was for her lifetime.'

'Oh, yes. I was thinking about that. I feel we could knock it down, fell the trees that are on each side of it and put the land to grazing or crop. We could gain another five or six acres.'

'What? No!' Surprised, John threw up his hands. 'Miss Wallis wants to stay on there and pay rent.'

'Rent? No, no. It is hardly viable. The old woman had that place for over fifty years. It is time to make some money on it.'

'And evict Miss Wallis?' The idea floored him, and he was alarmed at his own reaction.

'She is young. There is nothing stopping her from moving away. Perhaps into one of the cities.'

'She has no one, Des. We cannot be so heartless.' He had to fight for her.

Des shrugged. 'I doubt Miss Wallis will take it personally. In fact, she might thank us for setting her free to explore other avenues.'

A muscle ticked in his jaw. 'No one thanks you for knocking down their home.'

'Come, we should join the others.'

'I wanted to tell Miss Wallis that she had no need to worry. I told her she could stay.'

'Then you should not have said anything of the sort until you spoke to me. The estate needs to run efficiently, John, or we could go under as the Asquiths have done near Thirsk. Is that what you want?'

'Of course not. The Asquiths are generations of gamblers. We are hardly in their sphere of incompetence.'

'All it takes is one bad investment, a few years of poor crops and we could soon find ourselves in peril. I promised Papa that I would do everything I could to keep our wealth growing and I can only do that if I modernise and keep abreast of our expenditure and income.' Des took a deep breath. 'Let us have this discussion again some other time.'

'Tomorrow, then?'

'No, not tomorrow. I want us to travel to Rosewood Hall tomorrow. I want your opinion of it. Yardley is coming with us. Let us go through now, the ladies are waiting.'

John stayed behind as Des went ahead. He respected his brother's business sense in regards to the family fortune, and yes, they had to continually change and adapt to survive, but surely a simple cottage would not make or break them? He had to convince Des to allow Miss Wallis to keep the cottage. He also had to turn his attentions away from the lovely young woman and focus on other things. Annabelle Wallis was becoming more and more important to him and that was dangerous.

8

Placing the bouquet of roses and dahlias on Ma's grave, Annabelle then tidied up the dying posies left by well-wishers over the last two weeks. In the shade of the tree, the August sun didn't burn her as much as it affected the two gravediggers at the other side of the churchyard. Now and then they would stop the task, take off their hats and wipe the sweat from their brows.

Wearing all black, Annabelle understood the need to be in the shade, for summer continued to boil them all. The beck at the end of the cottage's garden was low now, the grass on the slope opposite brown and dry. Annabelle worked long hours to harvest the vegetables and herbs, working late into the night to make tonics, not that she was inundated with requests for Ma's remedies. Since Ma's death many orders had dropped off, as the villagers didn't trust Annabelle could make the same medicinal recipes as Ma, despite being taught by Ma all her life.

She had to do something about it. Visiting each customer and spreading the word that she was continuing Ma's work must be done, or soon she'd run out of money. How would she pay the rent without money? She was yet to walk to the manor and speak with

Mr Desmond Hartley about keeping on the cottage. Her courage failed her every time she thought about doing it. And Mr John Hartley she'd not seen since the day of the funeral, which saddened her more than she cared to admit.

'Ah, Annabelle.' Mrs Arnold, the baker's wife came along the path between the graves carrying a basket.

'Good afternoon, Mrs Arnold.'

'How are you keeping, dear?'

'Well, and you?'

'Oh, I'm fine as always.' Mrs Arnold peered closer. 'You should stay out of the sun, dear girl. You'll be the colour of nutmeg soon.'

'I have to be in the garden. It's how I earn money.'

'Speaking of which, what are you to do now Widow Wallis has gone?'

'Continue as I am. I know all the recipes for the tonics. Ma taught me the herbs to use and what ailments we can help cure. I can carry on her work just as she did, except the delivering of babies. Ma only took me to a few births. I'm not confident to be the local midwife.'

Mrs Arnold shook her head, setting the feathers in her bonnet bobbing. 'You must understand that Widow Wallis had a long life-time of experience. You do not.'

Annabelle bristled. 'She taught me well, though.'

'Yes, but you are young, a maid, an innocent. Folk around here won't have you wanting to know their private ailments. You're not wise in the world, lass. You couldn't attend to a man's illness, you who isn't married. Someone such as you can never be a midwife either, for you don't have the experience.'

'But the people of the village know me,' she defended, alarmed at what Mrs Arnold was implying.

'They do, but as someone who delivers their orders from Widow Wallis, not as someone they can call on to deliver their babies, or lance a wound, or listen to their woes as your ma did. They trusted Widow Wallis with their secrets, their concerns and I'm afraid you will not have the same respect for you haven't earned it.'

'I can still make up orders that people always ask for.' She felt wounded.

'Perhaps, for a while.' Mrs Arnold swapped her basket from one arm to the other. 'You need to plan for the future, Annabelle. A very different future to the one you hoped to have.' The older woman gave her a look full of sympathy before walking away.

Annabelle turned back to the grave, her hopes of continuing as she was fading fast. Without orders, she'd not be able to pay the rent and she'd lose the cottage, her home. Was Mrs Arnold right about the villagers not wanting her to attend to them? Of course she didn't have Ma's experience, but she could learn. She'd study all Ma's books. If they gave her a chance, she would show them she could do it.

'Ma, why did you have to leave me?' she whispered.

Sighing deeply, she left the grave and walked along the path.

'Miss Wallis,' Reverend Marr called to her as he came out of the church. 'I am pleased to see you.'

'Oh?'

'I was going to call on you. I have some news.' He clasped his hands together in front of him, pleased about something. 'The village have banded together a subscription for your ma's headstone. Mr Fletcher, the stonemason, will donate the stone and the sum collected will pay for the words inscribed. Isn't that wonderful news?'

Annabelle glanced back at Ma's simple wooden cross in amazement. 'A proper headstone?'

'Yes, indeed. Is it not generous? It shows how much the village thought of Widow Wallis.'

Joy filled her that the whole village cared so much for her ma.

'I'm happy Ma will have a fine headstone. She deserved one. I had hoped to pay for one myself in time. Will you thank everyone for me in your next service, please?'

'I will, happily.' He paused, his smile wavering. 'Is something wrong?'

She hesitated, wondering if speaking about her concerns would help. 'Mrs Arnold has dashed my hopes for continuing in Ma's place. The villagers won't accept me offering advice as Ma did.'

'Ah. Yes. That is very possible.' He clasped his hands behind his back, frowning in thought. 'You are too young, you see. You do not have any life experiences as Widow Wallis had. A married woman gains respect and knows about life far more than a young maid. It is no fault of yours, you must understand.'

'But I need to earn, Reverend.'

'You do, naturally. May I suggest you apply for service at Hartley Manor?'

Her stomach flipped at the thought of working at the manor and being so close to John Hartley. 'I know nothing of service.'

'You are qualified for sure, Miss Wallis. You have kept house. You know how to clean and mend, that sort of thing. Your cottage is a testament to your housekeeping skills. You would make a fine maid at the manor, or anywhere. There are a good many estates around, and then of course there are the towns where you might find work. Thirsk or Ripon, even York and Leeds. It is not all bad news, my child. All it means is a different life for you. Whatever you decide, I shall write you a character reference to take with you.'

She forced a smile and thanked him.

Walking home, her mind whirled at the enormity of Mrs Arnold's and the Reverend's words. To no longer work with herbs and deliver orders? She was breathless at the idea. And to work in service? At the manor? To go into service would mean giving up the cottage. Her home would house strangers. How would she deal with walking past it and seeing another family live there?

John Hartley said he'd talk to his brother about her staying in the cottage but that could only happen if she was earning enough to pay the rent on it. Perhaps she could take in washing or ironing?

Her head throbbed with the uncertainty of it all. To go into service and give up the cottage was like a knife to the chest, but to stay would depend on her finding a position out of service and the good nature of Desmond Hartley allowing her to stay and pay rent.

'Annabelle!' Dickie came loping up the road in the direction of the cottage. 'I just called on you and found the place empty.'

'I was visiting Ma's grave.'

He fell into step beside as they left the High Street behind and headed along the dirt road to the cottage. 'Sorry I've not been about much lately. We've been sorting the lambs ready for going to market.'

'You don't have to apologise, Dickie. You have work to do.'

'Aye, but I don't like to think of you being all alone at the cottage.'

'I'm fine. Ginny called for tea after church last week and I've been busy with harvesting in the garden.'

'The weather has been brilliant, hasn't it? Though we are in need of rain. The becks are running low and so is the river.'

'The beck at the bottom of the garden is barely running.'

'Aye, I noticed it as I crossed the stones just now.'

'Did you want some tea or something cold?' she asked as they left the road and walked down the path to the cottage gate.

'Any drink would be welcomed. I'm far parched. I've got the afternoon off. Did you fancy going for a walk or a picnic?'

She entered the cottage and untied her bonnet. Pulling off her gloves, she stalled in answering. 'I have too much to do.'

'Then I'll help you in the garden.'

'Not on your afternoon off, Dickie. Why don't you have a pint with your mates?' She donned a worn apron and took off her best boots and replaced them with her old gardening ones.

He shrugged and sat at the table. 'I'd rather spend the time with you.'

'I'll make some tea, then. Did you hear about the people in the village getting together a sum of money for Ma's headstone?' She busied herself making tea.

'No, I hadn't heard. I've been in the fields all week.'

'It's a wonderful thing. They thought so much of her. I wish Ma could see it.'

'Annabelle...' Dickie took her hand as she stepped past him. 'Sit down a minute, will you?'

Seeing the impassioned look on his face, she sat next to him. 'What is it?'

'We need to talk.'

'About?' She perched on the edge of the chair ready to jump up. She didn't want to talk to Dickie about anything serious. Her mind was too overwrought to think clearly.

'I want us to get married.' He squeezed her hand. 'Tell me you want that, too?'

'No, I don't, Dickie.' She winced as the words flew out of her mouth and his face fell. 'I'm sorry to be so hurtful. I don't mean to be, but I'm not ready for marriage.'

'Then I'll continue to wait. I'm getting good at it.'

Frustrated by his refusal to give up, her tone was sharp. 'No. I don't want you to wait. We keep going around in circles and, to be honest, I don't want the responsibility of making you happy or unhappy.'

His expression became desperate. 'We'd be good together. I know we would be.'

'You know more than me, then.' She went to the stove and took the boiling kettle off the heat.

'I would make you happy, Annabelle. I promise I'd spend my life doing so.'

'You can't make those promises, Dickie. Don't you understand, *I* don't know what will make me happy, so how can you?'

'All you want is to stay here, isn't it? If we marry, I can ask up at the manor for us to live in this cottage. I'm head shepherd and we can rent this place. I'm sure they'd let us.'

Annabelle gazed around the cottage, loving every bit of it. Yet, as much as she wanted to live here, she didn't want to marry Dickie to do so. As tempting as the offer was, she knew she'd not be happy married to him. She'd rather stay unmarried and move away than feel trapped in a marriage to a man who didn't make her go weak at the knees.

Dickie came to her. 'I thought with your ma dying, you'd be eager to marry me. You'd be safe with me.'

'I'm honoured you care about me so much, really I am, and I care for you...'

The light faded from his eyes. 'You don't love me, do you?'

She shook her head sadly. 'No, not in the way that you deserve. You're my best friend, Dickie, and I treasure that, but you want more, and I don't have anything to give.' She raised her hand as he went to speak. 'Don't say you'll wait for me to change my mind because I won't.'

'But—'

'If I wanted to marry you, I would have done so by now.' She kissed his cheek, but he gathered her into his arms and kissed her properly. For a moment she enjoyed being held, being kissed, but as his hands roamed her body, demanding more, she pushed him away and spun out of his arms.

Breathing heavily, Dickie hung his head. 'I'm sorry.'

'I am, too,' she murmured. For an instant she'd wanted to be held, but Dickie wasn't the person she wanted to kiss. John Hartley's handsome face came to mind and it hit her like a hammer that he was the only man she wanted, and the only man she couldn't have.

'I'd best go.' He grabbed his cap off the table and left via the back door.

Taking a deep breath, Annabelle sat at the table feeling miserable. She didn't want to lose her friend, and that's all he would ever be to her.

* * *

John walked the hills belonging to Rosewood Hall. From this height he could see most of the acres surrounding the farm buildings, which were hidden in a hollow from the main house. The Hall itself surprised him. He'd been expecting a small, sturdy grey farmhouse lacking style and comfort. However, the carriage had swept up a gentle hill to level out on a wide stretch of grassy fields edged with woods. The long drive afforded them a view of a pale sandstone two-storey dwelling with a fine gabled entrance and many windows on either side.

Inside, the front entrance showed the architecture of the original medieval Hall, but over the last century the previous family had enlarged the main house with wings on either side. Consisting of eight bedrooms upstairs and attics, and several reception rooms downstairs, John had liked the house immediately. It had the atmosphere of a home, albeit a home that was a little neglected and in desperate need of refurbishment.

Des hadn't been particularly bothered with the house but was more interested in the land. Sheep farming was a lucrative business, and Des wanted John's opinion on whether Rosewood Hall should be kept or sold.

'Well, what do you think?' Des asked, turning his back on the stiff breeze that blew over the hills.

'I like it a lot.'

'You do?' Des seemed surprised by his answer.

John squinted in the sunshine. 'We have the markets of York to the south, Thirsk to the north-west, Ripon to the west and Malton to the east and beyond Malton there is Scarborough on the coast. We are in an excellent position.'

'My thoughts exactly. We can run sheep and with a good manager, this place will not only pay for itself but add profit to the coffers.' Des grinned.

'We should run deer, too.' John could see the land full of healthy livestock.

'Deer, yes, I had not thought of that.'

'And we do not need to find a manager.'

'What do you mean?'

'I will live here.' John had made up his mind.

'You?' Des's eyes widened. 'Out here?'

'It is not that remote. Helmsley is a splendid village and only four miles from here.' John chuckled. 'Several places I have travelled to are so isolated you do not see another soul for days.'

'You may become friends with the Duncombes of Duncombe Park,' Des joked, but John detected a hidden hope in his voice.

'We shall see, brother.' John gazed at the view. 'Two hundred and fifty acres, you say?'

'Yes. Papa bought it for next to nothing from the Randalls who had this place, amongst many others, but who had lost a great fortune in some investment in Italy, of all places. The youngest Randall died a few years ago without an heir. His young widow sailed for Jamaica to be with her family there and instructed solicitors to sell the lot of it. Papa knew one of the Randalls from his

Oxford days. He sent for the sale catalogue of the Randall properties and bought this one. Heaven knows why.'

'Perhaps Papa wanted to become a sheep farmer?' John joked.

'All I know is that it is another knot in the noose around my neck. I have far too much to deal with and this place falls low on my list of priorities.'

'Well, I like it, especially on a sunny day such as today.' John watched a hawk hover high above them.

'It does have a pleasant outlook. We can have shooting parties here. A gamekeeper would be beneficial.'

'I agree.'

'And the house?' Des asked. 'You can see how much needs to be done.'

'I will be happy to oversee the upgrade.'

'It would ease my mind to have someone to bring the place into shape, but I never expected it to be you. I could do with your help at home, especially when I must go to London at times. The estate runs sufficient well enough under Yardley, but now I am a local Justice of the Peace, my time is even more constrained. Tomorrow I must start a tour of the district around the estate to file a report on the state of the roads and bridges in my local authority and I must attend the Petty Sessions next week at Easingwold.' Des rubbed his eyes.

John could see the strain on his brother's face. 'I have told you to give more responsibilities to me. Forget this place, I will see to it all. My inheritance will cover the costs of the refurbishment of the house and the restocking of new flocks and herds of deer. I shall put some of the lower pastures to plough, too.'

'Having Rosewood off my mind will be a great relief.'

'I need a home of my own, Des, and this place feels right for me.'

'That is true.' Des shrugged. 'So be it. I shall not stand in your way. I will have the deeds put into your name and have it separate from the estate, so it is always yours, no matter what. I shall write to Arthur and ask him if he is happy to have Dogwood Cottage in Derbyshire for his home whenever he leaves the army.'

'Arthur will be happy with that. He has always liked Dogwood Cottage, and its links to Mama,' John assured him. 'You must allow me to help you with the other concerns Papa has accumulated over the years.'

'There is a shareholders' meeting next week in York, regarding the railway company Papa invested in. He sold his shares in the canals, did you know that?'

'No, I did not.'

'Papa judged the railways were the future and would leave the canals behind.'

'I agree. The railways are opening up America and India like you would not believe. I have seen it first-hand,' John told him as they began walking back down the hill.

'Will you come with me to the meeting? You will have more insight into it than I.'

'Of course.'

'With both of us there we can be educated on the company. Penny will come with us as she wants to do some shopping and Eliza is staying with Joanna.' Des glanced at John. 'Do you trust Eliza is finished with all that nonsense concerning Morris-Hippleton?'

'She tells me that is so. We have to trust her. We cannot spend all our time worrying that the two of them are meeting up, it'll drive us into madness.' John gazed at the house and surrounding outbuildings and stables, his thoughts jumping ahead to how pleasant the Hall would look once he began the improvements. He could not wait to get started.

Back at the Hall, he walked around the drawing room, taking notes of the work needed.

'This house needs a woman's touch,' Des said, inspecting the faded wallpaper.

John's stomach lurched. Yes, he agreed. But the only woman who consumed his thoughts was Miss Wallis. He'd not been to see her since the funeral, despite wanting to. Every discussion he had with Des about the cottage turned into a minor argument. Des wanted the cottage gone – Annabelle, too. As much as John fought for her to stay, Des dug in his heels. In the end, John had stopped mentioning it. However, that didn't help Annabelle. He couldn't knock on her door and tell her anything good, so he stayed away in the hope that when he did see her, Des would have relented and agreed she could stay. He wanted to be the bearer of good news, not bad, not after the loss she'd suffered. Nevertheless, he wanted to see her. He missed her, which was foolish in the extreme. He'd only met her a few times, yet she was all he thought about. What the hell was he going to do?

9

Thunder made Annabelle jump as she sorted through Ma's winter clothes in the trunk. Kneeling in the cramped corner of the loft where the roof met the wall, she had waited four weeks since Ma's funeral to approach the trunk which stored the seasonal clothes Ma had worn. The dark green trunk sat in the corner and served as a table for Annabelle with the loft being her bedroom and also storage space. Every surface was useful to hold books or hats or whatever else Annabelle kept.

At the start of each season, Ma would fold her clothes and ask Annabelle to take them up to the trunk to store and bring down the next season's garments. On the floor surrounding her were Ma's thick petticoats, two woollen shawls, her woollen workday dress, the winter nightgowns and stockings...

Lavender scented the air as she moved the clothes. Sadly, this time she'd not be replacing the clothes with Ma's summer ones. Instead, she was giving all of Ma's garments to the poor relief collected by Reverend Marr. All she would keep was a heavy black shawl, which Annabelle couldn't part with for she'd bought it for

Ma one Christmas some years ago when she'd started earning money from selling Ma's tonics and herbs. Pinned to the shawl was a brooch in the shape of a rose, the red stones still glittered even though they were only glass and not rubies. Ma's husband had bought it for her, and it was a treasured token of his love. Ma said it would be Annabelle's one day and because of that promise she'd not pinned it on Ma's chest in her coffin.

The shawl and the brooch were the only two intimate items she had belonging to Ma, and she'd keep them always.

Thunder clapped again. Glancing out of the window in the roof, she was alarmed to see the angry clouds racing past. A storm was brewing.

Gathering up the clothes, Annabelle descended the ladder and placed them on the table. Lightning flashed outside the back door. Bobby's neighing added to the noise of the rolling thunder.

Dashing outside with a bucket, Annabelle went into the field and caught Bobby by his halter and dragged the protesting pony into the little stable. 'It's for your own good, you silly boy,' she scolded him. 'Do you want to be wet when you can stay dry? Now get in!'

Once he was in the stable, she went out to bring in Daisy, who followed her calmly into the shelter and stood beside Bobby as if to show him how to behave.

With them fed an armful of hay, she secured the door and then quickly herded the chickens into the coop. The wind lashed the trees, tossing the higher branches about and sending some leaves down. The trees hadn't begun to turn colour yet, but the storm showed which trees had dying leaves as a shower of foliage covered the garden.

Yanking her hair out of her eyes, Annabelle quickly grabbed two buckets and went down to the beck to fill them. If the storm raged all evening and night, she'd need the water to last until tomorrow.

Angry dark clouds blotted out the setting sun as she closed the potting shed door and secured it against the gale. Once inside the cottage, she closed the windows and stopped to stare at the storm, which was growing stronger. Suddenly, rain fell hard and fast, surprising her with its ferocity. Soon the path to the road was hidden by the heavy rain.

The warm sunny weather they had experienced for months turned grey and dismal. The temperature dropped and Annabelle added more wood to the fire in the main room and to the range. She'd make a cup of tea and heat up the beef stew she'd made yesterday.

Lighting the lamp and a few candles, the cottage became warm and cosy. She ate the hearty stew while reading the newspaper she bought in the village. Her gaze strayed to the small brown jar on the shelf above the range. It held all the money she had, which was not as much as she hoped. She had ten shillings and nine pence left. The orders had dried up from Ma's regulars, but she hoped she'd make a few shillings tomorrow at the Friday market in Easingwold a few miles away. Thankfully, she'd spent the morning cutting and sorting the flowers and herbs and they were tied and bound in baskets in the potting shed; the storm couldn't harm them. Bottles of tonics were in a crate in the scullery. She prayed the storm would have passed by dawn when she needed to be on her way with Bobby pulling the cart. He'd not behave in a storm all the way to Easingwold, that was for certain.

As darkness blackened the windows, the night sky frequently lit up with flashes of lightning. She closed the curtains and settled herself on the faded red brocade sofa before the blazing fire. Thunder still boomed like a giant hammer on an anvil.

Before Ma's death, she'd been knitting a pair of woollen socks to wear with her boots in the winter. In the sewing basket was the unfinished work Ma had been doing. Annabelle picked up the petticoat and traced Ma's fine stitching of the torn hem. Sorrow filled her.

The nights were the worst when she missed Ma. The evening hours seemed so lonely and quiet. During the day, she kept busy working outside. The garden had never looked so tidy, the potting shed never so organised. She'd collected reeds down at the beck and mended broken baskets or made new ones. The scullery had been whitewashed and scrubbed, fresh straw filled the hens' nest boxes and the stable had been mucked out.

She would spend the evenings knitting, and maybe her efforts would be something she could sell at the markets.

A bang against the front door made her jump violently. Not many people used the front door, the locals and friends came around to the back door. The banging came again. Was something blown against the door by the gale?

Annabelle went to the window and pulled back the curtain but saw nothing in the darkness. The thumping on the door became urgent. Alarmed, she stepped towards the door. She cracked the door an inch and peered through the gap. Something was blocking the view.

'Who is there?' Annabelle yelled, scared.

'Please... I need help...' The female voice sounded desperate.

Opening the door wider, Annabelle caught the figure as it fell inwards. 'Good heavens. Are you hurt?'

'I need help...' The hooded cape fell backwards off the woman's head.

Annabelle stared at Eliza Hartley. 'Miss Hartley!'

'Forgive me.' Miss Hartley gripped Annabelle's arms like a vice.

'Come in.' Annabelle slammed the door shut and helped her over to the sofa, but as Miss Hartley sat down, she groaned deeply with closed eyes. 'Where are you hurt?' she asked her unexpected visitor.

Miss Hartley's cape fell open and Annabelle had seen enough pregnant women to notice the swollen stomach and know what it meant. She might be an unmarried maid, but she wasn't a complete innocent. She'd helped Ma with a few births in the last year when Ma decided she was old enough to understand and aid her in the deliveries. Ma didn't believe in keeping her in ignorance and Annabelle was suddenly grateful for Ma's modern thoughts.

'I can go to the manor, Miss Hartley, and get help.'

'No!' Miss Hartley shouted, shocking Annabelle so much she took a step back.

'But Miss—'

'No one must know I am here.' Eliza Hartley's grey eyes screwed tight as pain bent her in two. 'You have to help me,' she panted. 'I came here as I thought you would be the best person to help me.'

'Yes, I'll help you, but your family will want to know you're here.'

'They think I am with a friend until tomorrow.' Miss Hartley leaned back, her hands on her stomach.

'How did you get here?'

'I caught a coach from Scarborough to Easingwold and then walked from there to here.'

'That's a long walk in your condition.'

Miss Hartley managed a wry grin and looked like John so much that Annabelle's heart skipped a beat. 'I could not walk another step if I tried. My feet have blisters.'

'How long have you had the pains?' Annabelle asked, fetching her a glass of water as rain battered the windows. She passed the glass to Miss Hartley and stirred up the fire.

'All day. Actually, last night I was most uncomfortable. I thought perhaps something was happening and suddenly I did not want to be alone. I thought of you and this cottage as somewhere safe. Was I wrong? Your mother helped so many people.'

'So, you don't want to go home?' Annabelle couldn't believe it. Why wouldn't she want to be with her family?

'No, God forbid. Anywhere but home. I came here as I thought you might help me, and you are not in the village. This cottage is tucked away in the trees, safe from prying eyes. No one saw me.' She grasped Annabelle's hand. 'I had nowhere else to go.'

'You need a doctor. I can run for Dr Henderson.'

'No, I tell you,' Miss Hartley snapped. 'No one must know, you fool.' Another pain made her gasp and moan. When it had passed, she looked at Annabelle. 'Forgive me for being rude. You have to assist me, please.'

'I will.' She tried to smile in reassurance but felt the opposite. How was she to help Miss Hartley? The woman needed to be at the manor with a doctor in attendance.

'I wish Widow Wallis was alive,' Miss Hartley murmured, panting through another pain.

'Me, too,' she whispered. Ma would have known what to do. 'Where is your husband? I assume you have married?'

'I do not have one.' Miss Hartley's stare became teary. 'This has been a secret I have kept from my family and friends. It is a secret that you must keep too. I will pay you well to do so.'

'How have you managed to keep it from everyone?' She thought of John Hartley. He'd be distressed to know his sister was in such trouble.

'I wore looser dresses and covered myself with shawls like this.' She held up the ends of a beautiful silk peacock-coloured shawl she wore under her cape. 'I barely showed for the first six months or so, but lately it has become more difficult. I sent for a maternity corset to help hide my stomach. I have spent the last two weeks in a hotel in Scarborough, out of the way...' She spoke through gritted teeth.

Summoning all her knowledge about births, Annabelle prayed for Ma to help her from beyond the grave. 'Right, miss. Let us get you comfortable for I think your baby will be born soon. Can you make it up the ladder to my bed?'

'No, I do not think I can.' Miss Hartley began to sob. 'What a mess, and it hurts terribly.'

'Calm down,' she soothed, holding her hand. 'You're feeling anxious and overwrought, but I'm here and we'll get through it together, yes?'

Miss Hartley nodded as tears glittered on her lashes.

'Good. I'll make a bed on the floor in front of the fire and put some water on to boil. We'll soon have you comfortable.'

Annabelle worked quickly. She went up into the loft and took the bedding Ma had used from the trunk. Downstairs she made a bed on the rug before the hearth and then raced out into the storm to the potting shed, where she collected a piece of calico to lay over the bed to protect the sheets from the mess of childbirth.

Miss Hartley bore through several contractions as Annabelle added more wood to the fire and then the range. She filled a bowl and a jug with boiling water and took fresh towels from the cupboard.

'Have some water, Miss Hartley,' she encouraged as she set up the things she'd need on the small table next to the sofa. Having watched Ma a few times, she knew she had to have clean hands and so she went into the scullery and scrubbed her hands with soap, then found scissors and twine.

Miss Hartley's screams brought her rushing back into the main room again.

'You need to get undressed, Miss Hartley.' She helped her remove her boots, the cape and pretty peacock shawl, her bodice, hooped skirt and the pregnancy corset, which looked like an instrument of torture to Annabelle with its fastenings and straps.

Miss Hartley sighed in relief when she wore only her chemise and under petticoat.

Without all the trappings of clothing, Annabelle could clearly see the small round bump. 'You're not very big, Miss Hartley. Is the baby coming early?'

'I would not know, Miss Wallis. I do not know how far advanced I am. I have no knowledge of babies, childbirth, or any of it.'

'Do you have an idea of when you last had a monthly show?' she asked gently, blushing at having to ask a lady such a question, but she'd heard Ma ask the same question many times when a woman came to the back door asking for a tonic.

'No, I cannot recall...' Miss Hartley, chin on her chest, groaned and strained.

'I need to check on the progress, Miss Hartley. Will you allow me to look?'

'Yes... Just get it out.'

Annabelle lifted the blanket and pushed back the petticoat. She gently touched the opening where she could see a small area of wet hair on the baby's head. There seemed to be a lot of blood. Was that normal? She didn't know and it scared her more than she cared to acknowledge.

She had never delivered a baby by herself and when she'd helped Ma, she'd been standing to one side out of the way, only there to pass Ma anything she needed and to learn. Now, faced with the prospect of being solely accountable for the safe delivery of a Hartley baby, she felt winded. An overwhelming sense of responsibility and alarm frightened her. With shaking hands, she pulled the blanket back over Miss Hartley's legs.

'How long do I have to go through this?' Miss Hartley asked, puffing away her hair that had come loose from its confining net.

'A while yet, but I can see the head,' she confirmed with an encouraging smile. 'Why don't you rest for a little while?'

The wind and rain battered the cottage as Miss Hartley dozed. Annabelle glanced at the little clock on the mantle as it softly chimed ten times. Quietly, she made a pot of tea and brought the tea tray to the table.

'May I have some tea?' Miss Hartley asked.

'Of course.' Annabelle poured her a cup and helped her to sip from it.

'You are exceedingly kind, thank you.'

'I'm worried, Miss Hartley. Your family should know you are here.'

'No. This is a secret. You shan't be in any trouble, I promise.'

'But I'm not a midwife.'

'No, but you must have some knowledge from your mother?'

'A little. Ma wanted to teach me the ways of midwifery, but she was taking the lessons slowly, waiting for me to grow older, or become married... Ma thought it would be a valuable skill for me to have.'

'Well, let me be your first, for I have nowhere else to go and I cannot possibly go home. My shame would destroy any love my brothers have for me. I cannot damage their reputations or the family name with my stupid foolish actions. Des will never forgive me, and Penny will be horrified I have been with a man...' She grunted as another pain consumed her.

She waited until the pain had passed and Miss Hartley opened her eyes. 'What about your brother, John? Will he understand?'

'No. He will only want to kill the man who put me in this condition, and I cannot let him harm the one I love.' Miss Hartley panted. 'Oh, it hurts so much!'

For the next hour, Miss Hartley pushed and strained as her pains grew stronger.

Annabelle coaxed and soothed her to push and relax when needed. Instinct took over as she worked, holding the baby's head as it came out. She remembered Ma's instructions on how to ease a baby into the world. Miss Hartley's deep groans echoed around the cottage as Annabelle manipulated the shoulders while Miss Hartley pushed until she was red in the face.

'I cannot do it!' Miss Hartley yelled.

'You can!' Concerned at the amount of blood Miss Hartley was losing, Annabelle used several towels to stem the flow.

'No...'

'Yes. Nearly there,' Annabelle encouraged as the baby suddenly slipped out into her hands on a rush of blood and water.

'Oh!' Miss Hartley sagged back onto the cushions, eyes closed.

'You did it, Miss Hartley.' Awed and utterly relieved, Annabelle wiped the baby's face and tied the cord and cut it. She vigorously rubbed the baby with a towel to bring life to its blue skin. 'Come on, little one.'

After a minute of rubbing, the baby squirmed and made a tiny squawk like a baby bird.

'It is alive?' Miss Hartley asked, not opening her eyes. She looked pale, sweaty and exhausted.

'She is.' Annabelle wrapped the baby in a warm blanket. 'She is tiny, but extremely sweet.'

'I need to sleep,' Miss Hartley said, tearfully. 'I am awfully tired.'

'You can sleep as soon as the afterbirth is out.'

'Afterbirth?' Miss Hartley's eyes sprang open. 'What in heaven are you talking about?'

'You aren't done yet, miss. I'm sorry.'

'Then get it out!'

'I can't, you must. Soon, I think. You'll feel another contraction. You need to push when you do.' She glanced down at the blood continuing to flow. Fear trickled down her spine. Why was this happening here in her home? She needed Ma desperately. 'It must be delivered, miss.'

'No! I shan't do it all again. This is torturous!' Miss Hartley wailed.

'Please, Miss Hartley, you must. Ma told me if it doesn't come out, a woman can die. Do you want me to fetch Dr Henderson?'

'No. Definitely not!' Crying, Miss Hartley buried her face in her hands. 'I just want it to be all over.'

'And it will be, soon. Here, hold your daughter while we wait. I'll make us some fresh tea.' She handed the baby to Miss Hartley, who gently held her daughter.

'I cannot keep her,' Miss Hartley sobbed. 'I must give her up.'

'That is for you to decide, miss.' Annabelle paused in tidying away some of the soiled towels. She was alarmed by the blood loss. When she'd attended other births, she couldn't remember seeing so much. Was it normal or not?

'I have decided. Long ago I made up my mind. This baby cannot stay with me. The shame and scandal will consume the family. I cannot do that to my brothers. I have created enough gossip in London. If people found out about her, I would be ruined forever. The baby is evidence to my shame, my undoing.'

'The father? Will he not marry you?' She dumped the towels in a bucket and went to wash her hands.

More tears fell from Miss Hartley's eyes. 'No. It is impossible.'

Annabelle put the kettle on to boil. 'You don't need to think about all that right now.'

'I wish I was dead!'

'You mustn't say such things, miss.'

'But I do. If I died, it would be so much easier, or if this baby died. The evidence would be gone.'

'You don't know what you're saying.' How could she speak of the baby being dead? The tiny little thing was perfect and the thought of someone, her own mother, wishing her dead shocked Annabelle to the core. Had her own mother thought that way about her?

'I need to return home and not with this baby.' Miss Hartley stared down at the little pink face. 'My brothers expect me to marry well, and I have been silly about a man I cannot have. They will want me to make a good marriage...'

'What do *you* want, though?'

'I want this all to be a nightmare I can wake from.' Miss Hartley cried silent tears. 'Miss Wallis, you will have to keep her.'

'Me?' She nearly dropped the teapot she held.

'Yes, yes, you. It can be done.'

'No, miss.'

'Listen to me,' Miss Hartley became excited, 'I will have an allowance made for the baby's needs and your own expenses, naturally. I have a house in Norfolk. It was bequeathed to me through an elderly aunt. You can live there with the baby. I will tell my brothers that I sold the house. It will be yours and the child's.'

'Miss Hartley, please. What you're asking isn't possible.'

'It is.' Miss Hartley sobbed broken-heartedly. 'No one must know about her, do you not see? I must protect my brothers from my stupidity. They do not deserve to be dishonoured by what I have done. You must help me, I beg you. Promise me you will not tell a soul about her being mine. Promise me!' She was becoming hysterical. Sweat broke out on her forehead and she looked pale.

Helpless, Annabelle knelt next to the anguished woman and held her tight. 'I promise. Your secret is safe with me.'

'You have to take care of her. I will pay you well. Then I will know she is safe and will be brought up by someone I know who is kind. Someone who will care for her. You will do that for me, won't you?' Miss Hartley began to shake. 'I do not feel well. Please say you will care for her.'

Annabelle placed the baby on the sofa. 'We'll work something out, miss. Rest now.'

'How can I rest? I must go home in the morning and pretend

none of this happened,' Miss Hartley snapped, then reached for Annabelle's hand, an apologetic expression on her face. 'I know you to be a kind and generous soul like your mother. She brought you up well and loved you, didn't she? Even though you weren't her child by birth?'

'Yes, she did.' Sadness filled her on remembering Ma, but also a wave of love followed quickly after. Ma had taken her in as an orphaned baby and loved her like her own. Annabelle had been saved from being left in an orphanage and to an unknown fate.

'That's all I ask for you to do. Please take care of my baby like your mother took care of you,' Miss Hartley pleaded.

'It's a big decision, miss, one that will change my life.' Was she mad to even consider it?

'But you were happy with your mother, weren't you?'

'Yes, but it was a different situation. Ma was a widow, I'm not married.'

'You will be well paid, Miss Wallis. In Norfolk you can say you're widowed,' Miss Hartley murmured, growing tired and weak. 'I trust you. You will love her...'

'But your brothers?'

'Must never know. Des will send the baby away, have it adopted by strangers... He will never forgive me... The condemnation would be too much. I will be forever tainted in his eyes. I could not live with their disapproval... The truth would get out and I would be ruined.'

'They would forgive you.' Annabelle was adamant that they would, surely.

'Des would not. You don't understand our society, there are rules that mustn't be broken.' Silent tears rolled down Miss Hartley's cheeks. 'I am a disgrace. My child a bastard. Only you can save my reputation and my child...'

An hour later, with the afterbirth delivered, Annabelle sat on the sofa with the baby sleeping nestled amongst the cushions. The night had been fraught with emotion and tension. Miss Hartley had fed the baby for a few minutes only before she passed her back to Annabelle, turned over and closed her eyes.

Annabelle stared at the other woman, who remained pale and clammy. The blood loss scared her. She was inclined to run for Dr Henderson, but she'd promised she wouldn't. Instead, she packed more towels between Miss Hartley's thighs and raised her legs, hoping that would be enough to reduce the blood flow. She feared the amount lost wasn't normal, but apart from giving Miss Hartley a tonic in her tea to give her strength, she didn't know what else to do. What if she was torn inside? But the minute she mentioned fetching a doctor it caused Miss Hartley to become agitated and sob that no one must ever know what had occurred.

Miss Hartley's wish for her to take care of the baby was ridiculous. She couldn't possibly keep a baby. An allowance and a house in Norfolk would mean leaving Yorkshire, her friends, the village where she'd grown up. She'd be alone, a stranger in a strange place with a child not her own. But then, Miss Hartley's other option of putting the baby into an orphanage was too distressing.

Gazing at the sweet, tiny face, Annabelle couldn't imagine leaving her at a cold and impersonal orphanage where she might be given to a family who mistreated her. How would she live with that on her conscience? The whole situation was upsetting and she felt out of her depth.

Tiredness drugged her into a doze. It would be dawn soon, but there'd be no chance of attending the market today. Miss Hartley would need to stay with her for a few days to recover from the birth.

Annabelle woke to the baby's cries. She picked up the baby to soothe her and frowned as she noticed the bed on the floor was empty.

'Miss Hartley?' Annabelle stood, wondering if the lady wanted to use the pot. Surely, she'd have wakened her to ask for help to do so?

The baby's crying increased, and she rocked her in her arms as she went outside and behind the potting shed where the privy was. 'Miss Hartley, are you in there?'

When no answer came, she returned inside, ignoring Daisy's bellowing to be milked.

On the table was a note propped against the teapot.

Dear Miss Wallis,

Thank you for all your help. I am in your debt and will forever be so.

I beg you to keep my secret for the sake of my family's repu-tation and my own. My disgrace should not tarnish my family. If you have any respect for them, I implore you to never reveal my secret.

The baby's fate lies in your hands. I will make no interference, except to send you some money for your trouble. No one must know of the link between the baby and me. I do not want her, and I know my family would have her adopted by strangers. At least this way I know she will be looked after by a good and caring person such as you.

You will not hear from me again as I will go away, perhaps travel to the continent. Rest assured, I will do the right thing for the child and send you the details of a bank account I will set up for the child and of the house in Norfolk.

Thank you for keeping my promise.

With sincere gratitude,

Eliza Hartley

PS I have left my shawl behind. It was a present from my brother, John. He bought it in India, and I treasure it dearly. I want

*the baby to have it as a reminder that I did think of her and
always will do.*

Stunned, Annabelle read the note twice before the words sunk
in. What in God's name was she to do? Panic gripped her as the
baby cried louder. She couldn't do this. She wasn't responsible for
this child. How would she take care of it when she was floundering
herself?

Should she go to the manor and give the child over? What if
Miss Hartley had left already? Would they believe her if Miss
Hartley denied the truth? How could she possibly turn up at the
manor and give them a baby? They'd think her mad and have her
locked in an asylum. Or they would think she was a fallen woman
and that the baby was hers. She couldn't bear to see the look on
John Hartley's face.

She stared down at the little red face, which, having cried
herself to sleep, was now calm and perfect. To give her to an
orphanage would condemn the child to a life of servitude and questioning her parentage. She'd be simply an unwanted child in a
building full of other unwanted children. Unloved and only cared
for in the most basic of terms. Could she subject this tiny little thing
to that terrible life? A life *she* would have suffered if it hadn't been
for Ma taking her in.

Was this some sort of test? Was it now her turn to do the same?
Had Ma saved her only for her to then save this little mite? Or had
she helped to bring this baby into the world only to give her away
like an unwanted puppy?

Was that the fate of their lives?

Daunted by the decision she had to make, she sat on the sofa.
Over the arm lay the peacock-coloured shawl. Annabelle ran her
fingers over it, feeling the soft silk. She gently wrapped it around
the baby.

Her fingers shook as she tenderly touched the baby's smooth cheek. She was so delicate, so tiny, and abandoned by her mother, left alone with a stranger just as Annabelle had been. Had Ma thought the same about her when she held her all those years ago?

Ma had done the right thing by Annabelle. Maybe now it was time Annabelle repaid the favour.

10

John came down the stairs, adjusting his collar. The smell of bacon wafting from the breakfast room made his stomach rumble. His step checked as Eliza came across the entrance hall, looking dishevelled.

'Eliza? You're home early. Is anything the matter?' He took her arm as she went to pass him. 'Eliza?'

'I need to go up, John,' she whispered.

'What has happened?' He took in the state of her cape and the dress beneath, which were crumpled and wet at the bottom. Her hair seemed not to have received the attention of a brush. For her to be out in public in such a state of disrepair shocked him. Eliza prided herself on being immaculate at all times.

Her smile was strained in a face devoid of all colour. She looked ill. 'Everything is fine. I caught an early coach. I... I decided to walk from the village.'

'Why?' he quizzed. Something was not right about her. What was she hiding from him?

She swayed and gripped the banister. 'It... it is a fine morning for a walk.'

'You look unwell.'

'A terrible headache only...' Dark shadows bruised under her eyes.

'Will you be down for breakfast?'

She held on to the banister and slowly went past him. 'No... I must rest. I shall be down later.'

'Do you want me to assist you to your room? Or send for Dr Henderson?'

'No! I just need to lie down...' She stumbled up the next step and John helped her to the top.

'Are you certain you do not need the doctor?'

'A headache, John, that is all.' She held on to the wall as she went along to her room.

Uneasy, John went in to breakfast. Havers was instructing Stevens, the footman, on the right temperature to set the warming pans on the sideboard and Des was seated at the table reading the morning mail, a newspaper at his elbow.

'Eliza has just returned home,' John told him as he helped himself to a plate of poached eggs, bacon and mushrooms.

'She has?' Des frowned. 'That is decidedly early.'

'She looked unwell.'

'Perhaps she has caught a cold or done too much while she was staying with Joanna.'

'She says it is a headache, but she seemed rather ill. We should send for Dr Henderson.'

'Is that necessary? If it is a headache, then a lie-down and some quiet is recommended.' Des folded the newspaper and paid attention to spreading jam on his toast. 'Yardley says the grouse numbers seem rather high this season. We have ten for the shoot on Saturday. Ferguson has pulled out.' Des indicated a letter near his plate. 'He writes he has to go to London instead.'

'Are you replacing him?' John asked as Havers poured him a cup of tea.

'No. I shan't bother. I do want to speak to Guthrie while he is here. He breeds fine gun dogs. I am thinking of buying a couple of bitches. Yardley's dog is a rather fine boy. We could breed with them.'

John nodded. 'I would like a sheepdog for Rosewood. Do you know of anyone who has a litter?'

'No, but perhaps Guthrie will know of someone.' Des sipped his tea.

John kept glancing at the door, his breakfast half-eaten. Eliza's appearance worried him. It was unlike her to be ill. Their mama always said her children had the constitutions of horses. He was rarely ill himself, even when travelling to foreign places and eating foreign foods.

'John?'

He snapped back to the present. 'Sorry.'

Des gave him a stern look. 'I was saying that we should travel to Inverness soon. The sawmill has changed managers and although I appointed the new manager by letter after reading his references, I feel we should go up there and introduce ourselves to the new man to make sure we are satisfied by him. What do you think?'

'Yes, it would not hurt to show our faces.'

'My thoughts exactly, especially as another sawmill has opened up only ten miles from ours. The competition is fierce. We need to be seen to care that our operation is important to us, or orders may be in jeopardy. Shall we go this afternoon?'

'This afternoon?' John frowned in surprise. 'That is short notice. We have only just returned from Rosewood.' He wanted to visit Annabelle, but he couldn't say that to Des.

'I want it over and done with. I have too much coming up next week that I must deal with. Going up there now suits me. I can cancel my other appointments for the next three days, can you?'

'Very well.'

'Good.' Des turned in his chair to Havers. 'See that our luggage is packed for three days away and have the carriage prepared for this afternoon. We shall leave for York train station straight after luncheon.'

'Very good, sir.' Havers bowed.

'I shall go up and see if Eliza needs anything,' John said, pushing his chair away from the table.

'We have maids for that job,' Des said. 'If Eliza is unwell, she can ring for her maid. I will ask Penny to check in on her after breakfast. We have Yardley coming in for a meeting in ten minutes. There is much to do today before we leave for Inverness, and I want your full attention.'

A muscle clenched in John's jaw. 'Des, I am more than happy to be a part of the family business and do my fair share, but I will remind you that I am not a servant, but your brother, so do not order me about like one.'

Frowning, Des glanced at him. 'I am not. Stop being so sensitive. I understand you have been free to please yourself for the last seven years but if you are here to help me, then remember that I am in charge.'

'I could hardly forget.'

'What does that mean?'

'It means I have ideas of my own. Ideas that you dismiss every time I mention them.'

Des scowled. 'Is this about that damn cottage again?'

As John was about to answer, a maid rushed in and whispered in Havers's ear. John recognised the girl from the funeral – Ginny, who had stood with Annabelle.

'Havers?' Des asked as the old butler fired quick instructions to Stevens and came to Des's side. 'Sir, Miss Eliza has been found on the floor in her bedroom.'

'Good God!' John raced from the room and across the hall to the stairs which he took two at a time.

Dashing into Eliza's bedroom, he pushed through the two other maids who were trying to wake Eliza.

John gathered her into his arms and placed her gently on the bed.

'Oh, my!' a maid cried at the amount of blood seeping through Eliza's dress.

'A doctor!' John yelled as Des rushed into the room.

'He's been sent for.' Des leaned over the bed on the other side and gripped Eliza's hand. He stared horrified at the blood. 'How has she been hurt? Was she attacked? Where is all the blood coming from?'

'I do not know.' John dragged a blanket from the end of the bed and covered Eliza. 'Who found her?'

'I did, sir,' Ginny answered. 'I came in to prepare the room for Miss Eliza's return and found her on the floor. I didn't know she'd come back, sir.'

'She was unconscious the whole time?'

'Yes, sir.'

'What could have happened?' Des muttered, wiping a hand over his shocked face.

'Eliza!' John shook her gently, terrified at her grey, clammy skin. 'Eliza, can you hear me?'

Gradually, Eliza's eyes fluttered opened.

'Dearest.' John wiped the dark hair from her forehead. 'You are safe now. Lie still.'

Her lips parted. 'John...'

'Yes, I am here. Right here. The doctor is on his way. We shall have you well again in no time at all.' He smiled brightly, willing her to take strength from him for she was as weak as a newly hatched bird.

'Forgive... me...'

He held her to him. 'There is nothing to forgive. Nothing.'

'All my fault...' Her eyes closed.

'Hush now.' He kissed her forehead. 'Rest.'

Des sat closer to them on the bed, his hand still holding Eliza's, which he kissed.

Eliza opened her eyes slowly. 'I love you all... so much... I'm sorry...' she whispered, then her head flopped to one side.

John stared down at her. 'Eliza!' He felt for a pulse. Nothing. His heart thumped against his chest. 'Eliza! Do not give up. I beg you!'

'John...' Des croaked, feeling for a pulse in her wrist. 'John, I cannot feel it.'

'Jesus Christ,' John swore, his fingers again at her neck, searching for a pulse, desperate to feel a beat no matter how light. No. It couldn't be. She couldn't be... No, he wouldn't have it. This couldn't be happening. Not to his sister, the beloved young sister he adored. 'Eliza! Wake up!'

'Dear God!' Penny hurried into the room wearing her nightgown and threw herself onto the bed. She pulled Eliza up, but she fell back limply. 'No! Eliza! Des, do something!'

Des took Penny into his arms. 'There is nothing we can do.'

John took Eliza back into his arms. 'Wake up, darling sister. Wake up for me,' he crooned, rocking her, but knowing she was lost to him.

'How could this have happened?' Penny asked tearfully. 'I do not understand.'

'None of us do, my dear.' Des wiped his eyes. He stood, disengaging himself from his wife. 'But I intend to find out and I will get the answers no matter what it takes!' He stormed out of the room.

'John?' Penny cried softly.

Gently, John laid Eliza back onto the bed. A searing pain knifed him in two as he arranged the blanket over her. He'd seen all the blood on her skirts. Eliza had done something unbearably foolish and kept it from them, he knew it.

He climbed off the bed and stood looking down at the porcelain white face of his beloved sister. The maids crying and Penny's anguish filtered through his grief, but he couldn't comfort Penny or say kind words to the maids for a rage of despair at the loss of Eliza consumed him. She was so young. What a waste of her life. For what?

Like Des, he wanted answers. He marched out of the room and downstairs. He found Des in the entrance, giving orders to Havers to have the carriage brought around.

'Des?'

'I am going to Joanna. She must know something.'

'No. Wait until Dr Henderson has been.'

'I cannot sit around waiting.'

'And rushing off will not help either. Not yet.' John took a steadying breath. 'You must write to Arthur. He must hear the news from us first. Send a letter immediately.'

They turned as the bell rang and Havers hurried to open the door.

Dr Henderson came in and took off his hat. 'I met your man on the road to the village. I was coming back from visiting a sick patient.'

'It is too late, Dr Henderson,' Des choked, and turned away.

Dr Henderson turned to Havers. 'Show me to Miss Hartley's room.' He paused by Des. 'I'll come down shortly.'

John went into the drawing room with Des and was soon joined by Penny, who'd dressed in all black. The sight of her in mourning chilled John to the bone.

Staring out of the window, John watched the gardeners weed the gravel driveway and rake the pebbles. Tea was brought in and ignored by the three of them. Like statues, they remained where they were, not talking, caught in their own sorrow.

Eventually, Dr Henderson returned and addressed them. 'I am deeply sorry for your loss.'

Penny sobbed.

'Can you tell how it happened?' Des asked him.

'Your sister haemorrhaged. The loss of blood was significant enough to end her life.'

'Why did she haemorrhage?' John choked back the simmering riot of anger and upset that threatened to strangle him.

Dr Henderson closed the door and came back to them. 'My examination revealed she'd recently gone through childbirth.'

Des swore. Penny gasped but John simply closed his eyes. What he had feared was true.

'Are you sure?' Des asked.

The doctor flushed slightly. 'I will not go into details of the examination, for you would not want to hear it, but all the signs are there. Haemorrhaging after childbirth can happen. I take it she was wearing her travelling clothes? That she has not been home?'

'She travelled home this morning from a friend's home,' John supplied.

Penny reached out a hand to Des. 'Then where is the baby?'

Dr Henderson sighed. 'From the state of Miss Hartley's stomach, meaning the swollen size of it, she was at least seven or eight months pregnant, maybe more. She has gone through childbirth, not miscarried an early pregnancy. Do you understand my meaning?'

'I do not understand how we did not notice,' Des fumed. 'How was our sister with child and we did not see?'

'Some pregnancies can result in small babies and some women carry their babies low. Their skirts can easily hide a small stomach.'

'I thought Eliza had put on some weight around her face...' Penny clasped her hands together. 'I never expected it was more than that. Her skirts were large, but that is the new fashion in London, and she wore a shawl all the time...'

'We need answers,' John muttered, feeling useless and guilty for not taking care of Eliza.

'The baby might not have survived,' Henderson mentioned. 'Or perhaps it has been given up. Either way, Miss Hartley assumed she could get on with her life after giving birth, but she failed to consider that she needed to rest and recover. For any woman childbirth is difficult, but the first baby is usually the toughest birth. I would say she gave birth within the last twenty-four hours. Obviously, something went wrong. If she had given birth with a doctor in attendance, then he has not done his duty in taking care of her.'

'You mean he has neglected her?' Des asked. 'She died because of his lack of care?'

Dr Henderson shrugged. 'I am saying that if she was attended by someone, then they should have stopped her from leaving. If that was a doctor or a midwife, who knows? Miss Eliza might have been totally alone.'

'Alone?' Penny gasped.

'Could we have saved her if she had been at home and had a doctor with her?' John asked him.

Henderson's look was full of sympathy. 'I cannot answer that, Mr Hartley. A doctor in attendance might have prevented the blood loss but there are times when even we cannot stop the flow. If the uterus does not contract, then there is little we can do. The body goes into shock and death occurs. I am deeply sorry. Unfortunately, we do not have any of the facts of what transpired and where. I can only surmise.'

'We have to find out what happened to the baby, Des,' Penny whispered.

'And we need to limit the gossip,' he replied. 'I will not have our sister's name sullied or our family brought into disgrace.'

'No one will ever know,' John murmured, shaken.

Dr Henderson looked grave. 'I will have to report the death, naturally.'

'No!' Des boomed. 'I will not have this family's name involved in a scandal. Imagine if the newspapers found out? The headlines would scream "Eliza Hartley, unmarried, dies from childbirth". I'll not have it, do you hear?'

'Des, calm down,' Penny cried.

'It is my duty, Mr Hartley.' Dr Henderson picked up his medical bag. 'But I will do my best to keep the report confidential. I've been a loyal friend to this family for years, you can rely on me to keep the details vague. Will that suffice?'

John shook the doctor's hand. 'Thank you, Dr Henderson.'

Once the doctor had said his farewells and left, John paced the room. 'Joanna Pritchard. Who did she marry?'

'Freeman, Gregory Freeman, I think,' Penny said, clasping her handkerchief. 'I remember reading it in the newspaper.'

'They have an estate near Leeds, Eliza told me.' John wracked his brains for more information he might have missed.

'Dalemere Court,' Des added. 'It is on the road between Leeds and Harrogate.'

'I shall go over there now.' John strode to the door.

'What if Eliza was not at Dalemere Court?' Penny asked. 'She might have made it all up and gone elsewhere.'

'Where is her maid?' Des asked abruptly. 'She would know

something for sure. If she had a hand in this, she will be dismissed without a reference.'

'Eliza's lady's maid, Bridges, did not accompany her to Joanna's,' Penny said, calmly. 'Eliza had given Bridges permission to visit her family in Harrogate as her father died.'

'Eliza has been gone for two weeks. Has Bridges not been with her the whole time?' John asked in amazement.

Penny shook her head. 'I do not know.'

Des rang the bell and a few moments later Havers knocked and walked in. 'Havers, is Miss Hartley's lady's maid, Bridges, here?'

'No, sir. She is still away in Harrogate. She has not returned to the manor since her father's death. Miss Bridges is to arrive in the village today on the twelve o'clock coach.'

'Thank you, Havers.' John noted Havers wore a black armband over his dark grey pinstriped suit and another wave of loss consumed him. He pulled himself together and addressed Des. 'That sounds more suspicious. Eliza did not want her maid with her. She gave her leave of two weeks. It is unheard of, even for a funeral.'

'I agree.' Des suddenly sat down. 'What a bloody mess. Eliza orchestrated to have her baby away from the house, but where exactly? And who was with her? She would have been too frightened to be alone while giving birth.'

'Whoever she was with failed to provide adequate care,' Penny said with a sniff of tears. 'They allowed Eliza to get out of bed and go on her way. They are responsible for Eliza's death.'

Sadness, worry and anger all mixed inside John. 'I shall ride to Dalemere Court. I must start somewhere. If Eliza was not with Joanna, then we need to ask at the train stations and staging inns for any information. Someone must know what happened to Eliza and her baby. I intend to find out!'

'Shall I come with you?' Des asked.

John stopped with his hand on the doorknob. 'No. I can manage it. You need to instruct the undertakers and send out notices.' Grief hit him again and he had to harden his heart against it, or he would never cope.

'Eliza could have stayed anywhere in the country, John,' Des fumed. 'How are we to find out where? You can't roam the whole of England!'

'I'll start with her friends. Send a note to Aunt Martha. She may have an idea of who Eliza would trust.'

'What will we tell people, the servants?' Penny fought back another sob.

'We tell friends that Eliza died suddenly from an unknown illness. There will be enough speculation at that. We must hope the servants do not gossip,' John said between gritted teeth. 'The truth remains between us three and the doctor.'

* * *

Annabelle rocked the baby in her arms, trying to calm her. But she knew the little thing was hungry and the cow's milk she half-attempted to suck through a soaked muslin cloth wasn't filling her.

Since Miss Eliza's disappearance that morning, she'd been half-mad with worry and indecision. She didn't know what to do for the best. The baby needed feeding and breast milk was the answer but how was she to get a wet nurse without arousing suspicion? Was there even someone in the village she could pay to do it? She had no clue.

She'd milked Daisy and, using her finger, she'd dipped it in the milk for the baby to suck on, but Ma had told her that cow's milk usually made newly born babies sick.

A knock on the door made her jerk. 'Miss Hartley?' she asked hopefully, then sagged as Dickie came in, his cap in his hands.

'Annabelle?' He stared at the baby in her arms. 'Who is that?'

Seeing him, Annabelle's throat tightened with emotion. 'Dickie...' She couldn't speak. She was deeply disappointed that Miss Hartley hadn't returned, but to have someone here made her feel less alone and scared.

'Whose baby are you looking after?' He peered at the tiny bundle in her arms.

'I can't say,' she replied nervously.

He frowned. 'Can't say? Why?'

'I need your help.'

'My help?'

'Yes, Dickie. Please, you must help me.'

He backed away suddenly. 'Is this *your* baby, Annabelle?'

She glared at him. 'My baby? How could it be my baby?'

'Is that why you won't marry me? There's another fellow? You've had his kid!'

Angry now and overwrought from lack of sleep and worry, she sneered at him. 'How could it be mine, you daft fool! Have you ever seen me with a large stomach? Or with another man for that matter? How could I have hidden being pregnant? I have always been thin.'

He scowled, uncertain yet knowing something wasn't right. 'I don't understand.'

'You won't do unless you let me explain.'

'I've come to tell you about the tragedy at the manor before I went up onto the moors and I find you with a baby. It was a surprise.' He sat down at the table, his expression one of shock.

Her heart thumped painfully. Had something happened to John? 'What tragedy?'

'Miss Hartley. She's died. This morning. Came back from her friend's place and died in her bedroom. Ginny found her.'

Annabelle's knees buckled and she sank onto the sofa. 'Died? Are you sure?'

'Aye, the whole estate is agog with the news. I was talking to one of the stablehands when the news came out to us. Poor Miss Hartley, so young and pretty.'

'It's not just a rumour, a horrid, evil rumour?' She prayed it was just a misunderstanding. Eliza Hartley couldn't be dead. She had to return for her baby!

Dickie frowned at her. 'Who would say all that? No, it's true I tell you. Mr John has ridden off in a great hurry. No one knows where. I went into the kitchen and the staff were all seated around the servants' table crying. Ginny said there was blood all over Miss Eliza's skirts. Mrs Knowles, the housekeeper, had a brandy in front of her for shock as she'd stayed in the bedroom with the doctor as he examined the young miss.'

'Oh, no... no...' Annabelle rocked the baby in her arms, frightened.

Dickie came and sat beside her. He put his arm around her shoulders. 'Don't take on now, lass. It's a tragedy, but don't be getting all upset.'

'You don't understand. Oh God, Dickie. This is a nightmare.'

'What? What's wrong?'

She closed her eyes, not knowing if she should tell him, but she needed help and Dickie was her closest friend.

'Annabelle, tell me.'

'You must promise on your mam's life that you'll not tell a soul.'

'What?' He reared back.

'Promise me!'

'Aye, all right. I promise.'

'This baby is Miss Hartley's.'

Dickie jumped away from her as though she'd thrown hot water over him. 'Are you mad?'

'It's true. She came here last night. She was in labour, but she wouldn't go home or allow me to get the doctor.'

Dickie paced the floor. 'You should have gone, anyway! Holy Christ, Annabelle, Miss Eliza has died!'

'I never thought she would leave the cottage. I fell asleep for only a short time, not even an hour, and when I woke, she was gone.'

'She must have left here and walked back to the house...' Dickie wiped a hand over his face. 'She had a baby... I can't believe it. Not a lady like Miss Eliza.'

'I couldn't believe it either when she came to my door last night.'

'You're going to have to go to the manor and tell them.'

'Miss Eliza said I wasn't to do that. She wanted me to take care of her baby. She said the family would give it up for adoption. Read her note. It's on the table.'

Dickie quickly read the note. 'No matter what it says here. Things have changed. The Hartley family needs to know what happened.'

'I can't. I promised Miss Hartley I'd keep her secret.'

'Annabelle, she is dead!'

'So? Can you imagine the scandal if I turn up at the manor with Miss Eliza's baby? Is that fair to the family? They might think I am making it all up.'

'They will want to know.'

'Will they? Will they want to know that their sister got herself into the worst kind of trouble and not only has she died from it, but there is a baby now to add to the gossip and disgrace?'

'That is for them to work out.'

'Miss Hartley begged me and made me promise to keep the baby safe.'

'Let the Hartleys keep it safe. It's their flesh and blood.'

'Miss Hartley said they wouldn't want her.'

'It's none of our business, is it?' he fumed. 'You can't keep her, Annabelle.'

Torn, she gazed down at the little sweet face. Could she hand her over, *should* she?

A knock startled them both.

Dickie's eyes widened. 'Are you expecting anyone?' he whispered.

Annabelle shook her head, heart thumping.

The knock sounded again. 'Annabelle? It's me, Ginny.'

Relief made her wilt like an old flower. 'It's Ginny.'

'She can't see the baby,' Dickie whispered.

The door opened an inch. 'Annabelle? Are you home?' Ginny stuck her head around the door jamb.

'Come in, Ginny.' Annabelle beckoned her in, light-headed with relief that it wasn't the police.

'I thought you were out.' Ginny smiled wanly at her and then brightened even more on seeing Dickie, then her expression dropped as she stared at the baby. 'Who is that?'

'Miss Hartley's baby,' Annabelle murmured.

'Why in God's name did you tell her that?' Dickie shouted.

'Heavens above.' Ginny clapped a hand over her mouth in shock. 'She had it here?'

'You knew?'

'I guessed. She was bleeding so heavily...'

'Yes, she came here last night in labour.'

Ginny started crying and Dickie helped her to a chair. 'I found her, you know.' She gulped. 'It was horrible. Blood everywhere. The carpet has to be removed and the blankets on the bed. It wouldn't stop.'

'I'm so sorry you had to go through it,' Annabelle said, rocking the baby as she started to whimper. She felt sick that

Miss Hartley had died, sick and terribly frightened. Was she responsible?

Ginny glanced up. 'Why did she come to you?'

'I don't know. Maybe she thought because Ma had delivered the village babies that I would know what to do to help her.'

'The house is going mad with speculation. We've all been told Miss Eliza died as a result of a short illness, but we know different. The Hartleys might be able to announce that to their friends and put that in a newspaper, but we knew something was up. Bridges, Eliza's maid, is heartbroken. She's just arrived back at the manor to the news her young mistress is dead.'

'Did Bridges know she was with child?' Dickie asked.

Ginny nodded. 'She had her suspicions. She's told us maids that Miss Hartley hadn't had her monthly show for over seven months, maybe longer. Miss Eliza ordered a new corset while in London and Bridges knew it was the kind that expectant mothers wear, though Miss Eliza denied it and said it was a new fashion. That's why all her new dresses were a different style, high-waisted, full skirts.'

'Well, we all know the truth now.' Dickie made a pot of tea.

'Annabelle.' Ginny came and sat beside her and glanced at the baby. 'The Hartleys are angry. The word in the house is that whoever Miss Eliza was with failed to keep her safe. They let her come home when she was too ill. The Hartleys want answers.'

Annabelle gasped. 'I did the best I could. Miss Hartley wouldn't let me get the doctor. I didn't want her to leave the cottage for days, but she went while I was napping.'

Dickie passed Ginny the note left behind. Ginny read it and then stared at Annabelle. 'What are you going to do?'

'I made a promise...'

'You need to give the baby to the family,' Dickie said, hands on hips. 'Explain what happened. You can't get in trouble for that.'

'Can't she?' Ginny questioned. 'She's kept a baby that isn't hers. A baby that belongs to a prominent family in the district.'

Dickie shrugged. 'They'll likely give it up for adoption, anyway. They won't want a bastard in the nest. How will they explain it to their friends?'

'She's a *she*, Dickie, not an *it*,' Annabelle snapped, tired and fraught with worry. 'Miss Eliza didn't want her family to know about the baby. She didn't want the shame of them knowing.' She turned to Ginny. 'Do the *family* think Miss Eliza had a baby?'

'No, I don't think so. Mr Havers told us that Dr Henderson declared that Miss Eliza had died from a short illness. That's it. Us girls between us think differently, but the family wouldn't know what we know from Bridges, unless Dr Henderson told them the truth.'

'He might have done. Why wouldn't he tell them the truth? He is their family doctor. They would trust him to tell them why she died.'

'What good would it do to announce their sister was a fallen woman?' Ginny sipped the tea that Dickie passed to her.

Annabelle tried to school her thoughts. 'Would Bridges tell them?'

'Well, she has no proof, really. She's searched the bedroom for the maternity corset, but it's gone.'

'She was wearing it last night.' Annabelle went cold. 'It must be here somewhere.'

Dickie resumed his pacing. 'I don't like any of this. Miss Hartley died shortly after having a baby in this cottage. They will blame you, Annabelle.'

'Me? Why?'

'You delivered the baby. If the family want to blame anyone, they will blame you for not getting help, for keeping the baby.'

A cold shiver ran through her. 'I was doing what Miss Hartley asked me to do.'

'But that's only your word against the daughter of the family and she is dead.'

'I have the note.'

'A note you could have forged.'

'For what possible gain?'

'Money?' He lifted his hands in the air. 'I don't know. All I do know is that this isn't going to shine well on you. Miss Eliza is dead, and you have her baby.'

11

'Have you decided what to do?' Ginny asked Annabelle, late the following evening.

'I promised Miss Eliza I wouldn't tell her family about the baby, and if they don't know she was with child, why hurt them with the painful truth of her downfall?'

'So, you're going to keep the child?' Dickie asked, having walked over with Ginny from the manor.

Annabelle sighed. She'd asked herself that same question repeatedly all last night and today. She'd thought of nothing else until she gave herself a headache. The fact was, she felt responsible for the baby. She'd given Eliza Hartley her promise to care for her child. A child small and dependent on Annabelle, one whom she was beginning to love.

She'd spent another sleepless night, trying to feed the baby a mixture of watery flour, which had soothed the baby a little better than plain cow's milk. She'd felt very alone during the long dark hours of walking the room, trying to rock the crying baby to sleep. She wished Ma had been with her, giving her solid advice.

However, she didn't have Ma. This situation had to be dealt with by herself.

'Annabelle?' Dickie prompted.

'I feel...' she faltered. 'I feel responsible for her.'

'That's ridiculous,' Dickie grunted. 'Miss Eliza meant nothing to you.'

'But her child does!'

Worry over what to do for the best was making her short-tempered one moment and teary the next. Handing over the baby to the Hartleys would solve some of the problems but also create others. Would they understand that she was only following Miss Eliza's instructions? The family didn't know her. Why would they trust anything she said? John Hartley might think kindly of her but in the end his beloved sister had birthed a child in her cottage, and she'd kept that from them all. Whatever kindness he might harbour towards her would be gone in an instant.

Ginny added sugar to her tea. 'Well, the house has been in a state all day. Mr John has ridden around the countryside yesterday and today looking for answers on Miss Eliza's last movements. They thought Miss Eliza had been with her friend, Joanna Freeman, but she was never there.'

Annabelle's stomach flipped on the mention of John Hartley. 'No, Miss Eliza told me she'd gone to Scarborough for two weeks alone.'

'For heaven's sake, Annabelle,' Dickie swore. 'You never told us that.'

'I didn't see why it would matter.'

Leaning closer, Ginny's voice lowered even though there was only the three of them. 'Miss Bridges has confessed her thoughts to the family about Miss Eliza being with child. She told me and Miss Nevin, Mrs Hartley's lady's maid, that Mr John asked her if she knew where a child might be.'

'So, they know,' Annabelle whispered, terrified. 'Why didn't you tell me that as soon as you arrived?'

'Bridges hasn't told any other staff except me and Miss Nevin. If gossip gets out, Bridges will be dismissed.'

'Does Bridges know Miss Eliza was coming here?' Annabelle tried to remain calm, but felt as though the walls were closing in on her.

'No, she doesn't. She was away in Harrogate. Anyway, afterwards, Mr Hartley assembled the servants in the hall at midday and said if we had any information on Miss Eliza's movements in the last few days then he wanted us to speak to him personally. Mr Havers then gave us a right lecture on how no gossip was to leave Hartley Manor, which of course is impossible to enforce. Everyone talks.'

'They are trying to retrace her last days,' Dickie told her. 'We've all been questioned on the estate by Mr John.'

Ginny nodded. 'Mr John and Mr Hartley are grieving, but with Bridges telling them what she believed, it's meant they have a baby to find. They said to her that they vow to find out the truth and if foul play or neglect is involved, they will bring the law down on that person.'

Annabelle shivered. 'I've done nothing wrong.'

'You're keeping the baby away from them!' Dickie shouted. 'For God's sake, will you wake up and realise this could all go very badly for you? Do you want to go to prison? You're holding a Hartley baby, which is wrapped in a silk shawl belonging to Miss Hartley.'

'Be quiet or you'll wake her up,' she snapped, glancing at the little sleeping face. 'I helped Miss Hartley, that's all.'

'And you've kept her baby.'

'As I was asked to do!'

'This is getting out of hand.' Dickie rubbed his hands over his face. 'Whatever you promised Miss Eliza, you need to forget it.

Hand the child over and then get on with your life while you still can.'

'Miss Eliza wanted me to care for her baby and not have it adopted by strangers. I can't go back on my word. Imagine if Ma hadn't taken me in when I was baby?' Annabelle planted a kiss on the baby's forehead. 'Do you want this child to be with strangers?'

'Who bloody cares? Let the Hartleys do what they want with the child,' Dickie scoffed. 'I don't care about Miss Eliza, but I care about you, and the longer this goes on for, the more trouble you are in. The police could charge you with stealing—'

'Stealing?'

'Yes, you have an expensive silk shawl that belongs to Miss Hartley.' He pointed at the peacock-coloured shawl the baby was wrapped in. 'Then kidnap. You have in your possession a baby that is not yours, and murder because you failed to report Miss Hartley's condition to a doctor who could save her. Bloody hell, Annabelle, you could be sent to Australia in chains for this.'

'Do they still do that?' Ginny gasped.

'How can I be charged with murder when she died due to the effects of childbirth?' she defended tearfully. Emotion choked her. No matter what she thought or did, she felt it would be the wrong thing. What was she to do?

Ginny gripped her hand. 'A secret birth you assisted with. A birth that you never went and got help for when you knew Miss Eliza was bleeding heavily. If the police are under pressure from the Hartleys to find the truth, they *will* find answers.'

Annabelle's stomach churned. 'Why would the family get the police involved? They won't want society to know of Eliza's downfall.'

Dickie once again started pacing. 'You'll not stand a chance against the police if they arrest you. The police can twist you into knots and the Hartley family want answers. Remember, Des Hartley is the local magistrate.'

Annabelle's head throbbed. 'Eliza Hartley made me promise never to reveal the baby's identity. I've told you, I can't hand her over for her to be given to strangers. Miss Eliza never wanted that.'

'Are you willing to go to jail to keep that promise?' Dickie asked angrily.

'I can't go to jail if they can't find me,' she suddenly decided, chest heaving.

'And you'll look guilty when suddenly you aren't here any more.' Dickie stared at her. 'Just give the baby up, I beg you.'

'No.' Ginny shook her head. 'If Annabelle confesses to her part now, they'll have her charged. We are working class, the police don't care about us, especially when it is a case with a family like the Hartleys. My brother died in prison after being arrested for poaching on the Leverworth estate. He didn't do it. He'd been out with some of his mates and was walking home when they went out again to check their rabbit traps. They got caught and the police knew Freddie was with them earlier in the night. They dragged him out of bed and took him away. We never saw him alive again.' Ginny's vacant gaze came back to the present. 'If you want to keep this baby, then you need to get away.'

'Then I will.' Annabelle nodded, feeling better at having made a decision. However, the unknown future terrified her so much she wanted to be sick.

'This is utter madness!' Dickie seethed. 'Where will you go?'

'York,' Ginny said. 'I have a cousin in York. You can stay with her. She's poor, mind, but she's a heart of gold and will take you in.'

'Thank you.' Relieved, Annabelle grasped Ginny's hand in gratitude. York. It wasn't that far away. She'd been there before so it wasn't an unfamiliar place.

'Have you got any money?' Ginny glanced around the cottage. 'You know you'll never be able to come back here.'

Annabelle's smile faded. To leave the cottage and never return wounded her deeply. She'd be leaving her home, the memories of Ma, the delightful gardens she enjoyed so much, her friends.

'See?' Dickie raged. 'Madness. You're leaving your home and friends for what? A child that isn't your responsibility. Why am I the only one to see this?'

'I can't give her up to strangers, Dickie,' Annabelle told him softly, her mind made up once and for all. No matter what, she would take care of this child and love her as her mother couldn't. 'I'm sorry you feel as though I'm not listening to you, but you don't understand. I brought this little girl into the world, and I'll not see her raised by people who might not love her as much as I could. The Hartleys won't keep her, not a bastard child to remind them of Eliza's disgrace. She'll be adopted and forgotten.'

'She's nothing to you.'

'Miss Eliza gave her to me. She *gave* her *daughter* to me. A precious life. Just as I was given to Ma. I can't imagine how my life might have turned out if Ma hadn't brought me home. I could have ended up in a horrible, cold, loveless orphanage, instead I grew up here in this wonderful place. I will keep my promise to Miss Eliza as Ma kept her promise to my mother.'

Silence stretched between them.

'Very well. I have an idea,' Dickie announced. 'You and me will get married, and we'll say the baby is mine.'

Annabelle jerked and twisted to look at him fully. 'Get married?'

'It's the best way. No one will question the baby then. We'll say she's mine and once we are married, the gossip will eventually die down that she was born out of wedlock. She'll grow up knowing no different.'

Ginny looked downcast. 'It's an idea.'

But Annabelle shook her head. 'No. Thank you, Dickie, for it's a generous offer and kindly meant, I know, but I won't lump you with a wife and a child.'

'I wouldn't suggest it if I didn't want you to. I could care for you both.'

'But to raise another person's child for years? No. I won't do it to you. The guilt would be too much, and I already carry enough burden on my shoulders. All this is my mess, and I will be the one to sort it out.' She kissed his cheek. 'But thank you.'

'We should pack some things for you.' Ginny stood and looked around the room. 'You're going to need money to tide you over until you have a job.'

'Well, if you're going through with this stupid idea, then I'll help you.' Dickie made a show of his disapproval by his scowl and tone. 'The best day for you to leave is the day of the funeral.'

Annabelle paused in taking out a large hamper basket from the cupboard beside the dresser. 'The funeral?'

'Aye, it's on Thursday. If you leave then, no one in the village will notice for they'll all be gawking at the rich outsiders arriving to attend it.'

'Yes, good idea,' Ginny agreed. 'Now, what can you sell and what do you want to take?'

'Anything you leave behind, I'll store at me mam's house,' Dickie said.

'I can take the cart with Bobby. We can carry my things in the cart and then, when I get to York, I can sell Bobby. That will give me some money to start with.'

'York is too far to walk with Bobby when you have a baby,' Ginny said. 'Leave him here. I'm sure Dickie can sell him for you.'

'Course I will.' Dickie looked upset.

Annabelle tried to put a brave face on it, but the knowledge that she was leaving her home and all that she loved was hard to comprehend. Yet she knew she couldn't stay. She was in too deep now to give the baby to the Hartleys.

'And Daisy?' Dickie asked.

'Take her to your mam. I know she'll value her.'

He nodded and turned away to study the books on the shelf.

Ginny rubbed Annabelle's arm in comfort. 'I know it'll be hard, but the alternative is even worse. Staying here might mean the truth coming out eventually, and if the police come asking questions, you might find yourself locked up.'

'I know. But this is my home. To leave it is so difficult.'

'You take the memories with you.' Ginny smiled. 'In the morning, I'll send a letter to my cousin, Nellie, and ask her to come here as soon as she can.'

'Why?'

'Our Nellie has five kids, the youngest is about six months old and Nellie is still feeding him. She'll be able to feed that one too.' Ginny indicated to the baby. 'I'm no expert on kids, Annabelle, but that baby is tiny and sick-looking, she needs breast milk, not whatever pap you're giving her.'

Her heart plummeted. 'I agree. I'm scared stiff she'll die soon. I can't get enough milk down her.' The baby's health was her main priority, everything else would be dealt with later.

Dickie swore under his breath. 'If that happens, then you'll be in even more trouble.' He grabbed his hat. 'Write a quick note, Ginny. I'll go to York tonight to your cousin and bring her back with me.'

'It's too late for that. There aren't any coaches at this time of the evening,' Annabelle protested.

'I'll walk.'

'Good idea.' Ginny found a piece of paper and a pencil. 'Nellie won't mind. We are close and if I need her, she'll come without question.'

'It'll be the middle of the night by the time you reach York.' Guilt weighed heavy on her. How could she ask him to spend the night walking to York and back again?

'I'll take Bobby and the cart.' Dickie pulled on his coat. 'I can bring back Ginny's cousin on the cart.'

The baby woke and started her feeble crying. Dickie bid them farewell as Annabelle warmed up some milk and Ginny started packing the books into a carpet bag.

While Annabelle struggled to feed the baby, Ginny emptied shelves and packed crates ready to be taken to Dickie's mam's house in the morning. With the baby struggling to feed, Annabelle concentrated on getting milk into her little mouth and ignored the quiet stripping of her home and the fear and worry gnawing at her.

* * *

The cockerel heralded the dawn with his raucous crowing, waking Annabelle from where she slept on the sofa. Moving carefully so as not to waken the baby, she went into the scullery and washed her face to wake up fully. She'd spent last night packing up the cottage and trying to feed the baby small amounts of milk, enough to stop her from screaming. The results were little sleep for either of them and the cottage held random piles of boxes and crates, half-filled.

She heard the voices before she saw them go past the window. Dickie came around the back of the cottage, leading Bobby and the cart. Sitting in the cart was a woman holding a child.

Quickly, Annabelle raked the fire and added sticks to the embers and put the kettle on to boil. She opened the door. 'You're back. How was it?'

'Not so bad. Bobby behaved, so that was good.' Dickie helped the woman down. 'This is Nellie, Ginny's cousin.'

'Thank you for coming.' Annabelle smiled at the woman, who looked much older than Ginny. 'I'm very grateful.'

Nellie wore a worn brown dress and a battered black hat with a faded red flower on the side of it. In her arms, she held a sleeping baby in a grubby grey shawl. 'Well, I don't mind. Ginny rarely asks for my help so I knew it must have been important.' She hitched the baby more comfortably with one arm and with the other hand she pushed lank brown hair up under her hat. 'Dickie has filled me in, and your secret is safe with me. I know how to keep secrets, I do.' Her smile was wide and warm and instantly put Annabelle at ease.

'I don't know what to say.' Annabelle blinked away threatening tears.

'There's nothing to say. If you're Ginny's friend then you're my friend now, too.'

Relief made her weak at the knees. 'Thank you. Come in. I'll make some tea.'

'That'll be grand. I'm fair parched.'

While Annabelle made a simple breakfast with the last of the ham and eggs she had, Nellie placed her chubby baby on the sofa and picked up the newborn, who looked like a tiny doll in comparison.

'My, she's small, ain't she? Not full term?'

'I don't know. The mother didn't tell me much information.'

'No, the wealthy young ladies barely know the facts of life as it is. They don't have a clue about the real details. Kept in the dark all their lives, most of them.' Nellie sat down and unbuttoned her bodice. She gripped her left breast and pushed the nipple into the baby's mouth. 'This one is weak, you know. She may not last.'

'Don't say that, please.' Annabelle's hand, holding strips of ham, was suspended over the frying pan as she stared at Nellie trying to persuade the baby to feed.

'I'm just saying, that's all. Little ones like this are touch-and-go when it comes to surviving the first few weeks.'

Dread gripped Annabelle's heart. 'I'm changing my life for her. I can't go through all this for nothing. She deserves a chance.'

It took several attempts for Nellie to get the baby to suck but, at last, the baby latched on to the nipple and drank contentedly.

Nellie beamed at Annabelle. 'That's a start. She'll need constant feeding to build up her strength, but I've enough milk for two and Sammy is eating a bit of food now.'

Dickie came in and washed his hands in the scullery. 'I'll have a quick cup of tea and then be on my way. I'll be back at midday to see you off.'

Annabelle nodded and passed him a cup of tea. Now she was going, she encountered a mixture of emotions – fear and relief and sadness. In a few hours, she would be gone from this cottage, gone from the village and starting a new life. It seemed completely unreal, like a weird dream.

After the baby had fallen asleep with her first full tummy, Nellie placed her on the sofa and walked around the cottage, eyeing up the boxes full of belongings. Her own baby, Sammy, sat on the floor chewing on a bread crust.

'Dickie says we should take the coach back to York. It's quicker. We discussed it on the journey here last night,' Nellie mentioned, eating her breakfast and sipping her third cup of tea.

'But what of my things?' Annabelle looked up from fastening a small trunk full of bedding.

'Take a couple of bags that we can manage, and the rest Dickie will have to bring another day.'

'Very well...' Annabelle began sorting through what she could fit into two large carpet bags. Apart from her clothes and the little mantel clock, she squashed in Ma's black shawl and brooch, but left books and kitchen utensils. She wouldn't need them until she had a place of her own.

'When you've got your own place, you can send for your boxes of plates and stuff.' Nellie stated as though reading her mind. 'In the meantime, I have enough for us to be getting by with, and besides, my place is bursting at the seams already without extra crates of things you won't need right away.'

'I really appreciate you taking me and the baby into your home.'

Nellie laughed loudly. 'Don't be thanking me just yet, you've not seen where I live.' She glanced around the cottage. 'It's nothing as pretty as this place, that's for sure.'

Before noon, Dickie arrived, looking tired. 'I can't stay long. I've the flock to move to another field later and Mr Yardley wants to walk with me to the low moor and inspect the stone walls. Are you all packed?'

'I am.' She pointed to the two large bags by the door. 'I'm taking those two as Nellie said you'd bring my things later.'

'Aye. I'll keep it all at me mam's.'

'Are you sure she won't mind?'

'Nay, I'll put it all up in the loft where I sleep. There's plenty of room up there under the rafters. I'll take Daisy to Mam's this evening, and I'll go to the pub tonight and see if anyone wants to buy Bobby.'

'You'll be lucky, the whole village knows what a menace he is.'

Dickie grinned. 'I might have to sell him cheap, then.'

'Anything will do to help me get by. What will you tell people?'

'I've thought about that today. It might be best if I say you've found work elsewhere.' Dickie rubbed his eyes, which were red with exhaustion.

'Yes, I agree. People will understand my need to find a position now Ma is gone. Will you come and see me soon?' Suddenly, Annabelle didn't want to go away. The prospect seemed too daunting. She was leaving everything behind for an unknown future. Was she doing the right thing or making a huge mistake?

'You know I will. I'll be over on my first day off, which is in about two weeks.' He smiled reassuringly. 'If you need me before then, send a letter to me.'

Annabelle hugged him to her, and he held her tight. 'You've been the best friend,' she whispered tearfully.

'You'll be fine. You're stronger than you think, remember that.' He kissed her cheek. 'I'd best go. Ginny can't make it to say good-bye. She ran out to me as I was crossing the stable yard. They are all going to the funeral, and she won't be able to get away after as a lot of folk are going back to the manor after the service. She said she'll come to you on her next day off.'

Annabelle took a step back and gathered her emotions. 'Tell her thanks for everything, won't you?'

'Aye, I will. Don't forget to write to Mr Hartley about letting go of this cottage, but leave it a few days so I can clear it out.'

'I'll remember. I'll leave the key under the first pot on the floor in the potting shed.'

His gaze held hers for a moment longer. 'It'll be strange not seeing you here.'

'I'll feel strange not being here.' She gave a weak smile.

'Take care, Annabelle.' He squeezed her hands.

'And you.' She swallowed back her tears. Now wasn't the time to cry.

'Bye, Nellie. See you in a couple of weeks when I visit.'

'Aye, Dickie, you'll be welcome, any time.' Nellie waved from the sofa where she was once more feeding the baby.

Once Dickie left, Annabelle put on her coat and hat. She went out and gave Bobby a carrot and a pat. 'I know we didn't always get along, but I'll miss you, boy.'

He nipped her hand and she jumped back.

'Maybe I won't miss you that much at all, you damn thing!' She stomped into the house and took one last tour, mentally saying goodbye to her home and remembering the years of happiness she'd had.

Solemnly, she put her two bags outside the door and then wrapped the baby up in the peacock-coloured shawl.

'My, that's beautiful.' Nellie admired the shawl, touching it lightly.

'It belonged to her mother. It's the only thing she has that was hers.'

'Then let's hope you never have to sell it.' Nellie gathered up her own baby. 'Let's be going if we're to catch the coach.' Nellie paused. 'In the village, if anyone asks, say I'm a friend and you're helping me with my kiddies. Here, you take Sammy until we get into the coach, for anyone who sees you with a baby of his size won't think anything the wiser.'

Locking the door, Annabelle hid the key in the potting shed and came back to Nellie, who held the baby and one of the bags. Annabelle took the other bag and with Sammy in her other arm she looked around the garden one last time. She saw Ma standing in the garden, deadheading the flowers, and took a deep shuddering breath. In the tall trees, the birds sang and fluttered among the branches. Never again would she listen to them chatter or sit by the beck and dip her toes in the water to cool off in the heat of summer. Never again would she break the ice of the water barrels in winter or spend hours in the potting shed drying herbs.

'Bye, Bobby. Bye, Daisy,' she murmured. 'Goodbye, home. Goodbye, Ma.'

12

John stood by the church's porch, shaking hands with those friends and distant relations who'd come to pay their respects. Eliza's coffin had arrived and seeing it made his gut twist in grief.

'We should go in,' Penny whispered, her face hardly seen under her heavy black veil. 'She's here.'

'Yes.' Des sighed and, taking Penny's elbow, they went into the church.

John waited a few seconds more, watching the pall-bearers lift the polished coffin out of the hearse. A groom held the horses' bridles, their long black feathers dipping as the horses' heads moved.

He nodded to those who walked past him and shook the odd hand held out, but he felt far removed from the event. As though he wasn't really attending his sister's funeral. How could he be? To say goodbye to Eliza, his funny, sweet, happy sister, seemed ridiculous.

Reverend Marr came to stand beside him and gave a nod to the pall-bearers. 'Mr Hartley?'

'Yes. I shall take my seat.' John turned and was about to walk into the church when he thought he saw Annabelle standing on the other side of the boundary wall. The coffin came closer, blocking his view. He shifted to one side for a better look, but she had gone.

'Mr Hartley?' Reverend Marr urged.

John walked into the cool dimness of the church, hoping it had been Annabelle standing there, paying her respects, but he couldn't be sure.

Murmuring voices filled the stone building, lifting up into the carved arches of the ceiling. A choir of boys sang a hymn, but John's throat was too full to sing.

Penny touched his arm in comfort as he passed her to sit on her other side. Des stared straight ahead at the altar, but John gazed down at his shiny black shoes, wishing the time away until he was back outside, away from this place, away from the sympathetic looks and the soft condolences.

As soon as he possibly could, he'd be away on Dash, galloping through the villages, stopping to ask if anyone had seen someone with a new baby, a baby that might not be theirs.

He'd never stop the search for Eliza's baby. He owed it to Eliza. He'd failed her in the past. She'd been with child, and she couldn't speak to him about it. That she had to hide her shame and be alone at a time of such uncertainty and fear made him sick. Somewhere out there he had a niece or nephew, he was sure of it, even though Des and Penny said the baby might be dead, but he had faith that the baby lived. Eliza had trusted someone. She'd have not done it all alone. He would find that person, no matter how long it took.

Thankfully, the service was short. John couldn't have stood the torture of it for any great length of time. He followed Des and Penny outside again. Eliza was to be buried in the family's crypt, joining their parents.

He held Aunt Martha's elbow as she cried gently into her black-edged handkerchief as Reverend Marr spoke again of a young life cut short. Jaw clenched, fighting his turmoil, John got through it, but didn't encourage Des and Penny to talk with the villagers for long. He wanted to get home, to spend as little time as possible making polite talk with distant cousins he'd not seen for years and then, when enough time had elapsed, he wanted to change into his riding clothes and be up on Dash's back and away.

'Let us go,' Des announced, heading the way up the path to the carriages on the road.

'It was such a wonderful turnout,' Aunt Martha said with a sniff once they were in the carriage. 'Are many coming back to the house, Des?'

'Just family relations, Aunt, and a few selected friends and those who've travelled far and need some refreshments before they go home.' Des looked out of the window as the crowds of villagers left the church grounds.

'At least it did not rain,' Penny murmured.

John remained silent, his mind closed to small talk. He didn't have it in him. They trundled along the High Street, and he nodded to those who doffed their caps as they passed.

'Our dear Eliza was well liked,' Aunt Martha said.

The carriage slowed to go around the stagecoach that had stopped outside the Black Bull Inn. Passengers were aboard and a horn blew, alerting everyone that the coach was to depart. Absent-mindedly, John looked into the coach as they passed. He saw a face he knew, or did he? It went by so quickly. Was it her, Annabelle Wallis? No, he must be mistaken. Why would she be in a coach? His mind replayed the vision of her white face, and she held a bundle in her arm wrapped in a blue-green blanket. No, it couldn't have been her. Over the last week, he'd thought a lot about her, especially during his sleepless nights. Perhaps it was wishful thinking that he'd seen her. Unless she was going away...

'John?' Aunt Martha tapped his hand.

'Sorry, yes?'

'I was saying that my cousin, Reginald, has arrived in India. He is to meet up with Arthur. Have you heard from Arthur lately?'

'No, Aunt, I have not received a letter since last month.'

'How sad he shall be when he learns about Eliza.'

Their carriage slowed and moved to one side of the road to allow the stagecoach to rush by at full gallop. John craned his next to see into it again. There, a flash, a face, her eyes...

'What do you think, John?' Des asked him.

'Pardon?' He'd missed the entire conversation. He was sure Annabelle Wallis was on that coach.

'What is wrong with you, John?' Des snapped. 'Aunt Martha asked you a question.'

Pulling himself together, he gave his attention to his aunt. 'Forgive me.'

She took his hand in her small one. 'There is nothing to forgive. It is a harrowing time, and no one could blame you if your thoughts wander.'

Five minutes later, alighting in front of the wide steps of the manor, John helped his aunt and Penny down from the carriage.

'What is troubling you?' Des asked him as the women went in ahead.

'I need to ride, Des. I cannot stay inside and make polite talk for hours.'

'Do you think I want to?' Des scoffed. He placed his hand on John's shoulder. 'Go. Ride. Gallop for miles for the both of us. I wish to God I could join you.'

'Thank you.'

'You have hardly rested since Eliza's death. Promise me that after today, you will ease up on the mad dashing about the county?'

'I shall try, but it is a promise I cannot make to you. I need answers.'

'I know. Me, too. But driving yourself half-mad with worry will not help you and I need you here.' Des rubbed his face as more carriages arrived. 'I shall talk to you later.'

John slipped around the side of the house and entered by the conservatory. He avoided the hall and went through another door into the library and from there out of another door into a small hallway and the servants' back stairs.

'Sir?' Mrs Knowles, the housekeeper, stopped in surprise, the keys at her waist jingling. 'May I help you?'

'Yes, have a note sent to the stables for Dash to be saddled, please.'

'You're going riding?'

He'd known Mrs Knowles all his life and felt instantly like a schoolboy again. They all knew it was Mrs Knowles and not Havers who ruled this house. 'I am, Mrs Knowles. I am not in the mood for polite company.'

She nodded, understanding. 'Indeed, sir. It is an incredibly sad day and no mistake. Shall I send Stevens up to you?'

'No, he will be busy in the drawing room assisting Havers. I can see to myself.'

'Very good, sir.' The housekeeper paused. 'Miss Eliza will be deeply missed. She used to light up every room she entered, whether that be a drawing room or down here in the servants' quarters, when she'd visit us for milk and cake or come to tell us something exciting. We admired her greatly.'

'Thank you, Mrs Knowles. I cannot tell you how much that pleases me to hear.' He coughed, choking up, and quickly mounted the staircase.

It took him little time to change and pull on his long leather boots. He left the house via the back entrance without encountering anyone but a kitchen maid.

Dash was waiting patiently for him, and he was as eager for a gallop as John. They ate up the ground. Dash's hooves thundered over the fields as grey clouds skidded across the blue sky, plunging parts of the countryside into shadow.

Skirting the village and tenant farms, not wanting to chat, John kept to the fields until he finally turned Dash about and slowly headed home. It didn't surprise him to find himself stopping at the top of the slope and looking down at the Wallis cottage. Had he really seen Miss Wallis in the coach or just imagined it?

He dismounted and led Dash down to the beck to drink, before he jumped the stepping stones and wandered up the path between the garden beds, scattering the hens from their pecking. The pony came over to the fence to be patted but the cow stayed on the far side.

No one was in the potting shed and the door was locked. When he knocked on the cottage's back door, he received no reply. He walked around to the side window and peeked in. He stared for a minute, taking in the stacked crates and trunks, the cleared shelves, the closed-up look to the kitchen and main room.

His heart sank to his boots.

Stepping back, he glanced around for any sign of Miss Wallis. If the animals were still here, but the house packed, then where was Miss Wallis? Something was decidedly odd about it all.

Had she left? Why else would the house be cleared? No smoke spiralled from the chimney. He went back to the potting shed and looked around. The working benches were swept free of dirt, dried flowers and herbs hung upside down from the rafters, the garden tools were propped in a corner, pots were stacked neatly, and several crates held Widow Wallis's well-known tonics.

Outside, he stood, undecided on what to think. He'd come here wanting to see Annabelle, to talk to her and see her smile. He liked her much more than he should, which excited and alarmed him in equal measure. When he'd been in her company before, he had wanted to take her in his arms and kiss her until they both lost their minds. Not that he would. He knew she'd been brought up decently. And a quick fumble wasn't what he wanted. Christ, he didn't know what he *wanted*, except an hour in her presence, talking, walking, would help ease the pain in his chest.

'Mr Hartley, sir.' The tall young man walking between the gardens took off his cap.

John recognised him but couldn't remember his name.

'It's Smithers, sir. Dickie Smithers, the estate shepherd.'

'Ah, yes.' John knew him to be the young man at Widow Wallis's funeral, the one who had stood on the other side of Annabelle. He wore a black armband, as all the estate workers did, in honour of Eliza.

'Was there something you wanted, sir?'

'As a matter of fact, I was wondering why the place looks abandoned?'

'Annabelle, er... I mean, Miss Wallis, is going to write to your brother, sir, about letting the place go.'

'Letting the place go?' John scowled in dismay. She had left, for good? Why? Why did she leave?

'She's moved away.'

'That seems rather sudden.' A fresh bout of anguish hit him in the chest. He had missed saying goodbye to her?

'She's gone to live with a friend in... Leeds. She's asked me to store her things at my house. I'm here to take the cow now so me mam can milk her.'

'When did Miss Wallis leave?'

'Today, sir.'

John clenched his jaw. He *had* seen her in the coach. 'Do you know of her forwarding address?'

'No, sir. She says she'll write to me when she's settled.'

'Do you have the key, Smithers? If Miss Wallis is not continuing her tenancy, then I need to check the place for damage before we let it out again.' He knew his tone was harsh, but he couldn't help it. Annabelle had gone and the news affected him more than he cared to admit.

'Aye, sir. Annabelle said she'd leave it under a pot.' He lifted a few pots in the opening of the potting shed before finding the key and passing it to John.

John unlocked the door and walked into a whitewashed kitchen with a large table in the middle. Crates were placed on top of the table and by the scullery door. In the main room, the embers in the grate were dead, and with the sun behind a cloud. the room was dim and cold.

He climbed the ladder to the loft and stared at the empty bed, the bare striped mattress. No doubt this was her bed. A sense of loss filled him. Why was he so interested in a village girl? He could have his pick of women, yet for some reason, Annabelle Wallis had crawled under his skin and gave him an itch he couldn't scratch.

Back down in the kitchen, he checked the range fire was completely out, not wanting a fire to destroy the cottage. He flipped through a few books at the top of one of the crates and a sense of pride washed over him that Miss Wallis could read and enjoyed books. There were several books on herbs and husbandry, but also some fiction, Jane Austen, Charles Dickens, Defoe's *Robinson Crusoe*, a book he'd read many times.

Red leather ledgers listed the years of trading by Widow Wallis. The earlier ledgers showed a different handwriting to the later ones, and it was these last ledgers that John took interest in. A few weeks ago, the entries stopped. In small handwriting was the last addition and a remark. *Ma died today. I am lost.* The simple words went straight to his heart. Annabelle suffered as he did, a beloved person gone from their life.

He replaced the ledger in the crate, but when he turned away, he noticed a piece of paper under the corner of the crate. He pulled it out and opened it.

Dear Miss Wallis,

Thank you for all your help. I am in your debt and will forever be so.

I beg you to keep my secret for the sake of my family's reputation and my own. My disgrace should not tarnish my family. If you have any respect for them, I implore you to never reveal my secret.

The baby's fate lies in your hands. I will make no interference, except to send you some money for your trouble. No one must know of the link between the baby and me. I do not want her, and I know my family would have her adopted by strangers. At least this way I know she will be looked after by a good and caring person such as you.

You will not hear from me again as I will go away, perhaps travel to the continent. Rest assured, I will do the right thing for the child and send you the details of a bank account I will set up for the child and of the house in Norfolk.

Thank you for keeping my promise.

With sincere gratitude,

Eliza Hartley

PS I have left my shawl behind. It was a present from my brother, John. He bought it in India, and I treasure it dearly. I want the baby to have it as a reminder that I did think of her and always will do.

John sucked in a breath. Eliza had a baby here in this cottage! He glanced around as though searching for some evidence of his sister or her child. There was nothing, of course. He rubbed a hand over his face, conflicted with emotions. Eliza had been here. She'd borne a baby here in secret. Did the child still live? Would Miss Wallis take care of it as Eliza wished, or give it to an orphanage? Why would Miss Wallis want to keep a child she had no connection with? Eliza had promised money for the baby's keeping. Was that Miss Wallis's motive to keep the child? Had Miss Wallis panicked when hearing the news Eliza had died? Was she fleeing her home to protect herself because she had allowed Eliza to suffer without a doctor?

He heard Smithers outside and slipped the note into his pocket and went out to him. 'Smithers, where did you say Miss Wallis has gone?'

Smithers ducked his head, trying to persuade the cow to move beyond the field gate. 'Er... I don't have an address, sir.'

'But she will not be coming back?'

'No, sir. She's gone looking for work. She said she'd try the cities.'

'Was she alone?'

'Aye, sir.' Smithers pulled the cow's halter. 'Come on, Daisy, you damn thing.'

'Were you particularly good friends with Miss Wallis?' John asked, watching him struggle.

'We've known each other since we were young 'uns, sir.'

'And you're keeping her things until she sends for them?'

'Aye. I offered as we've room in our loft.' Smithers finally got the cow beyond the gate and onto the path. He wiped the sweat from his brow with his forearm.

'Has anyone been staying with Miss Wallis lately?' John studied him. Was the man lying to him? Did he know more than he was letting on?

'Not that I know of, sir, but I didn't visit that often. I'm too busy in the summer.' Smithers closed and secured the gate.

'Miss Wallis was not in any trouble, was she?' John prompted, not letting the man leave until he had more answers.

'Not that I know of, sir. Why would she be?'

'No reason. It just seems odd she would leave her home.'

'Widow Wallis told her that the cottage was only for her lifetime, and that Annabelle would have to discuss staying here with Mr Hartley.'

'Why did Miss Wallis not come to my brother and speak with him, or me?'

'I don't know, sir. She said she was going to, but I don't think she got the chance.' Smithers grabbed the cow's halter. 'Annabelle did say that orders had dropped off since her ma died. She needed to find work if folk weren't going to buy the tonics any more.'

'I see. So, Miss Wallis will write to my brother about the cottage?'

'Aye, that's what she said, sir. Once she was settled like.'

'Leeds, you think she went to?'

Smithers kept his focus on the cow, adjusting the halter for no reason. 'That's what she told me. Leeds and if she has no luck there, then maybe Manchester.'

Inwardly, John groaned. Two huge cities. Searching them would take time, a lot of time. 'And you are certain Miss Wallis said nothing else about where she was going?'

'No, sir.'

'You are to let me know if you hear from her, understood?'

'Absolutely, sir.' Smithers bobbed his head.

John rode away from the cottage and into the village. At the Black Bull Inn, he asked the landlord the details of the midday coach.

'It was the York coach, sir,' the landlord told him as he wiped down the bar. 'It leaves once a day at midday. The coach for Scarborough leaves each morning at nine and the Harrogate coach at seven in the morning.'

'No diversions on the York coach?'

'No, sir. Straight to York. It leaves at midday so passengers can get the last trains to London or Leeds. Are you wanting a ticket, sir?'

'Not today, thank you. However, do you know of Miss Annabelle Wallis?'

'Aye, sir. Everyone knows of Widow Wallis's lass.'

'Did Miss Wallis purchase a ticket for the York coach?'

'Not that I'm aware of, sir, but I wasn't working this morning. Let me ask me wife. Wait one minute, please, sir.'

John sighed. The smell of stale ale was strong in his nose. Elderly men were seated around small tables, smoking and talking quietly. Would there be any point in asking them questions about Annabelle? He didn't think so. A young single woman wouldn't be friends with the older men in this public house.

The round, brawny landlord returned with his small, skinny wife. 'Sir, me wife says that Miss Wallis did buy a ticket. She said she was going away to look for work.'

'Did she...' John swallowed back his words about a baby. No one must ever link Eliza with a baby. 'Was Miss Wallis with anyone?'

'No, sir. She came in alone,' the wife answered. 'I was sorry to see her go as I buy the odd tonic from her. Nothing is the same now Widow Wallis has gone to meet her maker and now the young lass has left, too. Ever so kind she was, and always smiling.'

'Thank you. You have been of help. Good day.' John went outside just as the first drops of rain fell from a large, angry-looking cloud.

He rode home in the downpour, feeling miserable about the huge task before him. But at least he now knew of Eliza's last wishes and where she'd been in the hours before her death. Had Miss Wallis helped her to give birth or was the baby already born when

Eliza arrived at the cottage? Was Eliza unwell at the cottage? If so, why didn't Miss Wallis go for the doctor? Or send a message to the manor?

Did Miss Wallis have his niece, or had she left the village to give it away to an orphanage? Why would Miss Wallis want to keep the child? She had no personal attachment to Eliza. He had so many questions his head throbbed.

Des and Penny would need to read the note, which confirmed their sister's downfall. Why had she been so foolish as to lie with a man? Oh, she had been flirtatious and on occasion rather silly where men were concerned, but he never thought she'd take the ultimate step and actually give herself to a man so wholly unsuitable as Morris-Hippleton. That *devil* should be horsewhipped for taking such advantage. The day would come when the bastard rued meddling with the Hartley family.

Still, Eliza should have told them, or at least *him*, of her troubles. He would have helped her. He would have gone away with her so she could have the baby in secret and then they'd find a good home for him or her. Eliza could have then got on with her life, her shame hidden.

His despair boiled into anger as he turned into the manor's gate. If only Eliza had come to him. Instead, she went to an herbalist's ward, thinking she would save her. What had she been thinking? But she must have been petrified of being found out. Then to leave the baby with Miss Wallis and walking home when she was too weak to leave her bed. She was so ill... He remembered the sight of her climbing the stairs.

He closed his eyes at the senseless waste of it all. If Miss Wallis had only gone for help, maybe Eliza would still be alive! How much was Annabelle at fault, if at all? Why hadn't she come to him? Did she fear she'd be in trouble? She must have done to flee her home and leave Smithers to pack up the cottage.

He should have visited her more after returning from Rosewood, instead of staying away. Somehow he should have gained her
trust, given her reason that he was her friend, someone she could
come to when in need.

God, what a mess!

Well, he knew that out there somewhere Annabelle Wallis was
hiding with Eliza's daughter, and he would find them, no matter
what. After that, he didn't know.

13

Although Annabelle had been to York several times before, she had never been beyond the main shopping streets and the market in Parliament Street in the heart of the city. But as Nellie led her away from the busy thoroughfares, the crowds thinned along Goodramgate as they headed towards Nellie's home.

In the coach, the baby had slept peacefully, with a full tummy for the first time. Sammy had also behaved, content to look out of the window at the rushing scenery as they travelled at speed to York.

Nellie nodded, the midnight journey of the night before catching up with her, and so Annabelle had also dozed. The days since Miss Hartley's knock on the cottage door had taken its toll. Her nerves were so tightly strung she wondered if she might descend into madness at any moment. That she had left her home and was now totally responsible for a baby added to the fear. Had she done the right thing in leaving the cottage?

If she'd been half-asleep on the coach through the countryside, she was now wide awake, walking the narrow, grim streets within eyesight of the magnificent Minster. The cathedral towered above them in all its multi-windowed glory.

'Now, do you know much about this area?' Nellie asked her with Sammy on her hip and carrying one of Annabelle's bags.

'No, I don't.'

'Right, well, to the left of Goodramgate is Bedern. Do not go there for any reason, you understand? It's full of desperate Irish and disease and together it bodes ill to anyone who ventures into the snickets and yards. Understood?'

'Snickets?'

'The little cuts between the houses and buildings, alleys. Don't you have them in the country?'

Annabelle shook her head, thinking of the meandering dirt lanes of Hartleydale village.

'Well, in York we have snickets. Don't be caught down them at night,' Nellie warned.

They passed a group of young men, dirty and unkempt, smoking pipes. One fellow opened his trousers and flashed himself at Annabelle.

Nellie nudged her along. 'Don't gawp at them, for God's sake. They'll have you down a dark cellar before you can open your mouth to scream.'

Holding the baby tightly, and her other bag slung over her shoulder, Annabelle hurried after Nellie, looking neither left nor right.

'The Minster side is a little more decent, but always have your wits about you. Never show any money in the street or hold your purse in one hand. I'll give you some twine to tie it to and then shove it down your bodice or up your sleeve. Got it?'

'Yes.' Her timid response sounded feeble even to her own ears.

Nellie flashed a grin. 'You'll be fine. To start with, you'll only go out with me, or my Paul will go with you, until you know your way around. My lot will pester you to go with you as well.'

Annabelle knew that Paul was Nellie's husband, who worked on the other side of town at the railway works, and that they had four other children besides Sammy.

'Aldwark,' Nellie suddenly announced. turning left before the impressive tower of Monkgate, one of the original medieval entrances in the castle walls. 'This is our street. It's not as bad as Bedern, but not far off.' Within a few seconds, she stopped again at the entrance to a narrow cut between two brick terrace houses. 'We live down here, Monk's Yard. We go through this snicket, and it brings us out into the yard.'

Annabelle didn't have a free hand to cover her nose and had to breathe through her mouth to avoid gagging at the foetid stink. The yard was dirt and mud with a pump in the middle which young children played around. Surrounding the yard were the two-storey terrace houses at the front and down each side more dwellings, but they were only one-storey. At the end of the yard was an assortment of small storage sheds lined against the stone castle wall that surrounded the city.

'This is us.' Nellie stopped before a low wooden door in the single dwelling attached to the right side of the terraces.

The door opened at a push, and she went in and dumped Sammy on the floor by the table that filled the small room. A range took up half of the far wall and at either side of it were bunk beds. The floor was made of dirty grey stone flags of mismatched sizes, and the walls were whitewashed originally but now held a trace-work of mould and damp.

Nellie bent and added bits of rubbish to the smouldering fire in the range. 'I'll make us some tea. We'll use the stuff you brought as it's better than the weak scrapings I have in the pot.' Nellie winked, then, seeing Annabelle's shocked face, her expression changed. 'I know it's not what you expected. It's different to what you're used to, but you'll get used to it.'

Not knowing if she ever would, Annabelle nodded at her new friend and sat on a stool at the table. The bag and baby had grown heavy in her arms from the long walk.

'In the room next door is where me and Paul sleep with Sammy. The other four are on the bunk beds Paul built. He's so useful with his hands. He can make owt out of nowt.' Nellie rummaged through Annabelle's bags and found the little bags of tea leaves.

'Where will I sleep?' She stared around the dwelling, which looked no better than an animals' barn.

'On this bunk. Dora can sleep with Florrie up the top.'

'Thank you for putting me up.'

'I've told you a dozen times already, it's no problem. To be honest, another bit of money coming in will be grand.'

'I'll get a job as soon as I can.' Her stomach clenched at the thought of getting work in the city, but she had to do something to survive.

'Aye, course you will, and I'll look after the baby for you when you do.' Nellie reached for the infant. 'I'll give her another feed while you make the tea.'

Grateful to have something to do, Annabelle dumped her bags on the bottom bunk out of the way and then set to make some tea.

'Doesn't look as though they've left anything to eat.' Nellie frowned at the empty shelves by the range. 'I'll go out later and do some shopping.' She put the baby to the breast. 'Feeding always makes me hungry. Just check the cupboard next to the range and see if there's a scrap of anything.'

Annabelle searched the cupboard, opening two tin boxes, but both were empty. She also noted the mouse droppings in the corner of the shelf and shivered in disgust.

The door opened and in rushed four children, wearing ragged

clothes, with dirty faces and unkempt hair. They stared at Annabelle, and she stared back at them.

'Mam, who is this?' the eldest child asked.

'Florrie, this is Annabelle. She and her baby are staying with us for a while.'

Annabelle jerked at the words *her baby*. Yet that was the reality of the situation. She had become a mother.

'This is my unruly lot, Annabelle,' Nellie chuckled. 'Florrie, she's ten and the eldest, then there's my boys, Wilf and Ralphie, and then Dora.'

'I'm four!' Dora pouted. 'Ain't I, Mam?'

'Aye, my love. You were four a few days ago. You're getting my big girl.' Nellie hugged the small child against her legs.

'Baby?' Dora asked.

Nellie looked at Annabelle. 'What is this little mite's name? I've never asked.'

'She doesn't have one,' she replied. 'I never thought to think of a name. Miss Eliza should have mentioned one.'

The children lost interest in the adults' talk and disappeared out of the door again to play in the filthy yard outside.

Nellie swapped the baby over to the other breast. 'From what you've told me, I doubt the young miss was in any state to think of names for a child she didn't want. You're going to have to call her something. What was your mam's name?'

'Ma named me after my real mother, Annabelle, and Ma's name was Amy, so I'd rather not have another name starting with A.' She smiled as she mashed the tea. She found two chipped cups on a high shelf. There wasn't any sugar or milk.

'Well, let's think of something,' Nellie said, her stomach rumbling.

'It's hard to think on an empty stomach. Would Florrie show me where the best shops are?' Annabelle asked, pouring out the tea. 'I could go and buy some food.'

Nellie glanced out of the one window at the setting sun. 'We've missed the markets where I usually shop. You'll have to go to the Quakers.'

'The Quakers?'

'Aye,' Nellie gulped her tea, 'a shop in Goodramgate, Fox's, is owned by a Quaker family. Nice enough but, well, they keep themselves to themselves. Elias Fox is decent enough and doesn't rob you like other grocers. He's too honest to put sawdust in the tea to make the weights, or powder in the flour. He's pricey, mind, and won't haggle, but if you've the money to buy in his shop, you get better quality.'

'I'll buy some food, then.' Annabelle rose from the table and with a last sip of tea, she pushed the cup to Nellie to have since she'd already guzzled her tea despite the hot temperature.

'Take Florrie with you. There's a net bag hanging on the back of the door.'

Pulling on her coat, Annabelle grabbed the bag and her purse and went outside in the waning light. 'Florrie, can you come with me to Fox's, please?'

'Can I come, too?' Wilf piped up from where he sat on the dirt watching a beetle.

'Of course.'

'And me!' Ralphie jumped up and held Annabelle's hand.

'And me.' Dora wasn't to be forgotten.

'You can all come with me.' Annabelle smiled. She turned to Florrie. 'You don't mind helping me?'

The thin-shouldered girl shrugged. 'Nope.'

'Do you all go to school?' Annabelle asked as they walked through the snicket and onto Aldwark.

'I work now,' Florrie said proudly. 'I'm a washer in the kitchen at the Royal Oak. That's it there.' She pointed to the inn as they turned on to Goodramgate.

'How fortunate you have a job.'

'Me and Ralphie go to the Blue Coats,' Wilf answered. 'But as soon as I'm ten, I'll be working proper like, not just in the orchards in the summer as I do now. I was harvesting the fruit there today.'

'We all do that.' Florrie nudged him. 'You're nothing special, Wilf Baker.'

'At my old home, I had fruit trees, too,' Annabelle said wistfully.

'Why did you leave?' Florrie asked, stopping outside of Fox's Greengrocers.

'I had to give up my cottage as my ma died.'

The girl nodded in an adult way as though understanding that was a valid reason for leaving. She pushed open the shop door and they filed in.

Annabelle looked around at the neatly stacked shelves behind the counter and the boxes of fruit and vegetables arranged around the shop.

'May I help you, miss?' An older man came through a doorway leading to the back of the shop.

'Yes, please.' She strolled around the stock. 'I would like some vegetables – a couple of pounds of potatoes, a bunch of carrots, a string of onions, a few turnips, and I'll take a bag of apples.'

The children's eyes widened in surprise. Florrie sidled up to her. 'Can you afford all this?'

Smiling, she nodded. 'It's my first night so I'll treat us to a meal.'

'That lot will last us all week if we're careful.' Florrie nodded wisely.

Once paid, and the children loaded up, Annabelle sent them home while she went along to the Shambles to buy cheap cuts of meat for the stew she planned to make. Stopping by a sweet shop, she was just able to buy a penny's worth of hard-boiled sweets before they closed.

Darkness had crawled over the city as the sun fell behind the buildings. Alarmed at being out alone at night and remembering Nellie's warnings of the Irishmen who loitered in the snickets, she ran back along Goodramgate. The pubs were lit up and men's laughter could be heard through open doors. One fellow entering the Royal Oak stopped and whistled at her as she ran past.

Turning into Aldwark, she slammed straight into the hard chest of a man. Annabelle screamed.

The man stepped back and swore.

'I'm so sorry.' Annabelle shrunk back from him, heart in her throat, clutching the meat before her to ward him off.

'Nay, no harm done.' He smiled, his head tilted to one side. 'Are you Annabelle?'

'I am.'

'I'm Paul, Nellie's husband. I'd been sent to find you and walk you home.'

She sighed in relief. 'Thank you. I was a little frightened.'

'And you've a right to be. Don't be out at night around here unless you're looking for trouble. Come on, then.' He took the meat from her and turned to walk back to the snicket. 'You'll find the city a strange place after living in the country.'

'I'm sure I'll get used to it.'

'Why would you want to?'

In the dimness of the yard, she couldn't make out his expression, but he sounded friendly enough and although not a tall man, he was well built and seemed pleasant.

'I do thank you for taking me and the baby in,' she told him.

He stopped before the door but didn't open it. 'Nellie said you're a good lass who has had some trouble. It costs nothing to share an already cramped house with two more, but I'll be honest with you, having Nellie not earning, we could do with another person who can get a job and help pay for things. My wage only just covers rent and food.'

'I will start looking for a job tomorrow and pay my way.'

'That's all I wanted to hear. We'll get on well.'

Inside, the children were sitting around the small range listening to Nellie tell them of her adventure into the country.

Annabelle started to make the stew, chopping up the meat and vegetables.

'You can't be spending all your money the first night you're here, lass.' Nellie frowned at the pile of produce on the table.

'I thought to make a meal as a thank you for taking me in. You're feeding the baby, so I can feed you.'

'That's right kind of you, lass, but you've got to make your money last until you find work.'

Annabelle nodded and carried on with the meal. Making hearty stews to last for days was something Ma had taught from a young age, and she was pleased when Florrie offered to help, while Wilf brought in a bucket of water collected from the pump in the middle of the yard.

Later, after the filling stew had been consumed and she had doled out the sweets to the children before they'd gone to bed, Annabelle sat with a cup of tea at the table, holding the baby. Nellie, who this time was feeding Sammy, sat opposite. Paul had turned in, for he was up at five each morning.

'My lot haven't eaten like that in a long time. I do the best I can but it's becoming more difficult as they grow bigger. It's hard to fill them.' Nellie glanced at the sleeping children in their bunks. Florrie had happily shared with Dora, declaring it would be good in winter to have her sister to keep her warm.

'You have lovely children,' Annabelle said.

'Speaking of children. What name have you decided for that one?' Nellie indicated to the baby.

'Jemima Eliza Amy.' The name came suddenly, and she liked it.

'That's a mouthful, for sure,' Nellie chuckled. 'Jemima? That's pretty. I know a woman who attends church called Jemima.'

Annabelle sighed. 'You might think me macabre.'

'Why?'

'There's a grave not far from Ma's and I noticed it was a baby's grave. Jemima Price. Aged five days. I thought how that poor baby had never had a chance to live. So maybe this Jemima will have a good life in honour of that baby.'

'There's nothing macabre about that. It's nice. Our Jemima will live a life for two.'

'Our Jemima,' she murmured, her chest swelling with love for her. Annabelle gazed down at the little sweet face. Jemima was content and sleeping peacefully after the constant feeding Nellie gave her.

'You should get to bed, lass.' Nellie yawned. 'If you're to spend the day walking the streets for work, you need to rest.'

'Yes, good idea.'

'Lie Jemima between you and the wall. I'll come out and get her when she cries for a feed during the night.'

'Thank you.'

With the candles blown out and only the twinkling embers of the banked fire showing any light in the room, Annabelle huddled into the bottom bunk with Jemima snuggled against her, wrapped in the silk shawl. The thin blanket that Dora had used was little protection against the coolness of the night, so Annabelle threw her coat over the top of her and tried to settle on the thin mattress and equally thin pillow.

Her first night not sleeping in her own bed. The first night being away from the cottage. Hot tears rose as she thought of home and

Ma. The city's many church bells rang throughout the streets, and she counted ten rings. In the village, the church bells weren't rung at night past seven o'clock until four the next morning. Here the chimes seemed to echo between the castle walls and bounce off the buildings. It was one of the many changes she had to get used to.

Had she done the right thing in running away? She'd lumbered herself with the huge responsibility of a child that wasn't hers. Yet what else could she have done? The Hartleys would have sent darling Jemima away and likely had her arrested.

No, she'd had no choice. Eliza Hartley could rest in peace knowing her child was loved and cared for. Annabelle would protect Jemima with her life, just as Ma had protected her.

14

John ducked under a shop's awning on Briggate to pause while the heavy downpour sent people running for cover. He coughed into his hand and shivered. Summer had been replaced with a chilly autumn as September arrived with rain and gales, turning the colour of the leaves quickly before the wind tore them to the ground.

He'd spent the last three weeks in Leeds walking the streets, asking questions at every shop and business. He wrote down in a notebook each place and street he visited so as not to get confused. He wrote home to Des every few days giving him a brief report of his search, which revealed zero results on finding Annabelle or the baby.

From his pocket he took out the address of a private orphanage he'd been given at one of the inns he had called at. From his long days of walking the city, he knew that the address was out of the town centre. Ignoring the rain, he hurried along Briggate to the hansom cab rank and climbed into the first one available and gave the address to the driver.

'Kirkstall, sir?' the driver asked, rain dripping off his hat. 'It's two miles away.'

'Can you take me or not?'

'Aye.'

Sitting back, fighting the shivering that had come on him last night while in bed, John read through his notebook as the hansom edged its way out of the busy shopping area and onto Kirkstall Road.

Had he missed anything? John flipped the many pages, reading the ever-growing list of inns, boarding houses, shops, tea rooms, factories and mills he'd covered so far. He'd even visited two workhouses, which had left him shocked at the conditions some people were forced to suffer. He knew the workhouses were cold and forbidding to dissuade the poor from entering, but to see families separated, men away from wives, children away from mothers, brothers and sisters divided by walls... it opened his eyes to a way of life that gave him nightmares. What if Annabelle Wallis had gone into such a place with his niece?

Des had written to him at the inn he was staying at to inform him he'd spoken again to Dickie Smithers and again the shepherd had heard no news from Miss Wallis. John thought Smithers knew more than he was letting on, but the fellow was loyal to Annabelle and John couldn't blame him for his loyalty, even if it did hinder his own progress.

'Here we are, sir,' the driver called, slowing his horse.

John climbed down outside of a large, red-brick building standing behind double wrought-iron gates. The brass sign denoted it as Redhall Orphanage. 'Wait here, will you? I shan't be long.'

'Yes, sir.'

John entered the tended grounds of the orphanage and rang the bell beside the large black door.

It took some moments before a tall, thin woman opened the

door. She wore all black with a bunch of keys at her waist. 'Forgive me for making you wait. I have no idea where the maid is.' She smiled warmly. 'Please, come in.'

'Thank you.' John took off his hat, showering raindrops on the polished floor. 'I am John Hartley from Hartley Manor.'

'I'm pleased to meet you, Mr Hartley. I am Simone Harknall, matron of this establishment.' She held out her hand which he shook. 'Please come into my office.'

John followed her into a large room with windows overlooking the grounds. A walnut desk was placed near the windows, while on one wall ledgers filled the bookcase and a roaring fire gave out warmth from the opposite wall.

'How may I help you, Mr Hartley?' Matron Harknall went behind her desk and waved him to a chair in front of it.

'I have come looking for a friend of my sister's, who recently had a baby. We have been told this baby might have been put up for adoption and we would like to make the child a ward of our family.'

'How extremely fortunate for the child, if not for the mother.'

'My family are eager to find the child.'

'But not the mother?' Her eyebrows rose.

He held her gaze. 'Yes, and the mother, if that is possible.'

'And you have no proof this child has been placed here?'

'That is correct. I am visiting all orphanages in the area.'

Her expression showed her surprise. 'An impressive task. You must be truly devoted to this child?'

'I am.'

The woman studied him. 'And you would like to know if this baby has been brought here.'

'I would, yes.' John felt he was being examined and had come up short for some reason.

'What information can you tell me?' The woman opened the ledger in front of her.

'The baby is only a month old, a girl. The woman who might have given her up is called Annabelle Wallis.'

For several moments, the matron ran her finger down the ledger until she had turned two pages. She looked up at John. 'I am sorry – we have had no admissions of that sex or age in the last month.'

His heart sank and he slowly stood. 'Thank you for your time.'

The matron stood as well. 'May I be so bold to say, Mr Hartley, that you look like you could do with some rest?'

He snorted with good humour. 'Do I appear as bad as that?'

'Forgive me, but you do look unwell.'

John let out a deep sigh. 'It has been rather a trying time.'

She pushed a piece of paper towards him and a pen. 'Write down your address. If I hear of anything concerning this woman, or if she comes here, I will write.'

'You have my sincere thanks.' John wrote down his name and the address of the manor.

'There are many orphanages in the county, Mr Hartley. Do not despair of finding the child.'

'If only I was certain an orphanage was of interest. I am clutching at straws, so to speak. I have no clear idea of where they might be.' He passed the paper back to her.

She read the address. 'Hartleydale?'

'Thirteen miles north from York.'

'York? Why are you looking around here?'

'I was told Miss Wallis might come to Leeds to find work.'

'Have you searched York?' she enquired with a lift of her eyebrow.

He swallowed, his throat sore and head pounding. 'No, not yet.'

She smiled sadly. 'From my experience, a woman in trouble with a very young baby isn't going to travel far if she intends on giving the child away and getting on with her life. She will do it as quickly as possible, not traipse the countryside. I would return to

York, Mr Hartley, and search there.' She wrote on another piece of paper and handed it to him. 'These are a few orphanages I know of around York, which may be useful to you.'

'How exceedingly kind of you.'

She smiled, and he realised she was rather pretty, despite her unadorned garments and scraped-back hair. 'I hope you find the child, Mr Hartley, and the mother if she needs help.'

John bowed and walked out of the room with her. At the front door, he heard a bell ring and the scraping of chairs in the room on the other side of the wide hall.

'The older children are coming out of class,' Matron Harknall informed him.

'How many do you have here?'

'Fifty. Always fifty.' Sadness entered her blue eyes. 'There are always more children needing a roof over their heads than we have room for.'

John turned as a door opposite opened and a line of children filed out. The boys were dressed in uniforms of grey and the girls in green. After his visits to the miserable workhouses, it was a surprise to see an institution where the children were healthy-looking. None of the ones who walked past him seemed to be malnourished and a couple of the little girls gave him a cheeky smile. They looked clean and well behaved.

'They appear well and happy here, Matron.'

Matron Harknall straightened her back with pride. 'We try our best. The ages range from newborn to twelve years old, so we have much to do. We do our utmost, though, to make the children happy. They are never mistreated and are well fed. They learn skills to help them find work when they are older. Thankfully, we have an exceptional board of governors who genuinely care for the children and this orphanage, but of course the fundraising never fully stretches as far as I would like.'

'You will have a donation from me and my family, madam.' John smiled.

'Then you must return, Mr Hartley, and have a proper tour of the place.'

'I would like that.' They shook hands and John put on his hat and walked out into the rain. If Annabelle did give up the baby, he hoped she had chosen a respectable place such as this one.

'Back to Leeds, sir?' the driver asked as he approached the hansom.

'Yes. To the Golden Ram Inn. I shall collect my luggage and then will have you take me to the train station.' John coughed as he climbed into the hansom.

'Very good, sir.'

Sitting back in the seat, feeling hot and clammy, John thought of the matron's advice. It made sense for Annabelle to go to York first and perhaps stay there for a while. Why would she need to go to Leeds if in York she found work? He'd been foolish to start his search in Leeds first and not York, just because the shepherd had told him a small piece of information that might not even be true.

He would go to York and begin the search again there. Closing his eyes, he rested his head back, swallowing painfully. He didn't have the time to be ill.

* * *

Tired from traipsing the streets looking for work, Annabelle walked through the muddy yard in the rain to the place she still couldn't believe she called home. The grey, dismal weather had sent the children inside and the deserted yard looked unkempt and miserable. Everything looked neglected and dirty, such a contrast to the cottage and her lovely garden. How she missed wandering through the flowers, picking fresh vegetables, working in the potting shed, listening to the birds sing in the trees and the sound of the trickling beck.

In this poor part of York, the cottage seemed a paradise where she could go for days if she wanted without seeing another person except Ma. But not here. In this overcrowded area of the city, she heard screams and yelling, babies crying, and children playing day and night. There was no rest from the numerous factory hooters, the church bells, the ships' horns on the river, and the distant whistle of the trains. Hawkers shouted out their wares, the military shot cannons at the barracks and the constant traffic of carriage and wagons rang throughout the city. Not to mention the throb of people streaming through the streets. She couldn't get used to the noise of hooves striking the cobbles, the rumbling wheels, the banging of doors, of people, *strangers*, being wherever she went.

She longed for home. For Ma. For the life she used to lead. Here in the city, she became faceless, alone amongst the crowd. No one knew her and she knew no one. She had failed to find a job. Her skills were considered not worthy enough in the shops she applied to, nor did she have a reference for a maid's position in a decent house. Soon, all she'd have left to consider was working long hours in a bleak factory.

Annabelle opened the door to the dwelling; she couldn't honestly think of it as a house, for it was nothing more than two rooms attached to the back of another house.

'Here she is!' Nellie announced.

Happiness flooded Annabelle as Ginny and Dickie sat at the table surrounded by the children. 'I wasn't expecting you two.' She kissed them both on the cheek, excited to see two familiar faces that reminded her of good times.

'We both wrangled a half-day off at the same time so we could see you.' Dickie beamed as though he'd performed a miracle.

'Have you been waiting long?' Annabelle hung up her coat and unpinned her bonnet.

'Only ten minutes or so,' Ginny answered, cradling Jemima to her chest. 'Nellie says you've called her Jemima. My, she's come on, hasn't she? Right bonny, now.'

'She's fed well, that's why.' She smiled gratefully at Nellie. 'I can't thank you enough, Ginny, for bringing Nellie into my life just when I needed her.'

Ginny blushed. 'I'm glad it's worked out well.'

'They brought cake!' Wilf declared, eying up the sliced currant cake on the table.

'Aye, and you've already had some, so get that greedy look off your face, Wilf Baker.' Nellie slapped his shoulder. 'It had to be raining today of all days when we have visitors. I could have done with you all out from under my feet.'

'They're fine, Nellie,' Annabelle soothed.

'Always taking their side, she is. They have her wrapped around their little fingers, I'm telling you.' Nellie grinned to take the sting out of her words.

'Nellie says you've been out looking for work?' Dickie asked.

'Yes. I've had the odd day here and there washing pots in pubs when filling in for someone who is sick, but nothing that I can call my own.'

'The main thing is you're safe.' Ginny sipped her tea, giving Dickie a quick look.

'What is it?' Annabelle asked.

Dickie sighed. 'Mr John is still looking for you, or I should say looking for evidence of Miss Eliza's baby.'

Annabelle bit the inside of her cheek in worry. 'I thought they would think it a hopeless case.'

'Nope. Mr John has been searching in Leeds for weeks,' Ginny told her. 'The family keep it quiet, not wanting to draw attention or gossip, but Mrs Hartley lets things slip to Miss Nevin, that's her lady's maid.' Ginny added the last bit for Nellie's benefit. 'Mr John is determined to find some kind of evidence leading up to Miss Eliza's death.'

'Why Leeds?' Annabelle asked.

'Because that's what I told him where you might have gone when I saw him at your cottage,' Dickie admitted.

'He was at the cottage?' Her eyes widened in surprise. 'So that proves he's looking for me! He thinks I have something to do with Miss Eliza dying.' She began to shake.

Dickie nodded. 'Yes, you're probably right. He wouldn't go to Leeds otherwise.'

'Don't worry,' Ginny said, taking her hand. 'He doesn't know for certain that you have the baby.'

'But he must do! Why would he go to the cottage and then to Leeds? John Hartley wants to speak to me. He must know something.' Her stomach heaved at the thought. A man she admired, had even dreamed about, was searching for her, wanting answers. How he must hate her now. She felt sick at the thought of him having bad thoughts about her. Foolishly, she wanted him to like her, admire her, even. She hadn't imagined the looks he'd given her. But none of that mattered now. Whatever kindness he harboured towards her would be gone.

'He'll not find you here, lass.' Nellie refilled everyone's cups with tea.

'No, he won't.' Dickie gave her a small smile. 'I told him you'd gone looking for work in Leeds or Manchester. He won't search York. Did you write the letter to his brother about the cottage?'

She nodded sadly, remembering the day she'd written the note giving up the one place she loved. 'I sent it a few days after I arrived. Has anyone moved into the cottage yet?'

Dickie shook his head. 'No. It's still empty.'

Despair washed over her. John Hartley believed she was a link to his sister's death and her child. He wouldn't stop searching for her, not a man like him who'd travelled the world. She hated to think he was suspicious of her, or he thought ill of her.

'We brought you a bag of your things. A few more clothes, some books,' Dickie said.

'That's kind of you,' she murmured. The idea of wearing a different dress lifted her spirits a little. She'd been wearing the same two dresses for the last month.

'You mustn't worry.' Dickie caught her hand. 'No one knows you're here except us.'

The church bells around the city rang the hour.

Ginny handed Jemima to Annabelle and stood. 'We need to go if we are to make the last coach back to Hartleydale.'

'You'll come again soon?' Nellie asked Ginny.

'Aye, on my day off at the end of the month.' Ginny gazed at Dickie. 'Hopefully, we can both have the same day off?'

He slapped on his cap. 'I'll do my best.'

Annabelle watched Ginny, who kept her gaze on Dickie as he said goodbye to the children, making Dora giggle as he tickled her. It was clear to Annabelle that Ginny thought a great deal about Dickie, if her adoring expression was anything to go by. Seeing it surprised Annabelle. She hadn't anticipated Ginny falling for Dickie, not when she'd said when they first met that she didn't want to get married. But then why wouldn't Ginny find Dickie a suitable match? Dickie had a good job on the estate and a cottage he shared with his mam. He was decent-looking, tall and lithe, funny and kind. He was exactly the type of man Ginny or any woman should marry – but not her. Without a doubt, she knew she'd made the right choice. Dickie deserved someone who would adore him.

'Right, then. See you all.' Dickie walked outside, followed by Ginny. The rain had eased to a slight misty drizzle.

'It's been lovely to see you both.' Annabelle wished she were going with them. She ached to see her home.

They waved to her from the entrance to the snicket and then were gone.

'That was nice of them to come,' Nellie said.

Annabelle closed the door. 'It was.'

'You must miss your old life.'

She nodded, emotion clogging her throat.

Nellie's look was full of concern. 'You just have to make a new life, lass, that's all. Once you have a job and you find a room of your own, then you'll feel better.'

Annabelle nodded but wondered if she ever would feel better. A room of her own meant renting some squalid damp room in one of the big tenement houses, surrounded by hundreds of strangers. Her heart and mind rebelled at the thought.

15

'Lass!' Nellie rushed into the room, the October wind banging the door shut behind her.

Annabelle didn't glance up from where she sat on the bunk, changing Jemima's soiled napkin and clothes. 'You're back, then. This little one has made such a mess of herself. The others are out playing. Florrie took Sammy with her.'

'Aye, I just saw them.' Nellie thumped her shopping bags down on the table. 'You'll never guess what I've done.'

'No, what?'

Nellie beamed triumphantly. 'I've only got you a job!'

Annabelle finished dressing Jemima in a clean white smock that bore the stains of many children having used it before her. 'That's nice,' she finally uttered.

'Now don't be downhearted.' Nellie put the kettle on to boil. 'I know the last few positions have not been great, but this one will change all of that.'

'Not great? That's a joke, isn't it?' Annabelle placed the soiled garments in a tin bucket filled with water and caustic soda for such a purpose. She'd take it out to the pump and wash them later.

'True, the other positions you've held in the last month have been a little strange.'

'My first job was washing pots in a pub where the landlord only wanted to get his hands up my skirts. I lasted a week there. My next position was cleaning for Mrs Lane and her dog bit me everywhere I went in the house, until I was bleeding so much I was staining madam's floors and furniture. Mrs Lane sacked me after three days, blaming me for upsetting her dog. Then last week I got taken on at Humphries gun shop and he nearly killed me when a gun he was testing went off and just missed my head! He said it was my fault for being in the way and told me not to come back!'

Nellie laughed, because they could laugh about it all now. At the time, Annabelle had been upset that she couldn't keep a job for more than a few days.

'Well, that's all to change this time.' Nellie made them some tea.

'I'll remain doubtful until proven otherwise.' Annabelle cradled Jemima in her arms, pleased that the little one was growing more each week and starting to put weight on due to Nellie's constant feeding. At two months old, Jemima was a contented little thing who fed and slept and gave the odd smile when anyone cooed to her.

'Do you want to know what it is or not?' Nellie sat down and unpacked her bags.

'Go on, then.'

'I heard at the market that the Blewitts needs another house-maid,' Nellie declared as though that was all the information Annabelle needed to hear.

'And who are the Blewitts?'

'Mr and Mrs Blewitt own a nice house on Lord Mayor's Walk not far from here. They are an older couple. He's a retired teaching master and she comes from a good family.'

'How do you know them?'

'They are forever donating to different charities. Mrs Blewitt isn't happy unless she's trying to give her opinion on some committee or other, so they say anyway. At Christmas, the Blewitts put a table outside their house and give out presents to passing children and hot soup to those that are homeless.'

'That's kind.'

'Anyway, I heard from Mrs Owen, who owns the fish stall, that her sister-in-law's niece finished at the Blewitts' yesterday, to get married. I think you should go to the house before they find someone else. It's only up the road. First left after you pass under Monk Bar.'

'Yes, I know it. I've walked every street in York looking for work.'

Nellie took Jemima from her. 'Clean yourself up and put on that nice blue dress Ginny and Dickie brought in your bag of things. Get out of that mourning black. Your Ma would want you to look your best, wouldn't she?'

Doing as Nellie instructed, Annabelle changed into her blue dress and brushed her hair. She twisted and curled it up under bonnet and then pulled on her good coat, only to notice it had a mud stain on it.

'You can't wear that.' Nellie frowned. 'What have you been doing?'

'I let Florrie wear it the other day when it was raining.'

'And now she's ruined the front. It'll need sponging off.' Nellie grabbed the peacock shawl and passed it to her.

'No, not the shawl!' Annabelle held up the silk shawl that always reminded her of Eliza.

'It's the best thing we have for you to wear. My old shawl has more holes than a sieve. You have to wear it. It's not cold today and you can get away with wearing something fancy like that as you have the good looks to carry it off.'

'It's hardly what a housemaid would wear, though.'

'You'll be fine. It shows you have good taste.'

'I didn't buy it,' she reminded her, thinking briefly of John Hartley, who had bought it.

'They don't know that, do they? If you look respectable, you're halfway there.'

Sighing, Annabelle wrapped the fine silk around her shoulders and grabbed her purse, which held the reference from Mrs Lane. At last she had a reference, even if it was only a few lines.

'Good luck.' Nellie grinned. 'It's number nine.'

Annabelle walked through the yard onto Aldwark. The children came running over to her.

'Where are you going?' Florrie asked, Sammy on her hip.

'To ask for a job.'

'Where?' Ralphie took her hand. 'Can I come?'

'Lord Mayor's Walk and no, not this time, pet.' She smiled down at him. She had grown to love the five Baker children. They had accepted her into their home and family as though she'd always belonged, and Annabelle was grateful for it. The children's chatter and antics kept her occupied and gave her less time to dwell on missing Ma and home.

'Will you be back soon?' Ralphie asked as she let go of his hand at the corner of the street.

'I will. Go and play now.' She left them and walked towards Monk Bar and passed under the castle gate tower. The road to the left was the one she needed, and she walked along, thinking that if she got the position, she would be only minutes from Nellie's house and how easy that would make life, especially with winter coming.

She counted the numbers on the front doors, which led straight off the street. Outside number nine, she straightened her skirts and pulled at her cuffs, hoping she looked tidy, for Nellie didn't own a looking glass. Nerves twisted her stomach. She needed this position. Money was short at the Baker house, and she'd not been earning enough to help out. The proceeds from Bobby and the cow and the meagre wages she'd earned so far she'd given straight to Nellie for food and rent, but it had hardly made a dent in what was needed. So, Annabelle always made sure she didn't eat much to make the basic meals stretch further. If Nellie realised, she didn't mention it.

Behind her a carriage rumbled past, but she focused on knocking on the black painted door. This was it, her chance to gain a good position. She mustn't ruin it.

'Miss Wallis?'

The yell made her jump. She turned as John Hartley leaned out of the carriage travelling up the road.

Fear clamped her throat as the carriage stopped. Annabelle ignored the man who answered the front door and ran the other way down the street. She could hear Mr Hartley shouting her name.

She ran faster, heart thumping as she looked for a way to escape off the street. On her left was the rope walk and behind that the castle wall. To the right was the large and impressive building of the York and Ripon Training Institution for School Masters and she knew she'd not lose Mr Hartley going into the open grounds there.

Suddenly, the castle walls ended and ahead she saw open gates on her left. Without looking back, she hurried into a coal yard, searching for a way out beyond it. She had to get into the city streets and the maze of alleys and snickets, where she could lose Mr Hartley.

'What ye doin', lass?' an older fellow asked, chomping on his pipe as he came out of a shed. Mounds of coal were piled all over the yard, everything was black and filthy. A horse and cart stood to one side, the horse eating from a nosebag.

'I need to get away from someone,' she gasped, desperately

looking behind her and fully expecting to see Mr Hartley running into the coal yard at any moment.

'This way!' The man ushered her into a cabin and from there into another building. Annabelle blindly followed him, passing through rooms filled with tables and stacks of crates like some sort of warehouse.

He went out through another door into a cut. 'Go down there, lass. Turn right and there's a small gap in the fence. It'll lead you into the garden of a house, but they have a gate. Go through that to get to the walkway near the castle wall. Run alongside of that until you reach the next street. There are steps to get over the wall.'

'Thank you so much.' She smiled gratefully, picked up her skirts and ran along the cut until she reached the fence. Some of the timber panels were broken at the bottom like jagged teeth. She tightened the shawl about her shoulders, bent and crawled through.

On the other side, she stood in the back garden of a house but wasted no time in looking about and dashed to the gate on the other side. She unlatched it and slowly poked her head around. The walkway between the houses was clear and she could run up to the road, but that would expose her. Instead, she turned and walked along the back fence line of the houses until she reached the gate of a long yard. She cautiously opened it and went in. Barrels of ale were stacked along the fence and the smell of stale ale filled her nose. She was in the yard of a public house.

Pausing, she checked for anyone about. Her heart raced at the thought of being caught by John Hartley. It frightened her to think that he was in York, perhaps searching for her. Was he asking about her at every house and business? Would he search Aldwark? Was there anywhere safe? Should she leave York and go elsewhere? London, maybe?

Panting, she tried to remain calm and walked towards the door leading into a service area of the pub. Once inside, she stood in a short corridor, hearing the voices of those working in the kitchen.

A lad came out carrying a bucket full of slops. 'Hey, what are you doing back here?'

'I'm a little lost. I'm looking for a way out to the street. Can you help me, please?'

'Aye. You've gone the wrong way, miss.' He turned and pointed to the brown wooden door at the end of the corridor. 'Go through there and along past the snug and through to the taproom. Stay on the right side, though, the taproom on the left is for men only.'

'Thank you very much.' Walking as sedately as she could, and trying to catch her breath, Annabelle stepped through the pub without anyone questioning her. It was too busy with patrons to consider the out-of-breath young woman exiting the front door onto Gillygate.

Out on the street, Annabelle peered up and down. Not seeing a black carriage, she lifted her skirts and hurried down the long road. The hairs on the back of her neck stood up as a carriage turned into the end of the street.

She immediately went into the nearest shop. She stood by the front window, peeking over the display to watch the carriage drive by, but it was a green-painted vehicle, not black, and relieved, she let out a sigh.

'Can I help you, miss?' the man behind the counter asked.

Annabelle started and then blushed. 'No. No, sorry.' She stood in a bookshop, the smell of paper and leather and dust strong in the air of the cramped space.

'You look a bit flushed, miss. Are you all right?' The man came around the counter. His smile was kind in a clean-shaven face with soft green eyes behind his spectacles.

'Yes, thank you. I'm fine. I've had... had a busy day...' she babbled.

'Are you in need of a book?' he asked helpfully.

'I do like books...' Her voice trailed away as she knew she couldn't afford to buy a book. She glanced around the shelves, which were tightly packed. In fact, so much stock was held in the shop that piles of books were stacked on the floor beside the shelves. The table in the middle of the shop heaved with books.

'I'm Josiah Clement. Welcome to my bookshop.'

'Annabelle Baker,' she told him, not wanting to give her real name. She glanced out of the window when a horse and cart trundled by.

'Are you sure you are feeling all right?'

'Yes,' she lied. 'I was just on my way home and thought it might rain.'

He frowned for outside the afternoon sun was lowering in a clear blue sky. 'I don't think it will, not this evening.'

She blushed deeper. 'I should go.'

'You didn't look at any of the books.' His eyes held hers.

'I'll come again. I'm late.'

'If you are in trouble, let me help you.'

How did he know? She stared at him. 'I'm... I'm looking for work, that's all. I'm tired from walking the streets all day.'

'For work?' He frowned again, looking at the fine shawl she wore.

'Yes.' She didn't think he believed her. Wearing the shawl had been a mistake. The fine silk gave her the appearance of someone other than poor working class.

'As it happens, I have a position here. I need an assistant. My mother is not in good health and demands a lot of my time, which means I must close the shop continually. Can you read and write?'

'I can.'

'Well enough to work here in a bookshop?'

Surprised by the question, she blinked rapidly. 'Here?'

'What do you think?' His smile returned.

'You are offering me a job here?' She couldn't believe it. How could it be so simple after weeks of walking the streets, nearly begging for a chance?

'Yes, well, how about we do a week's trial and see how it goes? Would that suit you?'

'I would like that, I'm sure.' She nodded eagerly, wanting to take his hand and shake it.

'Shall I make us a cup of tea and you can rest a moment?'

'Thank you, that is kind.' She followed him out to the back room and sat at a table overcrowded with books while Mr Clement made the tea on a little stove.

'I do hope you like working here as I need to tend to my mother quite a lot.'

'Is she very ill?' Talking to him had taken her mind off John and steadied her racing heartbeat.

'Just her nerves, which are very bad. There are days when she will not leave her bed.' His shoulders slumped as though he carried a heavy burden. 'She is all I have in the world, Miss Baker. I cannot lose her.'

'My mother was an herbalist, Mr Clement. She taught me a great deal. Does your mother take any medicine or powders?'

His expression fell. 'I'm afraid she relies heavily on laudanum. Once it was simply smelling salts. Now...'

'That is sad. Does she drink camomile tea? It is very soothing.'

'She will only drink tea made in China.' He shook his head with a sigh. 'My mother is a trifle difficult, Miss Baker.'

'Try again with the camomile tea and wean her off the laudanum if you can. It can be ruinous if taken constantly.'

'Could you visit her and speak to her, tell her of your skills, your knowledge?' Mr Clement grew hopeful.

'I will, yes.' Annabelle brightened. Helping people pleased her and made her feel she was carrying on Ma's work. 'I'd like to help if I could. I could make her some tonics...' She faltered. She had no money for ingredients for tonics.

'Write me a list of what you need to make Mother a tonic and I will buy it all.' He found a piece of paper and a pencil.

Annabelle wrote down what she'd need to make a soothing tonic for Mrs Clement. 'Does she sleep with lavender under her pillow?'

'Not that I'm aware of.'

She added that to the list. 'Lavender under her pillow will help her sleep.'

They spoke for some time about herbs and healing, with Mr Clement serving the odd customer, until Annabelle noticed the light outside was fading.

'I must be getting home.' She gave Mr Clement a smile of thanks.

'Of course. I have enjoyed our talk, Miss Baker.'

'As have I. I'll start tomorrow?' she reaffirmed.

'Indeed. Let's say tomorrow morning at eight? That way I can show you around before the shop opens.'

She nodded eagerly, ridiculously happy when only minutes ago she had been desperate and scared. 'I'll be here.'

'See you then.'

Annabelle left the shop and, head down, hurried along Gillygate until she reached Bootham Bar. Without slowing, she rushed along High Petergate, but instead of walking past the Minster, she turned and went into the gardens to the north of it and then along College Street. Goodramgate was just ahead. She was nearly home.

Heart thumping, she felt sick at the thought that any minute someone would tap her shoulder and grab her. She kept her head down, her bonnet covering her face.

'Annabelle!'

She nearly collapsed at her name being called, but it was only Florrie, having finished working at the Royal Oak. She waved but kept walking fast.

Florrie ran to catch up with her. 'What's wrong?'

'I just need to get inside.'

Only once the door had shut and Annabelle was safe in the room with Nellie and the children did she relax. Slumping onto a chair, she closed her eyes.

'What has happened?' Nellie asked, quietening the children. 'Did the Blewitts take you on?'

Annabelle had forgotten all about the Blewitts. 'No.' She sat up straight, seeing the concern on Nellie's face.

They heard voices outside and Annabelle jumped up so quickly the chair flipped over. Her heart seemed caught in her throat as she stared at the door. Oh, God, he had found her already!

Paul came in, laughing at something his friend said outside. 'Nellie, love. I'm off for a pint at the Oak.' He gave her his wage and a kiss and went again. The men's laughter echoed around the darkened yard.

Annabelle's legs wobbled as she righted the chair.

'Here, Florrie, take this.' Nellie gave her daughter some coins. 'Run to the pie shop. Buy two meat pies, nothing more, mind. Wilf, go with her to help.'

Once the two eldest had gone, Nellie put Jemima to the breast while Annabelle poured weak milkless and sugarless tea into cups. Dora sat playing with a dirty old rag doll while Ralphie poked sticks into the fire.

'What happened, and why are you as jumpy as a thief in church?'

'John Hartley,' she could barely say his name, 'saw me outside of the Blewitts' house.'

'Sweet Jesus! Are you sure?'

'He called my name. I had to run. I've never run as fast as that in my life. I went into a coal yard, and a fellow there helped me to escape through some buildings. Then I ran behind houses and into the yard of some pub.'

'You got away from him, though?' Nellie held Jemima a little closer, eyes wide. 'He's not coming here?'

'No. Not here. I lost him. I'm sure I did.' She wiped a hand over her face. 'I was scared.'

'I can imagine, lass.'

'Walking down Gillygate, I thought it was his carriage coming up the road, searching for me. I ducked into the nearest shop. It was a bookshop.'

'Was it his carriage?'

'No, thankfully. But the man, Mr Clement, who owns the shop, was concerned about me.'

'That's nice.'

'In the end he offered me a job. I start tomorrow at eight for a week's trial.'

'Blessed girl, well done!' Nellie beamed. 'It sounds a decent position to work in a bookshop.'

'But what of John Hartley?' Annabelle couldn't get him out of her mind.

'What of him? It was a chance meeting that he happened to be driving past you. Who is to say it'll ever happen again?'

'But he knows I'm in York and I ran, which makes me look guilty of something.'

'True.' Nellie sighed. 'That's why you jumped up when you heard voices outside. You're worried he's going to knock on every door in York until he finds you.'

Annabelle stared into her tea. 'I believe he is the type of man who will do just that. I don't think I can stay in York.'

'No! Don't say that. You've landed yourself a good job. You can't throw that away.'

'Mr Hartley won't give up. What if he comes into the bookshop?'

'Right, well... then, if he does, you tell him you know nothing. Then, as soon as you can, you run home.' Nellie scowled as she thought. 'How about you go and live with Tess, Paul's sister, in Hungate?'

'Why there?'

'The likes of Hartley won't venture into the slums of Hungate, they'll lose more than their hat if they do. I'll keep Jemima here and we'll not tell the children where you are, just that you've gone away to work for a bit. Then, if anyone comes asking, they can't say owt, can they? I don't let my lot go visiting their cousins because Tess's boys are too big and rough, and they lead mine astray, so they won't know you're there and can't tell anybody.'

'Will Tess have room for me?'

'Not likely, but we'll sort something out. We'll go tomorrow once you've come home from the bookshop. At least if you're earning you can pay your way with her.'

'Can't I stay here with you?'

'If Hartley comes knocking or even asking in the street my lot will spill, you know what they're like, can't hold their own water, can they? No, it's best you stay with Tess, and we tell no one.'

'But for how long?'

'As long as it takes, lass, or at least until Jemima is on solid food. Once she's weaned from me, you can move away.'

'Yes, that's a good plan. A few months, that's all. I can hide until then.'

'You've found a good job.' Nellie nodded. 'Tess won't charge you much board, so save every penny you can for when you do go.'

Sighing, Annabelle sipped her tea. Her mind ached with thoughts.

Today, for a split second, she'd seen John Hartley. How had her sore heart not exploded with the conflicting emotions of it? Instinct told her he wouldn't give up searching for her. Now he'd seen her, and she'd run from him, he'd have reason to think the worst of her and that saddened her more than she cared to admit.

On top of that, she'd have to move to a slum area and live with Paul's sister. Somehow, she doubted Tess would be as nice as Nellie. Another stranger she'd have to learn to like and get along with and it would also mean she had to leave Jemima. At least she had her new job. Working at a bookshop was the only highlight in the last two months of stress and trouble.

John rapped the knocker on the door of the last house on Penleys Grove Street. As with all the hundreds of other doors he knocked on, he waited patiently for it to open.

He glanced along the street, his eyes always on the search for Annabelle Wallis. That he'd seen her yesterday and then lost her so quickly only inspired him to keep going. He was close, he knew it. However, the next time he saw her he had to act more calmly – yelling her name in the middle of the street was hardly the actions of a gentleman. Still, it worried him greatly that she had run from him like a thief. What did she have to hide? The baby? Information condemning her? Clearly it was something, or why else would she run from him? They knew each other, and he thought they had shared some sort of connection. Yet she had run like a deer before a gunman.

He'd tried to give chase, but she'd melted into the streets and lanes of the city within minutes. Driving around in the carriage for hours had only frustrated him, hoping to catch a glimpse of the peacock-coloured shawl – *Eliza's shawl*.

Miss Wallis knew what had happened to Eliza. He utterly

believed that. She wouldn't have Eliza's shawl otherwise. Annabelle had the answers he sought. He would continue to seek her, despite Des's pleas for him to return home and help him with running the family businesses. There was much to do at Rosewood Hall, too, but he couldn't concentrate on any of that, especially not now when he'd seen her. He only hoped he hadn't spooked her too much and she wouldn't flee York.

Although he accepted guilt for not easing Des's burdens, he couldn't return home and leave it to the police, who so far hadn't found a trace of her and didn't seem that bothered to continue the hunt. Des and Penny begged him to give it up, to stay home and rest for a while.

The door opened and a young maid smiled at him. 'Yes, sir?'

'Good day. I was wondering if a Miss Annabelle Wallis lived or worked here?'

'No, sir. No one of that name works here.'

'Have you heard of that name hereabouts?'

She shook her head. 'No, sorry, sir.'

'Thank you.' John turned away, fighting the feeling of hopelessness. He couldn't falter. He would find her.

Climbing back into the carriage, he sat for a moment and rested his eyes. The chest cold he'd suffered a couple of weeks ago still lingered slightly, sapping his energy. The shorter, colder days as winter descended wouldn't help him recover, either. He longed for a soak in a hot bath, some of the cook's delicious food, then an evening in front of the fire reading a book and a good night's sleep.

He consulted his map, ticking off the places he'd visited, the streets he'd explored, the houses he'd knocked on.

Reading his lists, he realised he'd searched all the decent streets and areas of the city, but not the slums, the areas riddled with poor families, vagrants, criminals, the homeless and the diseased.

His stomach knotted. Had Annabelle gone there to live amongst those people? Was his niece sheltered between walls running with damp, infested with vermin?

'Goldfinch,' he called to his driver.

'Yes, sir.'

'Goodramgate. I'll begin in the Bedern area.'

'Bedern, sir? Are you sure?'

'I am.' He had to search the poor areas. He'd been mad to not think of that first. It was the best place to get lost. Only he hadn't thought the likes of Annabelle, who'd been brought up decently, would ever consider entering the rough areas of a city. That's not where respectable young women ventured.

Within minutes, Goldfinch was halting the horse in Goodram-gate and John climbed down.

'Sir, don't take anything valuable in there.' Goldfinch pointed his whip to the cut leading down between two large houses that once, in their heyday, would have been beautiful homes for the wealthy but which were now multi-room housing, hosting thousands of the city's poor, mainly the Irish, who'd escaped the famine.

Emptying his pockets, John handed his leather wallet, gold fob watch and notebook to Goldfinch, knowing the driver would guard them for him. The man had worked at the estate for years and could be trusted completely, which was why he'd been chosen to accompany John this time.

'I shall return in half an hour,' John told him as the church bells rang six times.

'Sir, it's getting dark. Why not come back tomorrow?'

'This is the best time. People will be home for me to speak with.' With purpose, John walked down the cut and into the beginning of a warren of snickets, alleys and yards. The houses fronting the road rose some four storeys high, shutting out the waning sunlight and throwing long shadows into the deep recesses. Washing, grey and damp, hung like old garlands between the upper floors. Dwellings built behind the houses leaned on to each other as though to hold the next one upright. Add-ons and lean-tos gave way to open-sided shelters made of any material spare, creating a haphazard style of housing within the surrounding streets.

Dank hallways of the houses sheltered those who didn't have a room, while single rooms held large families who had nothing but a bed. John glanced into these rooms as he wound his way up the staircases, asking those that lingered in the stairwells if they'd seen or heard about someone called Annabelle Wallis. His questions were met with blank stares and muted silence.

John stepped over babies, mewing like weak kittens, wide-eyed children, their faces covered in sores, and men and women wallowing in stages of sickness or drunkenness. The stink of open sewers and rotting refuse made him gag. Animal manure littered the ground like fallen leaves and, mixed with strewn rubbish, the smell made John's eyes water.

'What have we here, then?' an older woman, her ragged dress barely covering her breasts, jeered him as he walked through a yard, treading carefully around piles of rubbish.

'I'm looking for a woman,' he said as a small crowd gathered around, forcing him to stop.

'Oh, aye, aren't they all?' the woman laughed. 'Maisie on the top floor will see to you for a shilling. For half a crown you can stay all night and she'll do things to you that would make the devil blush.'

The crowd tittered, nudging each other.

'Not that kind of woman,' John said tersely. 'I am seeking a young lady with a baby.'

'Did you hear that?' the woman crowed. 'He's only gone and got a lass with child.'

The rumblings of the people grew.

'I have not got anyone with child,' John defended, feeling the animosity of those around him. He tried to catch the eye of someone else, an old man with an unlit clay pipe stuck out of his mouth. 'Do any of you know of a woman called Annabelle Wallis with a small baby?'

'I'll be Annabelle Wallis for you, sir, any time you like!' came a saucy reply from somewhere at the back.

'There's no one here of that name,' the old man mumbled. 'You'd best be on your way.'

'She is in need of help,' John persisted. 'I must find her.'

'If she's here, then she doesn't want to be found,' another said.

Letting out a breath, he turned away, knowing he wouldn't get any aid from these people.

Scruffy, barefoot children followed him along the winding paths through the overpopulated tenements, pulling at his jacket, his arm, begging for coins.

'Give us a penny, mister.' They clawed at his clothes with dirty hands.

John ignored them, knowing that to throw out money would cause mayhem and more children would swarm him. He'd witnessed that before in India and wouldn't do it again.

The light had completely faded as he edged his way closer to the street and the carriage. No gaslight filtered into the murky nooks of this neighbourhood. The children fell away as he approached a dim covered walkway between two brick walls. He had a good sense of direction, honed from his travels, but the arched walkway ahead didn't look familiar. He stopped. Had he taken a wrong turn when dealing with the group of children?

Deciding to go ahead and hopefully find himself out on the street, he only noticed the men leaning against the walls when they moved out of the shadows. Four of them stood at the entrance to the walkway and blocked his way.

John's stomach clenched and his senses became alert. Moving only his eyes, he checked left and right for an escape. There was no way out. He'd have to pass the men or return the way he'd come.

'I do not wish for any trouble,' he said, eyes narrowing on the fellows in front of him.

'Then you shouldn't have come here,' the shorter of the men replied.

'I will leave you.' John turned and took two steps before he heard them come from behind.

The first blow struck his shoulder. The shock of being attacked halted him. He spun to face them to ward off the next punch. They surrounded him, punching and kicking. He held his arms up to protect his head, but that gave them easy access to his stomach. The blows to his chest and gut took the air from his lungs. He sucked in air, but another fist to the head sent stars bursting before his eyes.

John fought, landing the odd punch, but four against one were never good odds. He went down. The cold sludge splattered against his face, the stink in his nose. Pain filled him, crowding his brain. He curled up into a ball to protect himself from the boots kicking him.

The last thing he remembered was the church bells chiming.

He woke, shivering, something was pulling at his fingers. Frowning, not fully aware of where he was, he squinted through blurred vision into the darkness. A scream came from a distance. A sharp sting on his finger jerked him upright. A rat scuttled off.

He stared with one eye, unable to see clearly in the murky light. Pain riddled his body as he moved to sit up. Then he remembered. The attack. He groaned, sore and disorientated.

Feeling wet and cold, he realised he wore only his trousers and shirt, which were damp and stained with whatever filth he'd been lying in. They'd stolen not only his overcoat, but his tailcoat, waistcoat, cravat and hat. It was lucky he still had his boots!

Scrambling up, using the wall as a support, his head rang, and his stomach griped with pain. He needed to get out of here before others saw him and gave him a new beating.

Nightfall hindered his progress through yards, and only seeing out of one eye, he stumbled and fell over unseen objects. Shooting pains wracked his body and he speculated that some of his ribs were broken.

'Nay, look at the state of thee,' a kind voice echoed through a yard.

With his one eye, John made out a shadowy figure with a light coming towards him. 'Stay away!' He had no strength to go another round.

'No, sir. I'll not hurt thee.' The female voice sounded full of compassion. 'Hold me hand. There, let me take thee inside.'

John allowed her to lead him into a room lit by the stub of a candle and the flickering embers of a small fire in a little grate. The woman, petite with grey hair and a wrinkled face, helped him to the only chair in the room.

Shivering, his temperature rose, and his energy fell. Was he to pass out?

'Here, sir. Have a drink.' She held a cup for him to sip at.

He tasted the ale, but the act of drinking made the cut in his lip open and bleed. 'Thank you.'

'Can we send a message to someone, sir?'

'My carriage driver... is waiting on... Goodramgate.' His head swam and he swayed on the chair.

'Mickie, run to the gentleman's carriage. Quickly, now.'

Minutes later, Goldfinch entered the room, his expression one of shock and pity. 'God above. I thought something must have happened, sir. You've been gone an hour.'

'Get me home...' John's senses reeled. His head pounded and the pain in his ribs made it hard to breathe. He tipped sideways, his hand reaching for Goldfinch, then all went black.

* * *

'Well, what did you think of your first day?' Josiah Clement asked Annabelle as he closed the shop door and turned the sign around to *Closed*.

'I thought it very fine, Mr Clement,' she answered truthfully. The work and Mr Clement had proved interesting. The only problem had been her jumping in alarm every time someone entered the shop. She expected Mr Hartley to appear at any moment and as a result her nerves were on edge.

He smiled widely. 'How pleasing that is to hear. I am impressed by you. You're a quick learner, and look how tidy one wall is already?'

She turned and studied the far wall lined with bookshelves that she had rearranged and sorted into an easier system for buyers to search. 'I'm happy you are pleased with my efforts.'

'Soon, the whole shop will have benefited from your organisation.' He leaned over the front display and pulled down a large blind in the shop window. 'That alone is worth hiring you and, of course, the tonic you made today.'

'Making tonics comes naturally to me. I've done it every day for years.' The comforting feel of measuring and mixing ingredients gave her pleasure.

'I spoke to Mother about you last night. She is keen to meet you and is willing to try this.' He held up the little brown bottle. 'I pray it works, Miss Baker.'

'I hope it does her some good.' Annabelle wanted to please the kind Mr Clement and his mother. When she had arrived at the bookshop this morning, Mr Clement had already been shopping for the ingredients and set a fire in the stove for her to begin. She'd made the tonic in a pan and left it to steep and then concentrated on learning about selling books.

She stood by the counter, which she had polished to a shine this afternoon. The shop was in a sad state of neglect due to Mr Clement's time being divided between the shop and his ailing mother, but she could see the potential of it once she'd given her attention to the enormous task of sorting the books into some kind of order.

'Tomorrow, I shall be with Mother for the morning, as the doctor is visiting, but I shall come in first thing and unlock the door for you.' He took his hat and overcoat from a peg in the back room and waited for her to find her things and don her bonnet. 'Are you confident enough to be alone in the shop on your second day?'

'Yes, I think so. I manned our stall for years, so I can serve customers.' She walked back into the shop. 'I may not know of every title on the shelves yet, but I will do in time. While you're with your mother, I'll do some more sorting and that'll help me to become familiar with the stock.'

'There shan't be any deliveries tomorrow, so you've no need to worry about that.' Mr Clement shut the door behind them and locked it. He smiled at her in the golden glow of the street's gaslights. 'Well, it's been a most satisfactory day, Miss Baker.'

'I agree, Mr Clement. See you in the morning.' She hurried away, not wanting to linger on the street in case Mr Hartley should be driving past. Besides, she and Nellie were going to visit Tess in Hungate this evening. Head down and the collar of her coat pulled up, she strode quickly through the shadowy Minster gardens and along the darkening streets as the church bells struck six times.

Once at the dwelling, she had no time to sit and chat with the children as Nellie dragged her away, with Paul telling them to not be long as he wanted to go for a pint.

'Are you sure Paul is happy to watch the children, especially Jemima?' Annabelle asked Nellie as they crossed the empty wool market and into the equally empty hay market. On the corner, patrons of the Tower of London pub could be heard from its open door and light spilled out onto the cobbles.

'He's fine with it. As long as he gets his supper and one pint a night, my Paul is a contented man.' Nellie grinned. 'Now, we go down here, Havers Lane, and then onto Hungate. Tess lives on Carmelite Street off Hungate. You'll go straight through town, though, when coming home from work. You'll find a shorter route to walk than this one we've taken from Aldwark, or you can take the omnibus, but that will eat into your savings.'

'It will, but on an omnibus Mr Hartley won't see me as easily as if I was walking the streets home. Gillygate is the other side of the city.'

'Well, you decide. If Mr Clement pays you well enough, you might catch it a few times a week and walk the rest?'

'Yes. I'll work it out. How many children does Tess have?'

'Her boys, Bill and Geoff, are eighteen and nineteen, or thereabouts. They are all she has left. She lost her daughter, Minnie, when she was ten. Minnie drowned in the Foss. And three other little ones didn't make it past their first birthdays.' Nellie spoke matter-of-factly. Death of babies was common, half-expected amongst the poor, who had little money for decent food or good sanitation.

'How sad.'

'It's life. What's sadder is her feckless husband, Norman,' Nellie said with annoyance. 'The man can't keep in work for more than a week. He's selfish and lazy and spends all his time in the pubs spending money he doesn't have. Tess has had a rough life with him.' Nellie stopped before an open door halfway down Carmelite Street. The red-brick house was two storeys high and looked unappealing. The upper windows were broken, and when they ventured inside, the entry revealed a pile of rubbish on bare wooden floorboards caked in mud and dirt.

'Tess and her family live at the back. They have two rooms.' Nellie edged her way around broken shoes, holed and dented tin buckets and what looked like a dead rat. Going down the hallway, past the staircase leading up to the upper floor, shouts and yells echoed off the walls above.

Annabelle shivered standing behind Nellie, who knocked on the last door before stepping straight in.

'Nellie?' A small thin woman with straggly, grey-streaked hair stood at a range stirring something in a pot. 'What are you doing here at this time?'

'I've brought a friend, Annabelle, she's in a spot of bother and needs somewhere to lay her head for a few months.' Nellie moved to one side to reveal Annabelle behind her. 'She's a good lass from a decent home.'

Tess squinted in the dim light, the room lit only by the stub of one candle. 'Can she pay her way?'

'Oh, aye, she has a grand job at a bookshop on Gillygate.'

'That's fine, then. Bill and Geoff have moved out, so she can kip in their bed.'

'Moved out? Why?' Nellie sat at the small square table that rocked when she leant on it. 'Sit down, lass,' she instructed Annabelle. 'Do you have any tea in the pot, Tess?'

Annabelle sat on the stool next to Nellie and in the draught of the door, which had an inch gap under it.

'Aye, there's a bit of tea left...' Tess frowned. 'Not much, mind. There's not much of owt at the minute. Norman is out of work again and the boys have gone.'

'Where have they moved to?'

'They've...' Tess hung her head. 'They've not moved.' She sighed heavily. 'They've been arrested.'

'Not again.' Nellie scowled. 'How can they do this to you again?'

Annabelle sat in stunned silence. The filth and neglect of the room was worse than she could have imagined. Damp ran down the walls, and mould created a pattern that could be mistaken for wallpaper. The floorboards hadn't seen polish in forever, and the only window was thickly coated with cooking grease, while smoke had painted the ceiling a dirty yellow. The double bed in the corner by the window was heaped with thin grey-and-blue-striped blankets, the pillows flat and misshapen, the mattress bowed.

And now she learned that the place where she was to stay was also home to criminals. This had to be a nightmare she'd wake from soon.

'Aye, it's a long line of offences. They'll go down this time.' Tess sat down, the tea forgotten, her gaze vacant.

'When are they in court?' Nellie murmured.

'I don't know. The police tell me nowt. I'm not worthy of being informed. All I know is that they'll both have a long stretch this time. Years, probably. It'll be my luck that they send them to Australia and then I'll have no children left.'

'It won't come to that,' Nellie soothed. 'What did they do?'

'Stealing. It's always stealing.'

'Why didn't you tell me or Paul?'

'Because I'm tired of my business being common knowledge. All of Hungate know my boys are in the cells. I didn't want Paul getting involved, as you know he hates Norman, and it would only cause arguments and fights if Paul came around.'

'Well, we'll just have to hope that the boys get light sentences.' Nellie glanced at Annabelle. 'The good to come from this is that you'll have a room to yourself.'

'I'll want a shilling a week for it, mind,' Tess snapped. 'I'll not be taken for granted.'

Annabelle wanted to say the room wasn't worth a shilling a week, but she had no choice, not yet. Her wage at the bookshop was to be seven shillings a week, which left her six shillings to live off and save.

'A shilling a week is fine, isn't it, Annabelle?' Nellie nudged her.

'Yes.'

'She doesn't have much to say for herself, does she?' Tess eyed her as though she was an exhibit. 'And you'll behave yourself while under my roof.'

Annabelle nodded, wishing with all her heart she could go back to her lovely, clean and pretty cottage.

'She's a good lass, Tess, and she'll be company for you in the evenings.' Nellie stood. 'We'd best be getting home. Annabelle will move in tomorrow after work, all right?'

'Aye, fine.'

Leaving the house, Annabelle had nothing to say. Rain began to fall, making the cobbles slick and slippery.

Nellie put her arm through hers and grinned. 'Cheer up. It'll only be for a few months. After Christmas, I'll wean Jemima off me and on to cow's milk. She'll be eating food by then, too.'

'She'll only be five months old.'

'Old enough to take cow's milk. Then you'll be free to leave and settle somewhere away from the Hartleys.'

'Another new start,' Annabelle whispered to herself, not liking the thought. She had nothing to look forward to and was lost and adrift.

17

The rattle of a tea tray woke John. He opened one eye and peered at Stevens, who carried a lap tray.

'Ah, you're awake, sir. I was hoping you were so your food wouldn't get cold.' Stevens placed the tray on the dresser and opened the curtains, flooding the room with a pale light.

'What time is it?'

'Nearly ten o'clock, sir. You've been asleep since you were brought home last night. How are you feeling?'

'Like I have been run over by a carriage or two,' John muttered, painfully hitching himself up on his pillows.

Stevens hurried to help him, and John winced with every movement. Sweat broke out on his upper lip at the effort of not crying out at the pain from his ribs and back.

Stevens placed the tray over him. 'Eggs and toast, sir. The doctor said only something light for you to begin with.'

John didn't feel particularly hungry. Just breathing seemed to hurt.

The door opened and Des strode in, scowling. 'How are you feeling?'

'Bad.' He took a deep breath to try to relax.

'No bloody wonder!' Des fought to control himself.

Stevens bowed and made a quick exit.

'Des...'

'What were you damn well thinking of putting yourself in such danger? Are you mad? Dr Henderson says you have broken ribs, bruising on your spine, never mind the black eye and cut lip. You have cuts and grazes all over your body. You look like you have been trampled by several wild bulls!'

'It—'

'I nearly had a bloody heart attack seeing you brought in late at night, all bloody and beaten. Penny fainted!'

'I am sorry.' In truth, John remembered very little of the attack or the events afterwards.

Des paced the floor at the end of the bed. 'Goldfinch, bless the man, drove like a fiend through the darkness to get you back here. Then he went and fetched Dr Henderson. You owe Goldfinch your life, for you were in such a terrible state I fully anticipated attending another funeral of one of my siblings!' The distraught expression on Des's face upset John.

'It was stupid of me to venture into the poor area alone,' John admitted. 'I should have hired some men to accompany me.'

'Or just give it up!' Des fumed. 'It has been months, John. None of this is worth your life.'

'Only three months, brother, and it *is* worth it, how can it not be? Eliza's baby is out there.' John moved slightly and pain shot through his side. Weak as a kitten, he fought a moan, concentrating on Des.

'We have no proof of anything, John. Just a letter which could be interpreted in many ways. You must stop. I shan't lose you, too.'

'I saw her, Des. I saw Annabelle Wallis in York.'

Des halted and faced him. 'Did you speak with her?'

'No. She ran. I scared her.'

'Are you sure it was her?'

'She was wearing Eliza's shawl, the one I bought for her in India. I would stake my life on it.'

'Christ, John.' Des rubbed a hand over his face. 'None of this means she still has the child. Miss Wallis could have given her away.'

'I do not feel she would,' he defended. He'd thought of nothing but Annabelle Wallis for months and, as the days went by, he had started to believe that Miss Wallis would care for his niece. She would honour Eliza's wishes. She was kind-hearted and was once an orphan baby herself. She'd do exactly what Widow Wallis had done and take in another woman's orphaned baby.

Des studied a book's spine on a shelf but wasn't really interested in it. 'I have decided to visit the police in York. There is a police inspector I am aware of who I believe is discreet. I will ask him to send some men to search for Miss Wallis in the bowels of York's slums.'

'The newspapers will find out. They follow and pay the police for information for their stories. I began the search to avoid all that.'

'And I refuse to let you put yourself in danger again. I will try to limit the spread of gossip, but if you really think our niece is in York, then we have to find her.'

'Let me do it, Des. In a day or two I can resume the pursuit—'

'No. For one, Penny would never speak to me again if you once more put yourself in danger and, two, we need professional people to search. Those slum areas are not the places our class of people can easily venture into, even the police only dare to enter those areas in groups. Surely you see that now?'

'Miss Wallis will be frightened if she learns the police are looking for her. She will run again.' His mind replayed the vision of her terrified face as she recognised him and turned to flee.

'I will do all I can to make sure the operation is kept on the quiet as much as possible.'

'You cannot control such a thing. Rumours and gossip will abound once word gets out that the Hartleys are hunting a young woman.'

'It cannot be helped. As you say, we must find our niece. We owe it to Eliza. We have tried doing it your way and that nearly cost you your life. Now we do it my way.'

'Miss Wallis is only doing what she feels is best.'

'Really? Then why did she run from you? What has she got to hide?' Des glanced at his fob watch. 'I have to go. I am due in Easingwold. We shall talk more this evening.'

John rested his head back against the pillows, his breakfast cold and unwanted. He had to get back to York. He worried that the police would scare Annabelle away. But then, hadn't he also done that?

He groaned, dismayed at the thought of her living rough amongst the criminals and degenerate people of the slum areas. Did she and his niece have enough to eat? Did they have warmth and shelter? It was raining outside, were they cold and wet?

If only he hadn't been attacked, he could have continued his efforts. Now, the slightest movement hurt, his head throbbed, and his body ached with fatigue.

He glanced at the food. He needed to eat and rebuild his strength. Forcing cold egg into his mouth, he closed his eyes and swallowed. He would order chops for later, and a jug of stout. That would sort him out. Good food would soon have him up on his feet. Nothing would stop him from finding Annabelle, and he had to do it before the police did.

* * *

Annabelle opened the door to Tess's rooms and found her not there. Instead, a short, thin man sat on the bed, scratching his hairy chest. 'Oh, my! I am so sorry.' She stumbled back out into the hallway again.

Laughter sounded behind the closed door, and she squirmed in embarrassment.

Tess, coming in from the street with a bag of shopping, stared at her. 'You can go in if you like. It's your home now. It's never locked as there's nothing to pinch.'

'Your husband is in there.'

'Aye, he lives there too,' Tess scoffed.

'No, I mean he's not fully dressed.'

'God above!' Tess barged open the door. 'Norman, didn't I tell you that Annabelle was coming to live with us this evening? Where's your blasted clothes?'

Annabelle stood in the hallway, not daring to move as they shouted and yelled at each other for several minutes. Suddenly, the door swung open and Norman, now dressed, stomped past her, mumbling under his breath.

Tess came to the door. 'Come in, lass. He's taken some of my wages. We'll not see him now for a day or two. He'll end up drunk and asleep in some gutter somewhere.'

Gingerly, Annabelle stepped into the room. Patched sheets hung from a line stretched across the room. 'I don't want to cause problems.'

'You won't. He's his own problem. You'll be more help to me than he ever was. A shilling a week from you and what I can earn will keep us going, won't it?'

'If you say so.' She wasn't convinced. Living in this hellhole seemed hardly worth the money.

'Put your bags in there.' Tess opened another door, showing her the bedroom, which held two single beds and nothing else.

'Nails are in the wall to hang your clothes on. I washed the sheets for you this morning, but I had to go to work before they were fully dry.' Tess touched the sheets. 'They're not too bad now.' She pulled them down and bundled them up. 'It's not warm enough to wash the blankets, but at least you'll have clean sheets.'

'Thank you.' Annabelle took them from Tess and placed them in the cold bedroom on the end of one of the beds.

'I'll put some tea on, shall I? I got paid today so I've bought us a few things. Have you eaten?'

'No, not yet. I left work and went straight to Nellie's to get my things and came here.' Saying goodbye to Jemima had been difficult and she'd not stayed more than a few minutes so as not to prolong the upset. Even the children didn't understand why she was leaving and Ralphie had hung on to her skirts.

'Well, I've kidney pie for supper. I bought tea and sugar, too. A feast.' Tess raked at the embers in the grate and stuffed twisted bits of newspaper and thin pieces of wood into it.

Annabelle felt ashamed that Tess thought a pie with tea and sugar was a feast. Her heart went out to her. She thought Nellie's home had been poor, but at least Nellie provided a decent table, and the children were well cared for. Tess was so thin she was gaunt and had a stale smell about her as though washing her body was something she'd not done for some time.

'What can I do?' she asked, hovering between the bedroom door and the table.

'Will you fetch some water from the pump down the street? We need to wash up the plates. Norman would never do it.'

'Yes, of course.' Annabelle collected the empty tin bucket and went back onto the street where she'd seen the community pump on the other side of the road. A drizzly rain fell, shimmering on the cobbles and creating a golden halo around the one gaslight in the street. Men were walking either home or to the pub, but after a few curious glances in her direction, they didn't bother her.

Back in the room, Annabelle washed up the dirty plates and cups. A none-too-clean cloth was all she could find to dry them and, hating the thought of it, she used the inside of her brown skirt to dry them instead.

'This is nice, isn't it?' Tess's smile seemed a little forced.

'Are you sure you don't mind me staying?'

'To be honest, I worried all night and day about it.' Tess cut up slices of pie and put them on plates. 'I'm not used to strangers being here. But I need the money and that's the truth. I work two jobs as it is, because Norman is never in work. So having you here will help me out.'

A waft of smoke came back down the chimney, filling the room and making them cough.

'Does the landlord ever do any repairs?' Annabelle abruptly asked.

Tess laughed mockingly. 'Repairs? Not likely. His agent comes for the rent and buggers off as quick as a rat down a drain. If he lingered, he'd get a right earbashing from us all about the state of the place.'

They ate in silence for most of the meal, only talking a little of their day.

'You like the bookshop?' Tess asked, refilling her teacup.

'I do. More than I thought I would. It's quite different to anything I've done before, but I like books, and Mr Clement is nice.'

'Well, let me tell you, it's a far sight better than working in a mill or a factory. That's a good job and you don't want to lose it.'

'I'll try not to. I'll save to get my own room as soon as I can, so you're not put out having me here.'

'You'll not be a bother to me,' Tess told her, clearing away their empty plates. 'I go to bed early, as I'm up for five, and well, there's nothing to do at night. It's warmer in bed.'

Taking that as a cue, Annabelle helped clean the plates, said goodnight and then went into the cold bedroom.

By the light of a flickering candle stub she placed on the floor, she made the bed and unpacked her bag, hanging the few clothes she brought with her on the nails in the grimy wall.

A mouse ran out of a hole in the wall, and Annabelle stifled a yelp as it ran over her boots to another hole in the floorboards.

Freezing, she undressed to her shift, but with the sheets still slightly damp, she couldn't stop shivering. Pulling on her coat, she climbed back into bed, listening to the sounds from the floors above, the creaking of the stairs, the odd voice and a baby's cry.

The poor light meant she couldn't read. She could barely see her own hands, never mind the book's small print. Leaning over the side of the bed, she blew out the pathetic candle. Complete blackness covered her. It was darker than any room she'd ever been in. The windowless room resembled a coffin, or a prison cell, making her catch her breath.

She lay awake, forcing herself to relax as the church bells rang seven times. Seven o'clock. She'd not been to bed this early in years. A door slammed shut close by but in this windowless room, which seemed more like a prison cell than a bedroom, Annabelle couldn't tell where it came from.

A weight of sadness pressed on her chest. How had she come to this? Living in the slums of York without anyone she loved? She'd left her home for Jemima, and yet she wasn't even with the baby. If only John Hartley had not seen her. She had been content at Nellie's, whose natural warmth and kindness went someway to replacing Ma, if only a little bit. Only now, she was totally alone and bereft of Ma all over again.

Her thoughts drifted to John Hartley. Instinct told her he was still searching for her, and he wouldn't give up, not for anything. She had something that belonged to his family. Was Miss Eliza right when she said the family wouldn't take care of her baby? Had Miss Eliza misjudged them?

Annabelle's mind spun with thoughts. Had she also misjudged them? She'd believed Miss Eliza when she said the family would give the baby away. Annabelle had conjured up images of the workhouse and dismal bleak orphanages. Yet she had no proof that would be the family's response. Only Miss Eliza knew them better than she did, and if Miss Eliza was worried and begged Annabelle to take the baby, then she must have had her reasons.

Yawning, Annabelle shivered as she moved slightly in the cold bed. She had to find a room of her own and be with Jemima, otherwise it was all for nothing.

18

After church on Sunday, Annabelle spent the afternoon scrubbing the two rooms. Tess had gone to visit her ailing mother in Walmgate, and Norman had gone to watch a cockfight somewhere.

A week living surrounded by filth had nearly sent her mad, and with Tess and Norman gone for a few hours, she tackled the state of the rooms. It angered her that she was wasting her free time cleaning when she should be with Jemima, but she'd explained her anxiety about becoming ill with Nellie at church this morning and Nellie had encouraged her to clean and come and see Jemima tomorrow after work and have a bit to eat with them.

So, wearing her oldest dress, Annabelle carried bucket after bucket of water to the rooms and began the enormous task of cleaning years of filth. She started with the window and cleaned it inside and out, which instantly allowed more autumn light to filter through. Next, she raked out the pile of ashes from the fire and brushed down the grate before giving it a good blackleading.

She dragged outside Tess and Norman's mattress and her own where she bashed them with the broom. The cloud of dust she created made her cough. When she'd remade the beds, she washed the walls with caustic soda to try to diminish some of the mould, but it was a hopeless task. A history of dampness meant the plaster crumbed at her touch and she created more of a mess than when she started. Giving up on the mould, she swept the floor with an old broom she found under the stairs in the hallway and then, on hands and knees, scrubbed the floor several times until finally she got rid of the build-up of dirt and grime.

After a few hours, she reset the fire and lit it, needing a cup of tea. Without the bank of dead ashes, the fire drew better and sent out heat for the first time since Annabelle had arrived. She wiped down the table and set it with clean plates and cups for supper, though there was no food in the place and Tess had promised to bring home some food later.

After another trip to the water pump, Annabelle washed her underclothes in the bucket and hung them on a string across her room to dry. All her clothes needed washing but the tin bath she saw in the yard had several holes in the bottom and was neither useful nor ornamental.

A knock on the door halted her in pegging up her last pair of wet stockings. She went to the door, expecting a neighbour, but instead gaped in shock as two policemen stood in the hallway.

'Good day, miss. We are Police Constables Pierce and Gibbons. You are?'

'Annabel... Anna Belton...' She stumbled over the name.

'Miss Belton, we are inquiring about a young lady who is missing. Annabelle Wallis.'

Annabelle stared, her mouth suddenly dry, her heart beating like a threshing machine.

'She's about twenty years of age, with blonde hair. Have you heard of someone like that?' the second policeman asked.

She was so thankful she'd wrapped an old cloth around her head earlier to keep the dust out of her long hair. The policemen couldn't see the colour of her hair. 'I don't know anyone of that name, sir. Sorry.'

'Are you sure?'

She nodded, gripping the edge of the door. 'Wh-why are you looking for her?'

'That is confidential, miss. Thank you for your time.' Both policemen appeared bored to death and barely gave her another glance as they moved back to the bottom of the staircase.

'Shall we go up and ask upstairs?' one policeman asked the other.

'Nay, it's a bloody waste of time. I don't care what the sergeant says. I ain't spending all day searching in this filth for some toff's mistress, because that's who it'll be, you know.'

'You're probably right.'

'Aye, I am. And whoever it is, good luck to her. She obviously doesn't want to be found for whatever reason, and I ain't putting my life at risk amongst this rabble for her.'

'What will we tell the sergeant?'

'That we knocked on every door and no one saw her.'

'At least we aren't patrolling the Water Lanes,' the other said. 'Those slums by the river are the worst of the lot.'

Some children ran in and taunted the two policemen, who threatened them with a slap up the side of the head.

Annabelle heard no more as the two men walked outside. She closed the door and rested her forehead against it. The Hartleys had involved the police. Sweet Jesus, she was in such trouble.

She had to plan.

The door opened and Tess came in, carrying a basket. She stared around the room. 'What have you done?'

Still dazed by the policemen, Annabelle didn't answer. Surely it was obvious?

Tess slowly placed her basket on the table. 'You thought my home was filthy.' It was a statement not a question.

'I did some tidying.'

Tess's eyes narrowed with anger or hate, Annabelle didn't know which. 'I took you in, and this is the thanks I get?'

Annabelle frowned, not comprehending. 'What do you mean? I thought you would be happy I cleaned the place up?'

'Happy? Happy to be insulted?'

'Insulted?' Annabelle frowned. Had Tess gone mad?

'You must think of me as some slovenly slut. Someone who lives in filth. I'm sorry Miss bloody high-and-mighty that my home didn't come up to your standards!'

'No, no, it is nothing like that. I thought I was doing a good thing.'

'By showing me up with my unkempt housekeeping? By embarrassing me with my own filth?'

'I didn't mean for any of that. I simply cleaned.'

'Cleaned *my* mess. Yes, I can *see* that!' Tess heaved with anger. 'Get out!'

'What?' Annabelle reeled back at her rage.

'Get out. I'll not be shamed in my own home.' Tess advanced on her. 'Go on. Get!'

Annabelle ran into the bedroom and threw her few belongings into her bag as quickly as possible. In the other room, she heard Tess thumping things onto the table.

Packed, she went and stood by the door. 'I'm sorry, Tess. I thought I was helping you.'

Tess kept her back to Annabelle. 'I don't need to be degraded in my home, thank you very much. I know I live in a hovel, but I don't need the likes of you showing me that I lack housekeeping skills.'

'I wasn't, truly.'

'Get out.'

Frustrated, angry and totally fed up, Annabelle headed up the street. A whole day wasted cleaning that hovel, only to be turned out without thanks! She didn't fit in around here. She thought differently to everyone else, who were content to live in their own filth. Everywhere stank, the cobbles slick with refuse. Rubbish was piled high, wherever the wind drifted it. People walked through open sewers, not caring, not wanting to better themselves. Disease and sickness hung in the air like a cloud, while smoke choked throats. Dogs and cats fought; children screamed, faces covered with sores; men wobbled home drunk, relieving themselves in the open; painted women hung on corners beckoning customers like hawkers in a market.

This wasn't Annabelle's world. She'd been brought up in a sweet-smelling cottage with Ma's strict routine of washing and cleaning. Now she felt dirty all the time. Grime stained her dress collars and hems, caught under her nails. She longed for her old home, the soft tinkling sound of the beck, the birdsong, the whispers of the trees...

She had nowhere to go except Nellie's. Feet dragging, embarrassed at being thrown out, she walked the narrow streets and hoped the policemen had already knocked on Nellie's door. She'd have to keep inside as much as possible and only go out for work.

'Hey, lovely girl.' A man's voice brought her out of her thoughts.

She looked up at the man blocking her path. She stepped to the side to go around him, but he shot out a hand and grabbed her arm.

'Want a fun time, pretty lass?'

'No, thank you. I have to go.' She trembled at the drunken look in his eyes.

'Come on, a few minutes. I'll pay you well.'

'No.' She jerked her arm out of his grasp, but he grabbed her and flung her against the brick wall. She hit her head hard. Lights burst in front of her eyes.

'Listen, bitch, you'll do as I say or end up in the river, understand?' The foul breath flowed over her as he pushed himself against her, trapping her between him and the brick wall. His fingers gripped around her neck and one knee wedged between her legs.

'Please...' she begged. 'Let me go.'

'I'll let you go when I'm finished.' He panted, struggling to keep her still as he gathered up her skirts.

'No!' She banged her fists on his back and screamed.

His fist caught the side of her head, stunning her.

'Hey, you, fella! Get off her!' Another man came running towards them.

Annabelle was thrust to one side and fell to the cobbles as the offensive thug turned to fight her rescuer.

In the shadow of the building, Annabelle edged away from the fight, inching towards her bag. She had to get away. Suddenly, the man who had attacked her fell to the ground.

Annabelle spun around and looked up at the other man. 'Dickie?'

'Come on.' Dickie grasped her arm and hauled her to her feet.

Panting, they made a run for it into the winding lanes and snickets of Hungate.

They eventually made it far enough away to rest inside the boundary walls of Hewley's Hospital for Old Women. Annabelle couldn't speak for the stitch in her side.

'Are you all right?' Dickie panted, bent over.

'Yes. You?' She breathed deeply, trying to calm down.

He nodded. Leaning against a wall.

'How did you find me?' She rubbed her sore head where she'd hit it against the wall.

'Nellie told me.' Dickie straightened his cap. 'I'd gone to her place, and she said you were living with Paul's sister and told me the address. I was coming to have a chat when I saw that bast... er, man attacking you.'

'It's my fault. I wasn't watching where I was going and it's getting dark. I need to keep my wits about me, but I was upset and didn't even see the man until he was right in front of me.'

'Why were you upset?'

'Tess threw me out.'

'Why?'

'Because I cleaned her house.'

'What? That sounds crazy.'

'I agree.' She shrugged. 'I'm going back to Nellie's.'

They fell into step together away from the hospital and onto Saviourgate.

'I just saw Jemima. She's growing.'

Annabelle smiled for the first time that day. 'Isn't she? She's such a good baby.'

'Listen, I came to tell you some news.' He stopped walking and faced her. 'Two lots of news, really.'

'Oh?'

'I heard in the stables that Mr Hartley, Des Hartley, that is, has been to the police. The head groom took him in the carriage two days ago.'

'I know the police are asking about me. They came to Tess's place just an hour ago. I gave them my name as Anna Belton. They didn't seem that bothered in doing their job, but I *lied* to the *police*.'

'So, they are still searching for you. I thought they might give up after Mr John was bashed a few days ago.'

'John was bashed?' Her heart dropped to her boots. 'Is he badly hurt? How did it happen?'

'He was searching the slums, looking for you, no doubt. He went into Bedern at night. He got a right kicking. He's lucky his groom came and found him and took him home. Otherwise, he might have died in some snicket, and no one would know. His body would have been found washed up in the river.'

She gasped. John was hurt because of her. He could have died because of her. Tears filled her eyes. A pain tore through her chest at the thought of him nearly dying because of her. He didn't deserve any of that. She had caused this. Her knees buckled at the enormity of what she was a part of.

'I can't do this any more, Dickie.' Deflated, the strength drained from her. She couldn't continue being strong. Enough was enough. Her actions had put John in danger, could have got him killed. She had to stop this deception.

'Do what?'

'Keep Jemima from them.' She strode ahead, determination in every step.

'Annabelle!' Dickie hurried after her.

'Jemima belongs to the Hartleys, not to me. If John Hartley had been killed, then that would have been my fault. I can't live with this guilt any more. I took Jemima when I should have given her to them straight away, as you told me to.'

'But you could be in trouble, Annabelle. Arrested.' Dickie's face lost colour, his long strides keeping up with her quick steps. 'You can't take her back now. It's been months. They'll have you sent to prison.'

'Then let them. I'm tired of living this secret life. I jump at shadows. I hide my face during the day when walking to work or from work. I can't simply go to the shops without fear of meeting someone I know from the village. Every time I hear a carriage, I expect it to be the Hartleys. I can't even call myself by my own name any more. I found a good job, working for a nice man, and I've lied to him. He knows me as Annabelle Baker when, in fact, I'm Annabelle Wallis, a person in hiding with a baby that isn't mine! I have lived in the roughest slums, putting people out by being another burden for them to cope with. I'm done with it all.'

'But—'

'No, Dickie. You can't talk me out of it. Because of me, you had to lie to John Hartley. You could lose your position because of that if they ever found out. Ginny as well! I've been selfish, and it has to stop.'

'It's not selfish to take care of a baby. It was a dying woman's wish for you to do so, and you've made a promise to her.'

'Is that enough for people to risk their livelihoods or even their lives?' she scoffed. 'I should never had made that promise. I was silly and naïve. I thought I knew better. I thought I was being like Ma.' Her voice failed her as she swallowed back tears.

'Ma would be proud of you,' Dickie murmured, taking her hand. 'Are you sure you want to do this?'

'There is no other choice. Not if I am ever going to be content.'

They spoke no more until they reached Nellie's. The children were playing in the late afternoon shadows of the yard and ran to her.

'Are you back for good, Annabelle?' Florrie asked.

'No, dearest. I have to go away with Jemima for a bit. Come and say goodbye to her.'

Nellie opened the door. 'I saw you through the window. What are you doing here?'

'Tess has thrown me out.'

'What on earth for?'

'I cleaned her house.'

Nellie nodded, understanding what Annabelle didn't. 'She's a proud woman, is Tess. If you've cleaned, then she'd be offended that you thought her dirty.'

'The place was dirty!'

'Aye, but she doesn't need you pointing it out to her.' Nellie gave her a helpless look. 'Well, we'll just have to hide you here.'

'I'm not hiding any more, Nellie. I've come for Jemima. I'm taking her back. She belongs with the Hartleys.'

'Oh, no!' Nellie cried. 'You don't need to! Not after all you've done to keep her from them.'

'I do, Nellie. I've put out enough people. John Hartley was bashed near to death in Bedern. He was looking for me.'

'Nay!' Nellie gasped in horror. 'The poor man.'

Tears hung from Annabelle's lashes, and she brushed them impatiently away and picked up Jemima from the bottom bunk bed. 'No more hiding. Jemima is theirs, not mine.'

'But you'll get into trouble. Maybe even sent down.' Nellie looked at Dickie. 'Tell her, lad. Tell her she doesn't have to do this.'

'I think she does, Nellie. For her own happiness, she needs to live a life without this secret always hanging over her.'

Annabelle wrapped the sleeping Jemima in the silk peacock shawl.

'Will you come back?' Nellie asked, pulling Sammy to her from where he sat on the floor as though needing his chubby comfort in her arms.

'Aye. If they don't arrest me, I'll come back here, if you don't mind?'

'Of course, we don't mind.'

'Just for a few days until I find a room of my own. I have a good job, that is, if Mr Clement keeps me on once he knows the truth.'

'He will.' Nellie nodded with utter conviction.

Annabelle took a deep breath. 'If I'm free, I'll take the first stage-coach in the morning back to York. If I don't arrive, you'll know I've been arrested.'

Nellie hugged Annabelle to her ample chest. 'I expect to see you in the morning, then.'

Walking away from Monk's Yard, Annabelle kept her head up and Jemima held close to her. In mere hours she would never hold her again and so she kept hold of her even when Dickie offered to take her. She shied away from the thought of never holding Jemima again. To do so might break her, shake her resolve to give her up. She had to find the last of her strength to make it through the next few hours. She loved Jemima deeply, would protect her with her life, but she didn't belong to her.

They caught the last stage to Hartleydale, which thankfully didn't have many passengers.

'You didn't tell me the second piece of news,' Annabelle said to Dickie, wanting to focus on something else rather than the thought she might be sent to prison within hours.

'It's not important now.'

'That's unfair. You can't not mention it, you said there were two pieces of news. Is it good or bad?' Though she didn't think she could cope with more bad news. That John Hartley was beaten because of her sat like a lead weight crushing on her chest.

'For me, it's good news.' Dickie took his cap off and ran his hand through his short hair, then replaced the cap, looking uncertain.

'Then I really want to hear it, please.' She gave him a small smile.

'Ginny and I are getting married.' He said it in a rush, as though he wasn't sure of the reception he'd get from her.

Annabelle leaned over and kissed his cheek. 'That's the best news I've heard all year.'

Surprise registered on his face. 'It is?'

'My two best friends getting married? Of course it is!'

'I didn't know what you would say.'

'Why? Because you once asked me to marry you?'

'Yes, and we fooled about a bit last summer, didn't we?'

'It was a bit of fun, Dickie, nothing I would hold you to. I've said before, if I wanted to marry you, I would have snapped you up a long time ago. But it wasn't right for me.'

'I think I agree with you. Well, I do now. Ginny suits me far better.' He looked sheepish. 'Ginny understands me and, well... she loves me, and everything is just easy with her. I don't feel I have to prove myself with her.'

'Like you thought you had to with me?'

'Aye. You would always want more than I could give you. I'm not being nasty or regarding you as spoilt, but Ginny is happy to be a shepherd's wife. It would never have been enough for you.'

'Yes, that is true. I'm sorry.' She couldn't deny it. She didn't know *what* she wanted, but she did know what she *didn't* want.

'Don't be sorry. I'm happy. Happier than I ever thought I would be, really. Ginny is a grand lass.'

'She is. And I'm so very pleased you are marrying each other. Ginny will be a lucky bride.'

'I am lucky, too. I'm marrying a great lass and I still have you as my friend.'

'We'll always be friends, Dickie, no matter what.'

The sun was setting as they pulled into the village. Nervous at being back, Annabelle's legs wobbled a bit as she descended the stage's steps.

'You're fine?' Dickie asked.

Annabelle nodded; her throat too tight with emotion to speak. She was back home. She had missed Hartleydale so much. The air seemed cleaner, lighter, the sky wide and coloured a beautiful gold and dark orange as the sun set behind the hills. If only she was returning to the cottage.

They started the long walk through the village towards the estate. At this time in the late afternoon, the cool autumn weather had sent most people inside. The village High Street remained the same, yet she had changed so much. She had left here months ago as a naïve girl with a huge responsibility, fleeing from the home she loved. Now she was back as a woman, having experienced something of life beyond a country village. She'd seen and experienced things which had forever changed her.

At the church, she paused and looked over to where Ma's grave stood under the bare branches of the tree, its new headstone in place. Tears welled but she blinked them away. She couldn't weaken.

'Come on,' Dickie urged her on quietly. 'We don't want to keep this little one out in the cold.'

Heart laden, Annabelle made the walk to the estate, knowing that soon she'd face the wrath of the Hartley family, possibly jail. She glanced down at Jemima's sweet face, nestled amongst the silk folds of the shawl. She might never see her again.

'Ready?' Dickie asked at the estate's gates.

She pulled back her shoulders and lifted her chin. She would face the family, especially John, with courage, as Ma would expect her to do. She prayed silently that John wouldn't hate her too much.

A figure ran down the drive towards them and Dickie grinned. 'What are you doing outside, lass?' he asked Ginny. 'They'll see you.'

Ginny embraced Annabelle. 'I don't care. I saw you from an upstairs window and had to come.' She stared at Annabelle. 'What are you doing here?'

'Giving them Jemima.'

'No! Why?'

'It's the right thing to do.'

'But Annabelle...' Ginny looked as stricken as Annabelle felt.

'I have to, Ginny.'

'I'll come into the kitchen yard afterwards,' Dickie told Ginny. 'I'll let you know how it goes.'

'Good luck.' Ginny sprinted back to the service area, where she could enter the house and return to her tasks.

But Annabelle aimed for the front door. She wasn't a servant. Despite her knees knocking like a mad woodpecker, she would not be cowed into feeling like a criminal.

At the front door of the grand house, Dickie knocked.

Annabelle trembled. She felt sick.

19

John sat in the big wingback chair by the library fire, a book on his lap but unread. He stared into the flames, his mind lost to thoughts of how he could continue the search. Des had instructed the police, but John doubted they would find her. He doubted he would ever find her now. Annabelle would be long gone. Away to some other city, where she could be swallowed up into the heaving mass of humanity and never be heard of again. Why he should care about her, he didn't understand. The baby was his niece, and he wanted only the best for her, of course, but why the fascination over Miss Wallis? He could, within reason, have any woman he wanted in the county and likely beyond if he put his mind to it, but no other woman interested him as Annabelle did.

A mumble of voices outside the door made him turn in the chair. A knock preceded Havers.

'Ah, Mr John.'

'What is it?'

'Mr Hartley has asked you to join him in the drawing room, if you would, sir.'

John stood slowly, his ribs still causing him pain. His back ached also, but not as much as his ribs on the left side. Thankfully, the swelling over his eye had reduced enough so he could open it and have vision from both eyes, though the bruising was an interesting shade of blue, purple and green.

He heard a baby crying as he approached the drawing room and thought Nanny had brought Clemmie down from the nursery, but his step checked as he entered the room and saw Annabelle holding a baby and the shepherd standing beside her.

'Miss Wallis.' The sight of her took his breath away. Was he imagining it? But, stepping closer, he saw the anguish on her lovely face and his stomach swooped. She appeared crushed, broken. Instantly, he wanted to soothe her, care for her. One look at her and he knew he loved her. Perhaps he always had, from the very first moment.

Des and Penny stood on either side of the fireplace as if suddenly interrupted from a deep discussion. 'Close the door, John,' Des snapped.

John did it without thought, not taking his eyes off Miss Wallis, who looked as scared as she had when he shouted her name from the carriage. He had to take it carefully with her. 'Welcome, Miss Wallis.' He smiled, his tone gentle.

She stared at him, taking in his damaged face. 'I'm sorry you were hurt, Mr Hartley, because of me.'

'Ruffians did this to me, Miss Wallis, not you,' he said, hoping to reassure her. She looked terribly thin, with no colour in her face.

'John.' Des stepped forward. 'Miss Wallis has brought the baby. The baby she says is Eliza's.'

'Thank you for bringing her home to us.' John walked further into the room.

Miss Wallis held the baby closer as she fussed in her arms. 'I promised your sister I would look after her. She said I was to tell no one. She was ashamed of her disgrace and didn't want the family to suffer from it.'

'Eliza was foolish to make you promise such a thing,' John said. Standing closer to her, he was aware of her beauty, a beauty that living rough in the slums hadn't diminished.

'Your sister thought you would give the baby away to an orphanage and she would be adopted by people who might not love her or care for her as I would. I don't know why she thought this, but she did, and I couldn't refuse her. She begged me, nearly into madness, for me to take the baby.'

'Did she give birth to the baby in your cottage?' Des asked.

Miss Wallis nodded. 'She came to me in the middle of the night in a storm and already in labour. She refused to allow me to fetch Dr Henderson. I didn't want to leave her as she was close to having the baby.'

'But she left the cottage soon after. Why did you allow her to do that?' Des pinned her with a cold stare. 'You let her leave and she died straight after arriving here.'

'I didn't know she had left the cottage. I was asleep,' Miss Wallis defended. 'I would never have let her go. She was too weak. She'd lost too much blood. I expected her to stay with me for a few days and in those days we could talk about her plans, her wishes. But I never got the chance because she was gone by dawn, leaving me a note. I would have you read it, but I lost it when moving to York.'

'I have the note,' John said.

She whipped around to face him. 'You?'

'Yes. I found it in the cottage.'

'So you all know what your sister asked me to do?'

'Yes!' Des paced up and down in front of the fire. 'However, you still should have come to us! We are the child's family. You are nothing to her.'

'I brought her into the world. I love her. I've cared for her as if she was my own.'

'And you let her mother die!' Des shouted.

Miss Wallis stumbled back at the accusation, eyes wide, frightened.

John jumped to her side, furious at Des, but the shepherd was instantly holding Miss Wallis.

Angry, John shook his head at Des. 'That is unfair and unkind, brother. Miss Wallis was under the pressure of a dying woman's promise.'

'Nonsense! She should have come here immediately and told us what had happened.' Des glared at Annabelle. 'I hold *you* responsible, Miss Wallis, for my sister's death. I will lay charges against you on that account and also for kidnapping my niece.'

'No!' John stepped in front of Annabelle as if to ward off a physical attack from Des. 'You will do no such thing. Miss Wallis has cared for our niece, and she cared for Eliza. She has done no wrong here.'

'Eliza is dead. You could have died also, John, all because of this woman's actions!' Des pointed a finger at Annabelle.

'Miss Wallis didn't cause Eliza's death,' Penny suddenly said in her quiet way. 'Eliza went to the Wallis cottage for help. Miss Wallis did what she could and safely delivered her baby. It is not Miss Wallis's fault that Eliza left the cottage when, clearly, she was too weak to do so. I have had a baby, Des,' Penny raised a finger to him when he looked ready to explode, 'and I know what it is like to experience the pain and the trauma of giving birth and the fragility of my body afterwards. Eliza wanted to come home, to forget the whole event and get on with her life. Eliza made the choice to walk all the way here while her lifeblood drained from her. *She* made the choice! She did so to prevent scandal and gossip reaching the family. She walked away from her child. She gave it up! None of that is Miss Wallis's fault.'

John saw the emotions play across Penny's face and wanted to embrace her for her courage to speak out against Des, who was so used to getting his own way.

'May I hold her?' Penny asked Miss Wallis more calmly.

The baby was handed over and John watched as Miss Wallis sagged a little, tears filling her eyes and slipping over her lashes. His heart broke for her.

Des peered over his wife's shoulder. 'She looks like Eliza.'

'She is beautiful,' Penny said.

John stepped forward and gazed down at the little face, which did resemble his beloved sister, and he swallowed. Gathering his wits, he turned to Miss Wallis. 'You have done exceptionally well in caring for her when I imagine it would have been a frightening and difficult time for you.'

Miss Wallis stared at him. Her chin wobbled slightly. 'I was honouring Miss Eliza's wishes. I looked after Jemima as though she was my own baby. My friend was her wet nurse, and I made sure Jemima was always well looked after.'

'Jemima?' John grinned. 'That is what you called her, or Eliza?'

'I did. Your sister wasn't interested in naming her. I don't suppose she wanted to get too attached. So I called her Jemima Eliza Amy. The Amy is after Ma, who took me in as a baby.'

John desperately wanted to hold Annabelle Wallis. Could she feel his emotions when he looked at her? He stepped back, embarrassed by the strength of his feelings. 'My niece could not be better named, Miss Wallis.'

She smiled in relief, and he relished that he had made her feel a little better.

Des straightened. 'Now we must decide what to do, going forward.'

Penny looked up at him. 'Jemima stays here with us.'

'Is that wise?' Des frowned, clearly not happy at that answer. 'Anyway, we shall discuss it later and not in front of Miss Wallis and Smithers.'

Miss Wallis lifted her chin, a steely look in her hazel eyes. 'Forgive me, Mr Hartley, but I would like to know what is to become of Jemima. I promised Miss Eliza she would not be sent to an orphanage.'

'She will not be, I assure you,' John said, glaring at Des. 'The baby will stay in the family.'

'How do you propose we do that? By keeping her, it will undo all the hard work we did to keep Eliza's disgrace a secret. I am not saying we send her to an orphanage, but I am certain we can find a good, decent family to take her in. A family we research and know is worthy.'

'No!' John ran his fingers through his hair. 'That is not what we are going to do at all.'

'Please don't send her away, Mr Hartley,' Miss Wallis cried and looked ready to fall at any moment. 'Please don't give her to strangers. I beg you.'

'Do not distress yourself, Miss Wallis,' Penny said. 'She can stay here.'

'We cannot keep her *here*, my dear.' Des held up his hands as though it was obvious. 'I do not wish to be vulgar, but the child is a bastard, and she cannot be brought up in the same nursery as Clemmie or any future children we have. Do you wish to expose the baby and *our* children to ridicule?'

'But—' Penny started to speak but Des cut her off.

'No, Penny. It is my final word on that subject. Eliza's daughter will not live in this house.'

'Then she will live in mine,' John declared without malice. He understood that Des was considering the future and of his own children's upbringing. 'Des is correct. The scandal can be better controlled if the baby lives with me at Rosewood Hall. However, she will not be known as a bastard outside of these four walls. Is that understood?' He looked at each person in the room. 'We can tell our friends that Eliza married secretly to someone we did not approve of, and she had the baby while away on holiday on the coast. She died from an illness brought on by the birth. The husband went to live in... America, something like that.'

'Who will we say she married?' Des asked, not convinced.

'We'll consider a name and a history later.' Rather overwhelmed at what he'd just decided, John realised it was the right thing to do. Eliza would approve, he knew it.

'How will you cope? A single man with a baby, John?' Penny uttered in surprise. 'And what of any future wife you wish to have? She will have to take on the child as well. It is a lot to ask.'

'I shall deal with that when and if it happens, but for now...' He turned to Miss Wallis. 'Would you care to come and live in my home, Miss Wallis, and continue caring for Jemima? We can hire a wet nurse to help you, of course.'

The shock on her face was mirrored by everyone else, but John didn't care. He kept his gaze on Miss Wallis, willing her to say yes.

'You cannot ask Miss Wallis such a thing, John,' Penny said. 'She is a single woman.'

'What does that matter? I will have staff who are single women, why can I not have Jemima's nanny be a single woman as well?'

'Because there are rules, society's rules,' Penny jabbered. 'Nannies are older women, much older than Miss Wallis...'

It remained unsaid that most nannies weren't as pretty as Miss Wallis, too. John knew exactly what Penny was referring to, and he didn't care a jot. He'd make it about Jemima, but also he wanted Miss Wallis near him. He wanted to see her every day.

'Well, Miss Wallis?' he asked again.

Her shoulders went back, and her head came up. An inner light brightened her eyes, and she radiated joy. 'I would like that very much indeed, Mr Hartley. Thank you.'

'This is highly irregular, John,' Penny muttered.

'Everything about this whole episode is highly irregular, Penny,' he replied, smiling at Miss Wallis. 'But we have a chance to honour Eliza's memory by taking care of her daughter within the family. She will be brought up at Rosewood Hall and be happy. None of that can be wrong, can it?'

Penny softened. 'No, it cannot. I shall take this little one up to the nursery. Nanny and Josie, the wet nurse, can look after her until you are ready to leave for Rosewood.' Penny took a few steps but stopped in front of Miss Wallis. 'You have done this family a great service, Miss Wallis, as your mother did before you. It will not be forgotten.'

Miss Wallis let out a long breath once Penny had left the room. She glanced at Smithers and a jolt of jealousy surged through John.

'Miss Wallis?' John stepped forward, wanting her to only look at him. 'Shall we make plans? Would you care for some tea?'

'I must return to York, Mr Hartley. I have to let my friends know where I'll be and to tell my employer that I shan't be working for him any more.'

'I shall send for the carriage. It is late.'

She looked out of the window at the darkness. 'I have missed the last stage.'

'You can stay with me at my cottage, Annabelle,' Smithers said. 'Mam won't mind a bit.'

'No need, Smithers,' John said. 'I shall accompany Miss Wallis back to York.'

Clearly dismissed, Smithers hovered, staring at Miss Wallis.

She took his hand. 'Thank you for everything, Dickie. I will be fine now. I'll go and stay with Nellie and speak with Mr Clement in the morning.'

John stepped forward. 'And I shall collect you at say... ten o'clock? We can then go straight to Rosewood Hall.'

'Thank you.' Her eyes were back on him. 'I can meet you outside Clement's Bookshop on Gillygate.'

'I need a drink,' Des suddenly announced. 'I'll have the carriage sent for.' He left the room after a pointed look at John.

John ignored him. He knew what he was doing.

With Smithers gone, John handed Miss Wallis into the carriage and climbed in after her.

For some time, they sat in silence. John was acutely aware of her sitting beside him in the darkness as they rocked over the roads towards York. He had to break the silence.

'You must bring with you all that you wish to have at Rosewood,' he told her. 'You shall have your own room, naturally, next to the nursery.'

'Thank you.'

'Rosewood is getting redecorated. It needs more work, for it has been left for some years without any attention. However, the estate is pleasantly set in the hills near Helmsley and will be vastly improved...' His words dried up. Was he rambling? Did she even care about his plans for the estate?

'I'm sure Jemima will be most happy there...' She turned away from him to stare out at the black countryside.

They said no more until she gave his driver instructions to Aldwark. There, on the cobbled street, she climbed down from the carriage before he had a chance to open the door for her.

'Until tomorrow at ten, Mr Hartley. Goodnight.' She fled from him through a narrow cut between two buildings. *Monk's Yard*, the sign said. This is where she'd escaped to. He looked around at the men walking past, the drunken singing coming from a nearby alehouse. A ship's horn blew from the river.

John sat back and knocked for Goldfinch to take them home. Mixed emotions raged through him. As of tomorrow, he'd be living with Miss Wallis under his roof. It excited and terrified him at the same time. He was developing deeper feelings for the woman with every breath, but as of tomorrow he would be her employer. He had to keep a control on his sentiments about her, or she might run from him again.

20

The church bells were ringing as Annabelle let herself into Nellie's home. Her hands shook from spending the journey in John Hartley's presence and processing his offer to live with him as Jemima's nanny! God, she had nearly fainted when he suggested it.

The only light came from the fire, and in front of it, Nellie sat dozing on a chair, her chin resting on her chest. The older children were asleep, and the bedroom door was closed where no doubt Paul and Sammy slept.

Annabelle crept to Nellie's side and gently shook her shoulder.

Nellie leapt up, eyes wide. 'Hey, lass. You gave me a fright.'

'Sorry.'

'But you're home and safe?' Nellie looked behind Annabelle as though she'd been accompanied by an armed escort.

'They aren't arresting me, no.'

Nellie hugged her tight. 'Thank God. I've been so worried, couldn't eat a thing all evening. Sit down and tell me how it all went.' Nellie bustled about, putting the kettle on.

Annabelle relaxed for the first time that day. The strength

seeped out of her like a flood. She was exhausted in every way. 'The Hartleys were shocked to see me, of course.'

'Aye, of course.'

'And I think if Mr Des Hartley had his way, I might be in chains right now. Thankfully, his wife and Mr John were calmer and more understanding.'

'They should be thankful you took such good care of Jemima. After all, it was their sister's folly which created this whole mess.' Nellie was indignant.

'That is what Mrs Hartley told her husband.'

'Good on her. So, what happens now?' Nellie poured the water into the teapot and turned it around a few times to mash the tea leaves.

'Mr Des doesn't want Jemima living at the manor.'

'But why?'

'She is a bastard, and he doesn't want her living with his own daughter and future children.'

'It doesn't surprise me they don't want that. Jemima is living proof of Miss Eliza's scandalous past.'

'Miss Eliza was right to believe he would send the baby to an orphanage. I feel he would have, or at least found a family to take her in. He mentioned doing that this evening, but his wife stopped him.'

'The gentry must keep up appearances. Imagine how many unwanted babies are born to toffs who farm them off like newborn lambs, to never see them again?'

'Well, all I cared about was my lamb.' Annabelle smiled tiredly. 'I saved Jemima from that fate. I'd do it all again if I had to.'

'Aye, you should be proud of yourself. So, what have they decided, then?'

'Mr Hartley, John Hartley, is taking Jemima to live with him at his home, Rosewood Hall, near Helmsley.'

Nellie sat down and folded her arms. 'Now that's kind and generous. What a good and decent man. The darling little pet will stay within her family.'

'Yes. He didn't want her going to strangers.'

'We misjudged him?' Nellie's eyebrows rose as she poured the tea.

'I did misjudge him.' She sighed heavily. 'If I had known him a little more, I would have trusted him, but I didn't. I only had Miss Eliza's word to go on.' She shrugged, wondering how this all could have been different if she'd had more time to learn about the kind of man John Hartley was.

'It's done now. Jemima is safe with her family, and you are free to get on with your life.'

'John Hartley also offered me a position to be Jemima's nanny.'

'He what?' Nellie lurched forward over the table, nearly upsetting the teacups. 'You're to be Jemima's nanny? You said no, didn't you?'

Annabelle frowned. 'I agreed to the position. Why would I say no?'

'Because, lass, you've got your own life to live now. You've got a grand job with Mr Clement, and you can live with us. Why would you tie yourself any further to the Hartleys?'

Annabelle rubbed her hands over her face. 'I want to be with Jemima.'

'Is that all it is?'

She stared at Nellie. 'What do you mean?'

'Don't be coy with me. I've seen the way you speak of John Hartley. Your voice softens when you talk of him. You're keen on him, aren't you? Oh, lass. You mustn't go. John Hartley isn't the one for you. He's not of your class.'

'I like being with him, Nellie. I can't explain it.' Her heart soared when she thought of him. He was not only handsome, terribly so, but kind and decent, and she ached for him to look at her, to talk to her.

'Well, I can. It's called lust, girl. And you'll be in all sorts of trouble if you go to his house.'

'I'm there to look after Jemima, that's all,' she defended, blushing.

'And what if one day Mr Hartley tells you he's getting married? Can you stay then and see him with his wife? How will you leave Jemima then, when she's grown even more attached to you?'

John, marry? Like a punch to the chest, Annabelle realised she'd made a terrible mistake. She couldn't live in his house and raise Jemima while he found some woman to court and fall in love with. She knew she couldn't watch John Hartley marry another. The very thought brought her pain now, so how horrendous would it be in a year or two after living in the same house as him and falling more in love with a man she could never have?

'I'm right, aren't I?' Nellie asked softly.

Biting her bottom lip to stop herself from crying, Annabelle nodded. What an idiot she'd been. To even think she could create some kind of make-believe world with her, Jemima and John Hartley. She'd been dreaming, seeing a vision of a golden future that was impossible.

'Now then, tomorrow you tell him you're not going to be Jemima's nanny. You need a clean break.'

'How will I bear it?' Tears tripped over her lashes.

'With strength, just like you've done with everything so far.'

The following morning, after a sleepless night on the bottom bunk, Annabelle rose early and dressed even before Paul got up and left for the railway yards.

She dressed with care, wearing a deep-red woollen dress which had remained packed away in a bag she'd kept at Nellie's. Donning her black bonnet and gloves, she let herself out of the house and walked the cold, frosty streets, her mind and heart in turmoil.

The weak October sun gave no warmth as it slowly rose over the rooftops. The church bells rang out six times and gradually the city folk left their homes and ventured out into the chilly morning air to work. The quiet streets began to echo with hooves striking the cobbles and wheels rumbling along. Ships' horns blasted and smoke swirled from thousands of chimneys as women stirred fires for breakfasts.

Annabelle wandered without clear thought of where she was going. She stayed on the streets away from the parks, where the frost sparkled on the grass. Glimpses of the river showed a mist rising from the water, illuminated by the sun as it lifted higher.

Without the fear of being hunted, Annabelle could raise her face and see the real beauty in the city, perhaps for the first time. Church spires dotted the skyline, bare trees silhouetted against the pale blue sky.

Living here wouldn't be such a hardship. She could make a life now. As much as it pained her to never see Jemima again, or after today, to never look into the tender grey eyes of John Hartley, she would manage. Working at the bookshop would give her a decent wage, and she'd start exploring the available rooms to rent as soon as possible.

After an hour of roaming the streets, she went back to Nellie's, passing Paul on the way as he went to work.

Everyone was now awake, and the room filled with noise. Sammy cried on the floor, while Wilf and Ralphie argued over a holed sock. Dora ate a crust of bread at the table while Florrie was slurping her cup of tea before she went for her shift at the Royal Oak.

'There you are, lass.' Nellie turned from the range and passed her a cup of tea and a plate of bacon. 'Will you two stop that racket!'

she yelled at the boys. 'Wilf, find another ruddy sock, will you? Ralph, get dressed properly or you'll have no breakfast before school. Have you finished, Florrie, because if you have, get off to work.'

'I'm going!' Florrie flounced out of the room, muttering under her breath.

Annabelle sat at the table and stabbed at the bacon with a fork. She had to eat even if she didn't feel hungry. Nellie couldn't afford for food to go to waste, though the chances of any food not being eaten by the boys was slim.

After another ten minutes of mayhem, Nellie slapped the boys' shoulders for playing up and sent them off to school. She put Sammy on her knee and gave him some porridge while Dora munched through another bread crust. 'By heck, why are mornings such a muddle!' Nellie laughed. 'How are you feeling, lass?'

'I'll be fine. Once I've told Mr Hartley that I've changed my mind, I'll be able to get on.'

'Course you will.'

Finishing her breakfast, Annabelle washed and tidied herself and, taking a deep breath, waved goodbye to Nellie and headed for Gillygate.

She was early. Mr Clement, depending on his mother's health, was usually on time or at least only a few minutes late.

As the church bells struck the half hour of eight, he came rushing up Gillygate, a look of apology on his face. 'My apologies, Miss Baker.' He unlocked the door for them to enter. 'Mother is not her best this morning. I shall have to leave you for an hour or two as the doctor is calling.'

'I'm sorry to hear it, Mr Clement. Did she take the tonic?'

'A little, but she received news that a dear friend had died yesterday and she is grieving. Nothing I can say or do seems to lift her.' He looked defeated. 'Perhaps you could visit her this afternoon? She might listen to you and your tales of your Ma would be pleasing.'

'I would be happy to, Mr Clement.' Annabelle untied her bonnet and pulled off her gloves. 'There is something I would like to speak to you about, Mr Clement, if I may?'

'Is it important, Miss Baker?' He rushed about the shop getting it ready for opening. He drew the blind up from the front window.

She knew she had to get it over and done with or she'd lose her courage. He could dismiss her for lying to him and she needed to know if he was going to do it sooner or later. 'Mr Clement. My name is not Annabelle Baker. It is Annabelle Wallis.'

He paused in counting coins into the money drawer under the counter. 'I don't understand?'

'I told you a different surname because people were searching for me, and I didn't want to be found.'

'Why were they looking for you?'

'It is a long story, but basically, I had to run from the village where I grew up because I had to care for someone's baby. The mother sadly died but had begged me to care for the child. She didn't want her family finding out.'

'I see.' His eyes narrowed behind his glasses. 'And what has changed for you to tell me the truth now?'

'The family have the baby. I gave it back to them last night. I can be called by my real name.'

'Did you steal the baby?' he accused.

'No! Not at all. She was entrusted to me by her mother.'

'So, you aren't a criminal? The police aren't after you?' He seemed angry.

'No. There are no police involved.'

'I am surprised by this confession, Miss Ba... Wallis. I thought you to be a sensible and honest person. I feel you have tricked me!'

'I am sensible and honest.'

'Are you? Really? You have lied to me. You gave a false name. In fact, your story sounds ludicrous.'

'I did it to protect the baby, that's all.' Her stomach churned. This was not going well.

He scowled, as though weighing up whether to believe her or not. 'I confess this has shocked me. I have left you in charge of my shop, my money and stock. My trust has been broken!'

'I am not a thief, Mr Clement.' This job was slipping away from her.

'You just admitted to taking a baby.'

'At the mother's behest.' Deflated, she twisted her bonnet in her fingers.

Mr Clement checked his fob watch. 'I must return to Mother, but I shall be back as soon as possible. Can you be *trusted* to mind the shop, Miss *Wallis*?'

'Yes. Absolutely.'

'I hope so. I'll think about everything else when I return.' He gave her a long look and quickly left the shop.

Sighing, she sagged onto the stool behind the counter, knowing full well that the genial rapport she had with her employer was shattered. He might have left the shop in her care for an hour, but he didn't trust her any more, it was clear on his face. Would he keep her on, or dismiss her?

She had to show him she was worthy of his business. She wrapped an apron around her waist and began sorting and cleaning the shelves. An order arrived, and she dealt with it easily. Each book was packaged and matched to the customer's name and placed in a large wicker basket behind the counter.

Busy wiping a shelf free from dust, she heard the doorbell tinkle. Two lads of about eighteen entered, their eyes shifty and their clothes dirty.

Instantly, Annabelle was on alert. These lads weren't here for books. 'Can I help you?'

'Can you?' one boy smirked, rubbing his nose.

Annabelle bristled. 'I don't want any trouble.'

'Then give us the money in the tin and we'll be on our way,' the other sneered. 'Where's Clement?'

'You should leave.' She went to stand behind the counter.

The shorter fellow of the two pulled out a box of long matches from his pocket. He lit one, going cross-eyed as he held it up and watched it burn. 'We've come for our money from Clement.'

'Money?'

'Aye. Now give it over or we'll burn the place down.'

Alarmed, Annabelle grew nervous. The shop would go up in minutes and the thought angered her so much she strode around the counter and over to them. 'Put that down, for heaven's sake, and behave!'

Not expecting her to confront them, the tallest fellow grinned. 'You've got spunk!'

'And you'll have a thick ear if you don't stop your nonsense. Off with you!'

'Nah...' The taller fellow stepped towards her, a challenge in his eyes. 'We could have some fun with her, Tony, what do you say?'

Tony screwed up his face. 'What ye mean?' He blew out the match as it burned down close to his fingers. 'Shall we light the place up, Mel?'

'No, you idiot. We're going to take this pretty lass out the back for some fun.'

The blood drained from Annabelle's face. 'Get out! Go on!'

The shop door opened, and they all turned as Mr Clement walked in. He jerked to a stop on seeing the two fellows. 'What's going on?'

'Good of you to join us, Clement.' The lad named Mel grabbed

Annabelle's arms. She squealed and fought but he was strong. 'We're going to take this one out the back for some sport, Clement. Care to join us?'

'Take your hands off her.' Mr Clement came forward, brandishing his umbrella. He struck Tony on the head and swung for Mel, who used Annabelle as a shield.

She struggled to free herself and, with Mr Clement wielding his umbrella, she was able to yank her arms out of Mel's cruel grasp and run to the other side of the shop. Holding on to the table, she tried to catch her breath as Mr Clement waved his umbrella like a sword.

'You'll pay for this, Clement!' Mel yelled as he and Tony lunged for the door and dashed away.

Panting, Mr Clement turned to Annabelle. 'Are you hurt?'

'No. I'm fine.' She rubbed her arms, which were a little sore. She was a bit shaken and utterly amazed at the whole incident.

'I am sincerely sorry this has happened. I wasn't expecting them to come this week.'

She frowned at him. 'What do you mean?'

He flushed a ruddy hue and took off his glasses to wipe a hand over his eyes. 'They are my nephews, Miss Wallis.'

'Nephews?' She couldn't be more shocked if he said they were his own children.

'Yes. My brother's sons. My brother, Rodney, got himself mixed up in a rough crowd when he was young. He ran away from home and ended up travelling the countryside, never keeping a job. He was murdered a few years ago by some men who he owed money to. His wife came to my mother for help. But the whole family are a lost cause. Mother's nerves worsened after their visit. She gave them some money for them to go away but...' He sighed deeply. 'The boys keep returning for more money. They've grown up wild and unmanageable.'

'And you give them money?'

'Yes. Every month. If I don't, they threaten to go to Mother and I can't have that at any cost. Another visit from them will probably finish her off.'

'I'm sorry to hear of it, Mr Clement.' She was shocked by his revelations. He seemed such a quiet, studious kind of man with an ailing mother and a quiet, non-eventful life. She remembered Ma saying often that you never know what goes on behind closed doors. In this case, it seemed Mr Clement, the bookish man, had an unsavoury family who gave him angst unless he parted with money.

'And I am sorry you have become involved. They usually come at night when I'm closing up, but since I employed you, I told them to meet me on the corner. My fear was of you being brought into my nasty family business. Naturally, they didn't listen.'

'Shall I make us a pot of tea?'

He smiled gratefully. 'That would help, Miss Wallis.' He followed her into the back room. 'Will you forgive me for my treatment of you this morning? You see, trust is important to me, especially having a family such as I do. When you told me your story, I simply did not want to deal with more strife.'

'I fully understand.' She added wood to the small range tucked into the corner of the room where they could heat up hot water for tea.

'I do hope you will stay on, Miss Wallis, despite the awful confrontation just now. You will not be troubled by my nephews again. I will see to that. However, I completely understand if you would wish to leave.'

'I will stay, Mr Clement. Though I believe you should speak to the police about your nephews. Such threats can't continue.'

'True. They have ruled me for too long.' His tone was full of self-loathing. 'I will go to the police after I've drunk my tea. The sooner I sort this mess out, the better, especially now they know about you.'

She turned away from him and concentrated on making the tea. She didn't want him to see her unhappiness, because it had nothing to do with him but everything to do with refusing John Hartley's offer.

Minutes later, the church bells tolled ten times. The incident with the Clement boys had given her a short reprieve from agonising over meeting John. Only, now as she put down her teacup, the sadness overwhelmed her.

'I need to go outside for a moment, Mr Clement.' She left him and walked through the shop. Outside the window, the carriage pulled up, loaded with luggage.

She opened the door as John stepped down from the carriage, his face breaking into a wide smile as he saw her. His eyes were full of happiness as she approached. 'Are you all set? Jemima and the wet nurse are in the carriage.'

Her heart thumped so hard she was certain he could hear it.

'Miss Wallis?' His smile faltered. 'Is something the matter?'

'I...' She swallowed back the sudden tears that sprang into her eyes. 'I can't go with you,' she barely managed to whisper.

'Why ever not?' He reached for her hand, and she let him take it, though it broke all social rules.

'It would be better if I stayed here.' His touch went straight to her broken heart.

'Better for whom?' He searched her face, looking for answers.

'For me. For Jemima. I will get too attached to her.'

'No one is stopping you from becoming attached. It would please me for you to love her.'

'But she's not mine. I will simply be the nanny. I need to have my own life.' It broke her to speak the words to him. Words that would send him and Jemima away.

John took a step back, but still held her hand tightly. 'What has changed your mind? Last evening you were keen to take care of Jemima.'

'I've thought about it since then. All night, really, and it is for the best if I break from her now.'

His expression was of shock and something else she couldn't identify. 'But surely you want to watch her grow up and be a part of her life?'

'She doesn't need me. She has you and your family. You'll hire a good nanny for her. I will only complicate things. I'm not a nanny, Mr Hartley. I'm nothing to anyone.' She forced a smile, though her chest was tight with a pain so sharp she expected to die from it. 'I have to say goodbye.' She nodded firmly, tears rolling over her lashes and down her cheeks.

'No, please. Miss Wallis. This is not what I want.'

'We don't always get what we want, Mr Hartley.' She turned and fled back into the shop. She went through to the back room and out into the small courtyard and to the privy, where she shut the door and cried, her heart broken.

She sobbed for all she'd been through since Ma died. The grief of losing Ma, of experiencing the frightening birth of Jemima, then having her to care for, not knowing what she was doing or why, then leaving the cottage, her sweet home, to live amongst strangers in the wretched slums. Her tears wouldn't stop, and she clapped her hands over her mouth to stifle the moans that broke from her. She wept for the loss of John Hartley, the man she could never have. The man she was foolish enough to want when he was so far out of reach.

It had all been too much and happened all together, giving her no relief to deal with each event as it happened.

'Miss Wallis?' Clement's timid voice broke through the agonising wretchedness that consumed her.

Annabelle swallowed, gulped back the torrent of tears. Wiping her eyes, she straightened. 'I'll be out in a moment.'

'Very good.'

Taking deep breaths to calm herself, she patted down her dress, wiped her eyes again and opened the door.

Grateful that the yard was empty, she wiped her face again. The pain still lingered, and she believed it would always do so, but it had to be buried deep within her.

Squaring her shoulders, she lifted her chin. 'Enough,' she whispered. No more would she cry. The days and weeks to come would be endured until, hopefully, a time came when she found some happiness.

21

Standing on the brow of a hill overlooking Rosewood Hall, John held the drawings tightly in his hands as the cold breeze threatened to rip them away. Beside him, his newly hired agent, Phil Enderby, was studying a map of the whole estate that John had recently commissioned.

'What do you think, Enderby?' John asked him, viewing the rise and fall of the hills around the house.

'It's a sensible plan, sir. If we drain the bottom fields into the proposed lake, it will help with flooding. We can bring the sheep down to the lower fields in the winter to shelter them from the worst of the bad weather.'

John nodded. He had liked Enderby from the first meeting two weeks ago. Enderby had been the second man he'd interviewed for Rosewood's land and stock agent position. Enderby was a local man, yet had a high degree of education and seemed sensible.

Consulting the drawing of the house and acres immediately surrounding it, John tapped a spot on the drawing. 'I feel if we create a park between the house and the new lake, we can build a grand walking area. We'll plant dozens of trees.'

'It'll be a stunning place in time, sir, but what of the old Home Farm? It's in a sorry state.' Enderby pointed to an area on his map. 'With you buying Low Ridge Farm, we now have the opportunity to annexe that farm to the estate and make it the primary Home Farm for the estate and perhaps do away with the old one.'

'Exactly. That is why I purchased Low Ridge last week. As soon as the tenants move out, I want the whole of Low Ridge Farm transformed into a modern concern. The buildings will be updated, especially the pigsties and dairy. The field boundary walls need repairing. The farmhouse will be yours to live in, Enderby, if it suits you?'

'It would, sir, very much. I may even marry my Edith, if she'll still have me.' He grinned.

John patted him on the back. 'I am certain she will. Though she may not want the house. It is in need of repair, which I will fund, obviously, but it is not high on my list at present.'

'Oh, I'm sure we'll cope until you get around to doing it, sir. I'm handy and can spend my spare time on doing some repairs.'

'Good man.' John turned for Dash, who grazed contentedly, and mounted. Enderby mounted his horse and they trotted into the cold November wind that buffeted them as they descended the hill.

For the last three weeks, John had been up before dawn and worked well into the night on the estate. He oversaw all the improvements, interviewed new staff, for the Hall needed both indoor and outdoor staff to get the place back up to standard. He travelled back to Hartley Manor to aid Des in whatever he needed, as well as attending business meetings and inspecting livestock to build on the breeds already grazing at Rosewood.

He met with builders to repair the house, for it needed a new roof and inside needed modernising with better plumbing for the kitchen. The new cook deemed it a magical wonderland to have running water piped into large sinks in the scullery. A new, larger range was installed to add to her delight. The outbuildings also needed attention. The stables were in various states of disorder and the barn looked ready to collapse.

But all of this activity was just a ploy to stop him wondering about Annabelle. He'd hired a nanny, Mrs Carruthers, an older woman with a kind manner, and along with the wet nurse, Jemima was well cared for. Yet even spending an hour with the baby each afternoon and seeing her sleeping before he went to bed caused him unease that Annabelle wasn't with her. Was Jemima missing her?

Three weeks had passed since she refused his offer and every waking moment seemed like three years. He had to accept it, of course he did, but by God it was difficult. He yearned to see her, this young woman who, really, he'd didn't know all that well but who, unbelievably, had burrowed beneath his skin and into his heart and mind, leaving him disturbed and looking for something – he didn't know what.

All he knew was that when he was with Annabelle Wallis, contentment and joy filled him. She made him feel alive. For her, he wanted to be a better man than he was, the sort of man who made her smile and laugh. He had no right to feel these things, but he did. Meeting her had changed him. It was as though he had met the other half of himself, which sounded insane and something Lord Byron would write about. But how else could he explain this obsession with her? This constant need to be with her?

Had he, for the first time in his life, fallen in love properly? And if he had, he was a damn fool to pick someone who didn't feel the same in return. Miss Wallis was totally unsuitable in every way. She was not of his class, and she had the wisdom to accept that. Whereas he ignored common sense and allowed his heart to rule his head.

What in God's name was he to do about it?

He parted with Enderby at the stables, crossed the yard to the service outbuildings and entered the back of the house. The servants went straight into the scullery, but he had his own entrance, which opened into a large boot room, where Timmy sat at a table along the wall, melting candle stubs down to make new longer ones. Timmy, an orphaned local lad, had come knocking the other day looking for work and John had taken him on as a general dogsbody to any of the staff needing his services, but mostly Timmy worked in the boot room, cleaning John's boots and sponging down his overcoats, or refilling the lamps and trimming the wicks, collecting wood, and fetching and carrying for Mrs Ainsley, the cook. The boy was always smiling and happy to please. He'd been roaming the roads for the past year, getting work where he could. To be taken on at the Hall had given him hope for the future.

'There you are, sir.' Timmy stood. 'I was just told to come and find you, but I had to finish with this melt first as I'd already started the pour.'

John sat on a timber bench, ready to take his boots off to replace them with house shoes. 'Come and find me? Why?'

'Mrs Ainsley said Mrs Carruthers wanted you in the nursery.'

'I am wanted in the nursery?' John confirmed, slipping his feet into the shoes.

'Aye, sir.'

John left the boot room and went along the corridor, past the butler's pantry and the small gun room. He heard voices coming from the kitchen, a girl's laughter and the harder tones of Mrs Ainsley, and he smiled softly. The house had come alive with the hiring of staff. And if he felt the quietness at night when he dined alone then he only had himself to blame. He needed to meet more people in the area.

He took the stairs two at a time, only to pause at the top when Mrs Rawlings, his new housekeeper, came along the corridor.

'Oh, Mr Hartley!' Her Scottish accent grew thicker, he noticed, when she was either displeased or enthusiastic; in the last three weeks, he'd seen her express both emotions on several occasions.

'Yes, Mrs Rawlings?'

'It's the wee bairn, sir, Miss Jemima. She's poorly and we, Mrs Carruthers and I, feel the doctor should be called for.'

John's stomach twisted and turned in alarm as he raced into the nursery. By the cot, Mrs Carruthers held Jemima, who looked feverish and limp. 'What's happened?'

'A fever, sir. It started last night. I thought it might be her teething, but this morning she's grown worse.'

'Send for a doctor, Mrs Rawlings, immediately,' John snapped, taking Jemima into his arms. 'Can you not advise anything, Mrs Carruthers?'

'I've tried everything I can think of, sir. I've tried to give her water or have Josie feed her, but she rejects it all.'

John's heart thumped in his chest. Jemima looked terrible. Her little face, usually so sweet and smiling, was blotchy and hot. Her little body lay limp in his arms. Petrified something would happen to her, he paced the floor, rocking her gently. 'Now, little one. Uncle John wants you to get well.' What did one say to a baby? He had no experience with babies. The only baby he knew was Clemmie, and he'd not spent much time with her at all since arriving in Yorkshire.

In what seemed like hours, but was only forty minutes, the doctor from Helmsley village entered the nursery and examined Jemima. He declared her to be suffering from a simple fever and he didn't believe it was anything more dangerous, such as diphtheria or scarlet fever, but they must watch the baby carefully and call him again should they feel Jemima was worsening. His final words were that she should be kept quiet and warm with small amounts of water or milk given. They were to watch for rashes and congestion of the airways. The next day or two would be critical.

John saw him out, feeling less in control than ever. He had flash-backs to Eliza dying in his arms and the blood drained from his face. He couldn't let Eliza's daughter die. He owed her to keep the child alive, well and happy.

What could he do? He paced the drawing room, which was sparsely furnished due to it being repainted and wallpapered. The bare walls seemed to close in on him. The responsibility for Jemima weighed on his shoulders. Is this what parenting was all about? Such highs when a baby smiled and such lows when they were sick? Helpless, he couldn't imagine how Miss Wallis must have suffered while living in the slums and trying to provide for a baby.

Miss Wallis.

Suddenly he knew he had to fetch her, bring her to the Hall and let her tend to Jemima. She would save her. He knew that without a doubt.

'Mrs Rawlings!' he yelled for the housekeeper, running into the front hall.

'Yes, sir?' She came hurrying up the corridor that led to the kitchen.

'I need to go to York and fetch a friend who can help Miss Jemima. Have the carriage sent around. I'll be as quick as I can, but if Miss Jemima takes a turn for the worse, send for the doctor immediately.'

'Of course, sir.' She turned and scurried away.

John, not really a praying man, sent up an offer to whoever was listening. He just hoped Annabelle hadn't left York.

* * *

Closing the bookshop door, Annabelle locked it and pocketed the key, just as Mr Clement walked towards her. He waved a hand in greeting.

'Oh, I am too late.' He smiled kindly, as was his way. 'I thought I might be able to help you finish up for the day, but Mother kept me busy running errands. At least now I'm free tomorrow and can be in the shop all day with you.'

She handed him the key. 'It's been a busy day.' And, to confirm the fact, she yawned. 'Oh, forgive me.'

'I'm working you too hard, Miss Wallis.'

'Not at all. I enjoy being busy and working here makes me happier than I expected to be.' It was the absolute truth, for being completely occupied kept at bay her melancholy for Jemima and heartsickness for John Hartley. Keeping busy until she dropped into bed was the only way to remain sane.

'Perhaps I can walk you home?' he offered. 'We could stop somewhere for a cup of tea?'

'I'd like that. How is your mother today?'

'Much better, thank you. She says you are a miracle worker. It is much less often that she is down in spirits now. Your tonics help her greatly, but I think it is your visits that she enjoys just as much.'

'I'm so pleased I can be of assistance. Your mother is a dear woman.' Annabelle called on Mrs Clement once a week and they would chatter for an hour about all sorts of subjects, but Mrs Clement was keen to hear about Annabelle's childhood in the country.

'She thinks most highly of you,' Mr Clement said warmly.

A carriage came racing up Gillygate, the horses' hooves striking the cobbles as they were brought to a halt before the bookshop.

Annabelle stared in utter surprise as John Hartley jumped from the carriage to her side. 'Mr Hartley!'

'Miss Wallis, please, you must come,' Mr Hartley implored her. 'Jemima is ill, and I considered you would want to be with her.'

Her world seemed to implode at his words. Jemima ill? The darling baby she brought into the world and cared for so diligently was sick? How could that be? She had given her into the Hartleys' safekeeping.

Wordlessly, she stared at him. Her first thought was to climb into the carriage and race to be with Jemima, but she wasn't free to do as she pleased.

'Miss Wallis, Annabelle, please?' John Hartley's suffering expression made her heart lurch with love for this man she couldn't stop thinking about.

Mr Clement took Annabelle's elbow. 'Miss Wallis, it sounds as if you are needed.'

'But, my work, the shop...' she dithered. She couldn't just leave the bookshop, and for how long? Mr Clement depended on her. Not only that, but she couldn't run to John Hartley's house every time Jemima was ill. She would never get over the child if she did.

'That is not important!' Mr Hartley snapped. 'Jemima needs you!'

'Take as long as you need. I can manage.' Mr Clement gave her a gentle push. 'Go.'

'I have to tell Nellie.' She hesitated, not knowing what to do. She was at sixes and sevens, her mind whirling. To be thrust back into Jemima's life when she'd been so distraught for the last few weeks without her was a shock. Was she strong enough to say goodbye again?

Mr Clement walked with her to the carriage. 'I'll inform Mrs Baker of what's occurred. Do not worry. Your position is safe. Come back when Jemima is well again.'

'Thank you.' She climbed into the carriage. How lucky was she to find such a kind employer?

'I hope all is well and you return soon.' Mr Clement spoke sincerely, his gaze not leaving Annabelle's.

Mr Hartley nodded his thanks to Mr Clement and shut the door. The horses jerked forward and once more Annabelle was in a carriage with John Hartley – something she thought she'd never do again.

'Have I taken the correct action in fetching you, Miss Wallis?' Mr Hartley asked sternly. 'I thought perhaps Jemima would mean more to you than a bookshop?'

In the dim interior of the carriage, she couldn't see his face clearly. 'Yes, she does, Mr Hartley, of course. I'm pleased you thought to come and get me. However, Mr Clement has been a good employer to me, and he relies on me greatly.'

Mr Hartley's face tightened. 'Do you have an understanding with him?'

'No.' She turned to look out of the window at the lengthening shadows of the cool autumn evening. The thought of Mr Clement being an admirer had entered her head recently. Mr Clement, when he had the time away from his mother, was considerate of her sadness at losing Jemima and had been kind and thoughtful. When they worked together, he'd keep her mind off her sorrow with interesting conversations about books and travel, his studies at Oxford, and the early death of his father, which had brought him home from Oxford. They'd discuss authors, and he'd encourage her to read the books he lent to her.

She liked Mr Clement and he liked her. She could do worse than to reject Mr Clement should he offer marriage. She would be the wife of a respected business owner and live in a nice house. Indeed, she could do a *lot* worse. However, the prospect never really took root in her heart. She was not ready to forget John Hartley.

Mr Hartley sat forward to get her attention. 'The doctor told me that tonight and tomorrow are the most critical times for Jemima, and I immediately thought of you, that you would want to know.'

Annabelle's breath hitched. Poor darling Jemima. 'Thank you.'

'Don't thank me, Miss Wallis. It seemed as natural as breathing to come and collect you and bring you home. Jemima needs you...'

His soft tone held something in it that caught at her heart and tugged. She wanted to reach for his hand and hold it, which was ridiculous to even dream of such a thing. She clutched her hands together in her lap. 'I would hate for Jemima to be ill without me there to help care for her, but I gave up that right, if I ever had it in the first place.'

'You have the right, in my mind, and as Jemima's guardian that's all the approval you need.'

'I never expected to see either of you again. The shock of Jemima being ill and seeing you again is difficult to accept.'

'I understand hearing the baby is sick is distressing, but I hope seeing me is the opposite?'

She glanced at him, not knowing what he meant by that. 'I'm not distressed seeing you again, Mr Hartley.' In truth, she was a little, but she'd rather eat broken glass than admit it to him.

'I cannot tell you how much that pleases me to hear, Miss Wallis.'

They passed through a wood and the darkness in the carriage became complete, saving Annabelle from the embarrassment of her blushes. What did he mean by that? Being in his presence sent her stomach twisting and her mind became fanciful for his smile, a look, his touch... all the things she would never have and all the things she so desperately wanted from him.

It was fully dark by the time the tired horses pulled to a stop in front of the house. A cold wind tugged at their clothes as they stepped down from the carriage and to the door, which opened immediately.

A woman dressed in dark grey stood by and took their outdoor clothes.

'Any change, Mrs Rawlings?' John asked, ushering Annabelle to the staircase.

'No, sir,' Mrs Rawlings answered gravely.

Annabelle had no chance to take in her surroundings. Some rooms they passed were in differing states of rebuilding or redecorating, but she gave no thought to them as they entered the nursery, which was boiling hot like a furnace.

She rushed to the cot by the fire and picked Jemima up and cradled her in her arms. The baby was flushed and wheezing each breath. Hot to touch and sweating, Annabelle took her away from the fire and sat down on a comfortable chair near a table.

'Miss, you mustn't let her get cold,' said the older woman, who Annabelle took to be the senior nanny.

'Get cold?' Annabelle snapped. 'It's like the fires of hell in here. She's sweating being so close to the fire. She needs to cool down.'

'Miss Wallis, this is Nanny Carruthers,' Mr Hartley spoke. 'She is a diligent carer. Jemima has been well looked after.'

'Maybe she has, but I have had a lifetime of teachings from Ma and her knowledge was often better than a doctor's,' Annabelle replied, moving the thick woollen blanket off Jemima's legs. She cried out in surprise to see two black fat leeches on each of them. 'What in God's name!'

'The leeches are to suck out the evil blood and poisoned vapours,' Nanny Carruthers defended. 'The doctor said we were to keep them on her until they dropped off.'

Annabelle glared at the nanny. 'Evil blood? Are you mad?' She laid Jemima on the table. 'Please fetch me a lighted taper, Mr Hartley.'

He did as she asked and soon the heat on the back of the leeches made them drop off the baby's legs.

Wrapping Jemima up loosely, Annabelle sat back down. 'Has she been drinking?'

Nanny Carruthers shook her head. 'I can't get anything down her.'

'I need cool boiled water infused with feverfew,' Annabelle instructed. 'If you don't have feverfew, then ginger if you have that.'

'I shall see to it.' John left the room.

'A tepid bath will help bring her temperature down, too.'

'A tepid bath?' Nanny erupted as though Annabelle had asked for her to tie a rope around the moon and bring it down. 'A bath will kill the child.'

'It won't. My mother was an herbalist, Nanny, and she revived more sick children than you've had hot dinners – now, please, do as I ask.'

All night, Annabelle ignored everyone around her and concentrated on Jemima. She bathed the baby, noting that Jemima had grown in the three weeks she'd been away from Annabelle. Her chubby little legs and arms showed she'd been feeding well.

Josie, the wet nurse, tried to feed Jemima, but the baby was too weak to suck. Annabelle sent Mr Hartley and Nanny to bed, for she needed to be alone with Jemima and their presence distracted her. All through the long night, she sat in the chair for hours, dripping water into Jemima's mouth, or sponged down her hot little body.

Dawn broke with Annabelle sponging the baby's body again. Outside, the countryside came awake to a cold blustery November day, but Annabelle remained focused on Jemima. She walked the floor with her, singing or telling her stories about Ma.

Josie woke and tried to feed Jemima again, but the baby lay limp and uninterested, eyes closed and crying softly as though even to cry was too much effort.

Mr Hartley entered the room, dressed and shaved, his face solemn. He looked like he'd not slept. 'Any improvement?'

Tired, Annabelle shook her head. 'But she hasn't got worse.'

'That is some good news.' He gave her an endearing smile. 'You must be exhausted.'

'I'll sleep when Jemima is better.' She took the baby from Josie and sat down to drip more water into her mouth.

'I shall have breakfast sent up for you.' He hovered by her shoulder. 'Is there anything I can do?'

'No. Only time will tell.'

'I feel rather helpless and useless.'

'We all do.'

'Not you. You are inspiring.' His eyes showed how proud he was of her.

She was too tired to blush at his compliment.

He hesitated on leaving. 'I have urgent business to attend to this morning, only for an hour or so and then I will be back, but if you need me before then Mr Enderby, my agent, knows where to find me. I will be as quick as I can.'

She nodded, staring up at him, wanting him to stay.

Annabelle spent the next couple of hours watching Jemima breathe. The doctor came and took a short examination of Jemima, before declaring it could still go either way, and then he left.

Angry at his dismissive behaviour, Annabelle redoubled her efforts. Jemima would not die. She refused to allow it.

Mr Hartley returned and sat with Annabelle. He took the baby from her, urging her to rest, but she couldn't. Instead, she sat and gazed at him as he walked up and down the room, holding Jemima.

'Will you not go to bed, Miss Wallis? There is a room ready for you across the hall.' His grey eyes were soft with concern.

'I couldn't sleep, Mr Hartley, but thank you.' Despite the tiredness aching her body, her mind was on the handsome man in front of her. Seeing him tenderly caring for the baby brought a lump to her throat. Seeing Jemima nestled in his arms gave her such joy. It also made her acutely aware that soon she would have to walk away from them both.

He turned at the end of the room and then stopped and stared at the baby in his arms.

Annabelle's heart lurched with dread. She jerked to her feet, staring in horror at him. 'What is it?'

'Look...'

Dreading what she'd find, she stepped across the room to his side and peeped at Jemima. The air left her body as Jemima's blue eyes stared at her and then she smiled, a tiny hand reaching up from the blanket towards Annabelle.

Taking the little fingers in hers, hot tears burned behind Annabelle's eyes. 'Darling, you're awake,' she crooned. With her other hand, she touched the baby's forehead and it seemed not as fiery as before. Jemima's colour had changed from blotchy fever red to a more even pink.

Annabelle glanced up at John, but he was already looking at her with such a look of love and thankfulness in his eyes that Annabelle trembled at the raw emotion.

'You saved her,' he whispered.

For one wonderful moment, she thought he was going to kiss her, but he leaned back as though stopping himself just in time.

Gathering her scattered emotions, she stepped away. 'We must ring for Josie. Jemima might suckle now.' She rang the bell pull by the fireplace, for Nanny and Josie were in the staff dining room, having their tea.

'You must get some rest, Miss Wallis,' John said, his voice strained. 'I insist.'

With the crisis over, Annabelle deflated like a leaking ball. She sagged against the table. 'Yes, I might take a nap, if that is all right?'

'Sleep as long as you need.' His gaze locked with hers as though he wanted to say more.

The door opened and Josie and Nanny came in and fussed over Jemima as John told them the good news of her fever breaking.

Josie took Jemima into the adjoining room and began to feed her. Nanny reported back that she was drinking hungrily.

Feeling exhausted, but utterly relieved, Annabelle left them and crossed the hall to the bedroom. Fully dressed, she lay on the bed and sobbed into the pillow.

She was so grateful Jemima had recovered, so happy the darling little girl would be healthy once more, and she cried in gratefulness of the miracle that she hadn't died. Yet she also cried because she never wanted to leave this house. With Jemima well, she had no reason to stay. Again, she'd have to say goodbye to Jemima and to John Hartley, who stupidly she loved more than words could describe. She would have to return to York, to Nellie, and the bookshop and to Mr Clement.

22

A noise woke Annabelle. She opened her eyes and blinked at the brightness of the sun streaming through the window. A maid came in, carrying a bucket of wood.

'Oh, I'm sorry, miss. I tried not to wake you. But the fire needs wood.' The girl, about sixteen, pointed to the low fire in the grate.

'Please, come in.' Confused, Annabelle rubbed her eyes to wake up properly. 'What time is it?'

'It's midday, miss. A beautiful day outside. Sunny but cold.' The maid fed the fire small pieces of wood.

'Midday?' Annabelle frowned.

'Aye, miss. You've been sleeping since yesterday afternoon. Mr Hartley said we weren't to disturb you for anything, but Mrs Rawlings said for me to not let the fire go out or you'll be cold in here, and with all your hard work in saving Miss Jemima, we didn't want you to get sick, as well.'

'I can't believe I've slept so long.' Amazed, she climbed from the bed, feeling fuzzy-headed from such a deep sleep.

'Well, you must have needed it, miss. Shall I get you a tray?'

'No. I'll check on Jemima.' Annabelle realised she was still fully dressed. She longed to have a proper wash.

'Would you like a bath, miss?' the maid asked as though reading her mind.

'I would, very much.'

'Leave it with me. I'll sort one out for you.'

'Thank you. What is your name?'

'Lucy, miss.'

'Thank you, Lucy.' Annabelle felt like a queen, being attended to by a maid. She slipped across the hallway to the nursery and let herself in. Nanny was sewing by the window while Josie rocked Jemima in the chair by the cot.

'How is she?' Annabelle asked, creeping closer to the baby, not wanting to wake her up.

'Champion.' Josie beamed. 'She's slept nearly as long as you.'

'Forgive me. I didn't mean to.'

'Nonsense. You deserved it.'

Nanny eased herself up and nodded in agreement. 'She's right. You did all the hard work, Miss Wallis. No one would begrudge you a good long rest.'

'Has she been drinking?' Annabelle asked, casting a studious eye over Jemima.

'Aye. Not much at first during the night, but this morning she drank for ten minutes.' Josie preened as though it was a miracle.

'Well done.' Annabelle patted her shoulder. 'And Mr Hartley? Has he been up?'

'Oh, aye.' Nanny cocked her head to one side in a knowing way. 'He's been in and out of here all evening and then again all this morning. He kept asking if you would be all right. I told him you just needed to sleep.'

'I should go down and speak with him.' Annabelle forced a smile and left them.

Along the corridor, she braced herself to face him. Now Jemima was well, she would leave. The sooner the better, really, for staying would only cause her more heartache and, to be honest, she couldn't cope with it. Yet again she would have to say goodbye to Jemima, to John.

Downstairs, she peeped into several rooms, noting the half-finished decorating, or the improvements being made with new plaster or moulding. Despite the work, no builders were about. She went into the largest room, which she assumed to be the drawing room, like the one at the manor.

'Can I help you, Miss Wallis?' Mrs Rawlings asked with a kind smile.

'I was looking for Mr Hartley.'

'He's in his study. This way.'

Annabelle followed her down the hall beyond the staircase. Mrs Rawlings knocked on the door and when John replied to enter, she opened the door and stepped aside for Annabelle to go in.

Nervous, Annabelle walked into a dark green wallpapered room with a large walnut desk in the centre in front of a wide window.

John immediately stood. 'Miss Wallis.' The gentle way he said her name made Annabelle's legs go weak. 'Come, sit down.'

Knowing she must look a fright, Annabelle put a hand to her hair and despaired of it appearing neat. Why didn't she look in a mirror before coming down? She should have bathed first.

'You are well rested?' he asked, sitting back at his desk.

'Yes, thank you. I have checked on Jemima, and she seems so much better.'

'We were incredibly lucky. Do you not agree?'

'I do.'

'And it was all down to you.' His gaze held hers.

'Not really.' She blushed.

'Do not be modest, Miss Wallis. You cared for Jemima better than anyone.'

'I love her. I wouldn't stop until she was over the worst. I just used the knowledge Ma taught me. I didn't think I knew what to do, but it was instinct.'

'The best kind.' He smiled. 'Now, you must be hungry. I will ring for Mrs Rawlings to add another place at the table. You will join me for luncheon?'

She clenched her hands together. 'I'm not really dressed to join you at your table, Mr Hartley. Lucy is preparing a bath for me, if you don't mind, and then I shall have to make my way back to York.'

'York?' He stood abruptly. 'You wish to leave so soon?'

'I've been away two days. I have to return to York.'

'Why? You must stay as long as you want.'

'That is not possible.' How she wished it could be.

'I thought you would wish to stay a little longer and make certain that Jemima is fully recovered?'

'Mr Hartley, what I wish for is not in my power to have.'

He frowned. 'Meaning?'

'Nothing.' She shook her head, annoyed at herself for revealing anything. 'I have no clothes with me. Besides, Jemima is well attended with Nanny and Josie. I'm not needed.'

'You are by me,' he blurted out. He strode to the window and looked out.

Annabelle waited, heart beating uncontrollably.

After several moments, John glanced over his shoulder at her. 'Will you come and have a look at this, Miss Wallis?'

Intrigued, she joined him at the window. She stared out at the gardeners planting trees and the workmen levelling the driveway.

'I am making many improvements to this estate. In time, there will be many gardens, a deer park, a lake and better stables. In the house I am redecorating each room and modernising where I can. I want this estate to be one of the best in the county, if on a modest scale. What do you think?'

She stared at him. 'What do *I* think? Does it matter?'

'Yes, it does, to me.'

'It will be a credit to you when it's finished. Something to be proud of. A legacy to you and your family.'

'Something for me to leave to my children and Jemima.'

Her stomach dropped. 'Yes. How fortunate they will be. Jemima will grow up in a delightful home.'

'I need a wife for all that. A woman to be the mistress of Rosewood Hall.'

Annabelle couldn't take her eyes from his.

John took her hand and her whole body tingled at the touch. 'Will you be willing to take on the role of mistress to Rosewood Hall?'

'Me?' she croaked.

'I admire you greatly, Miss Wallis.' His voice deepened. 'Would you be averse to becoming my wife?'

'You want to marry me?' It seemed too unreal, too fanciful to be true. Was she dreaming? Would she wake up to the real world soon? If so, she never wanted to open her eyes. She wanted to stay in this fanciful land where John Hartley wanted to marry her.

'Would that be distasteful to you?'

She gazed at him, hardly taking it all in. Was he really saying these words to her?

'Miss Wallis, have I shocked you into silence? Does my offer seem unpleasant?'

'No, but how could it ever be? I am not of your class, Mr Hartley. Your family would judge me and find me wanting. I bring nothing to such a marriage. *I am nothing.*'

John took both her hands in his and brought them up to kiss them. 'You are *everything* to me.'

Her stomach fluttered and her heart seemed to be thumping so hard it felt as though it would burst from her chest at any moment, or she'd drop dead at his feet with a heart attack. It was all too much. He was holding her hands, offering marriage. How was it even possible?

'Annabelle...' His head lowered closer to hers and she raised her face to his, as naturally as breathing. His kiss was all she wanted at that moment, even more than air.

His lips touched hers softly, reverently, like the whisper of a warm summer's breeze. She wanted to arch into him, needing more, aching for more.

'You must know I adore you, my darling Annabelle,' he murmured against her mouth.

'You do?' To have his love was the substance of her dreams.

'All day, every day, all I do is think of you. It affects my work, my eating, my sleeping... I want Rosewood to be our home, filled with love and happiness. Perhaps you can come to love me in time?'

She squeezed his hands, the only part of them touching. 'I don't need time. I feel the same,' she whispered on a sigh. 'I never imagined I could ever have your love. I dreamed of it but knew it to be foolish.'

'It's not foolish to fall in love.'

'You are the only person I've wanted since the day you caught Bobby after he ran away. I tried to fight my feelings...'

'You and me both, but it's meant to be.' He touched her face gently, and softly kissed her again. It was a kiss that made her body tingle and her spirit soar.

When they parted, she smiled, feeling like a glow was shining from inside her body and radiating outwards to encompass the whole world. 'You are the only person I want to marry. Never did I think you would feel the same.' She wanted to cry with happiness.

He grinned, his handsome face showing his elation. 'I had

hoped but dared not consider it might happen, that you would have me.'

'But what will people say? I'm the ward of an herbalist, an orphan of unknown origin. It has never bothered me before because I had Ma's love and I was happy, but it might be a problem now, for you. People will say I'm not good enough for you and they'd be right.'

'They, family and friends, will be happy for us, or they will not be in our lives,' he declared, cupping her cheek and smiling into her eyes. 'All I want is you.'

Annabelle pulled back slightly to search his face. She needed his words to be true. And there in his eyes was the ardent love she sought, the simple truth she wanted. It would be a rocky road ahead, fraught with many obstacles, but she was strong enough to overcome them if John was by her side.

She leaned forward and kissed him boldly. 'You can have me, John Hartley, willingly.'

ACKNOWLEDGMENTS

Dear readers,

Thank you for reading *The Orphan in the Peacock Shawl*. I want to thank all the readers who support me and who buy my books. I truly appreciate your support. I really love receiving messages from readers who have enjoyed my stories.

Also, a shout-out to all those who review my stories on social media and websites, it means a great deal to me. Thank you!

Thank you to the whole team at Boldwood Books, especially Emily Ruston, my editor, who is so encouraging in making the book shine. I really enjoy working with you.

Last but not least, a big thank you to my husband and my family for their love and support. They make my life overflow with love and laughter and pure joy – most of the time, anyway!

MORE FROM ANNEMARIE BREAR

We hope you enjoyed reading The Orphan in the Peacock Shawl. If you did, please leave a review.

If you'd like to gift a copy, this book is also available as an ebook, digital audio download and audiobook CD.

Sign up to AnneMarie Brear's mailing list for news, competitions and updates on future books.

https://bit.ly/AnneMarieBrearNews

ABOUT THE AUTHOR

AnneMarie Brear is the bestselling historical fiction writer of over twenty novels. She lives in the Southern Highlands in NSW, and has spent many years visiting and working in the UK. Her books are mainly set in Yorkshire, from where her family hails, and Australia, between the nineteenth century and WWI.

Visit AnneMarie's website: http://www.annemariebrear.com/

Follow AnneMarie on social media:

twitter.com/annemariebrear
www.facebook.com/annemariebrear
bookbub.com/authors/annemarie-brear
instagram.com/annemariebrear

Sixpence Stories

Introducing Sixpence Stories!

Discover page-turning historical novels from your favourite authors, meet new friends and be transported back in time.

Join our book club Facebook group

https://bit.ly/SixpenceGroup

Sign up to our newsletter

https://bit.ly/SixpenceNews

ABOUT BOLDWOOD BOOKS

Boldwood Books is a fiction publishing company seeking out the best stories from around the world.

Find out more at www.boldwoodbooks.com

Sign up to the Book and Tonic newsletter for news, offers and competitions from Boldwood Books!

http://www.bit.ly/bookandtonic

We'd love to hear from you, follow us on social media:

facebook.com/BookandTonic

twitter.com/BoldwoodBooks

instagram.com/BookandTonic